THE
PINK FAIRY BOOK

THE MAIDEN BRINGS THE COAT OF HAIR TO THE GIANT

THE
PINK FAIRY BOOK

Edited by

ANDREW LANG

With Numerous Illustrations by

H. J. Ford

DOVER PUBLICATIONS, INC.

NEW YORK

This Dover edition, first published in 1967, is an
unabridged and unaltered republication of the work
originally published by Longmans, Green and Company in 1897.

Standard Book Number: 486-21792-2
Library of Congress Catalog Card Number: 67-17984

Manufactured in the United States of America
Dover Publications, Inc., 31 East 2nd Street, Mineola, N.Y. 11501

PREFACE

ALL people in the world tell nursery tales to their children. The Japanese tell them, the Chinese, the Red Indians by their camp fires, the Eskimo in their dark dirty winter huts. The Kaffirs of South Africa tell them, and the modern Greeks, just as the old Egyptians did, when Moses had not been many years rescued out of the bulrushes. The Germans, French, Spanish, Italians, Danes, Highlanders tell them also, and the stories are apt to be like each other everywhere. A child who has read the Blue and Red and Yellow Fairy Books will find some old friends with new faces in the Pink Fairy Book, if he examines and compares. But the Japanese tales will probably be new to the young student; the Tanuki is a creature whose acquaintance he may not have made before. He may remark that Andersen wants to 'point a moral,' as well as to 'adorn a tale;' that he is trying to make fun of the follies of mankind, as they exist in civilised countries. The Danish story of 'The Princess in the Chest' need not be read to a very nervous child, as it rather

P   a

borders on a ghost story. It has been altered, and is really much more horrid in the language of the Danes, who, as history tells us, were not a nervous or timid people. I am quite sure that this story is not true. The other Danish and Swedish stories are not alarming. They are translated by Mr. W. A. Craigie. Those from the Sicilian (through the German) are translated, like the African tales (through the French) and the Catalan tales, and the Japanese stories (the latter through the German), and an old French story, by Mrs. Lang. Miss Alma Alleyne did the stories from Andersen, out of the German. Mr. Ford, as usual, has drawn the monsters and mermaids, the princes and giants, and the beautiful princesses, who, the Editor thinks, are, if possible, prettier than ever. Here, then, are fancies brought from all quarters: we see that black, white, and yellow peoples are fond of just the same kinds of adventures. Courage, youth, beauty, kindness, have many trials, but they always win the battle; while witches, giants, unfriendly cruel people, are on the losing hand. So it ought to be, and so, on the whole, it is and will be; and that is all the moral of fairy tales. We cannot all be young, alas! and pretty, and strong; but nothing prevents us from being kind, and no kind man, woman, or beast or bird, ever comes to anything but good in these oldest fables of the world. So far all the tales are true, and no further.

CONTENTS

THE
PINK FAIRY BOOK

THE CAT'S ELOPEMENT[1]

ONCE upon a time there lived a cat of marvellous beauty, with a skin as soft and shining as silk, and wise green eyes, that could see even in the dark. His name was Gon, and he belonged to a music teacher, who was so fond and proud of him that he would not have parted with him for anything in the world.

Now not far from the music master's house there dwelt a lady who possessed a most lovely little pussy cat called Koma. She was such a little dear altogether, and blinked her eyes so daintily, and ate her supper so tidily, and when she had finished she licked her pink nose so delicately with her little tongue, that her mistress was never tired of saying, 'Koma, Koma, what should I do without you?'

Well, it happened one day that these two, when out for an evening stroll, met under a cherry tree, and in one moment fell madly in love with each other. Gon had long felt that it was time for him to find a wife, for all the ladies in the neighbourhood paid him so much attention that it made him quite shy; but he was not easy to please, and did not care about any of them. Now, before he had time to think, Cupid had entangled him in his net, and he was filled with love towards Koma. She fully returned his passion, but, like a woman, she saw the difficulties in the way, and consulted sadly

---

[1] From the *Japanische Märchen und Sagen*, von David Brauns (Leipzig : Wilhelm Friedrich).

with Gon as to the means of overcoming them. Gon entreated his master to set matters right by buying Koma, but her mistress would not part from her. Then the music master was asked to sell Gon to the lady, but he declined to listen to any such suggestion, so everything remained as before.

At length the love of the couple grew to such a pitch that they determined to please themselves, and to seek their fortunes together. So one moonlight night they stole away, and ventured out into an unknown world. All day long they marched bravely on through the sunshine, till they had left their homes far behind them, and towards evening they found themselves in a large park. The wanderers by this time were very hot and tired, and the grass looked very soft and inviting, and the trees cast cool deep shadows, when suddenly an ogre appeared in this Paradise, in the shape of a big, big dog ! He came springing towards them showing all his teeth, and Koma shrieked, and rushed up a cherry tree. Gon, however, stood his ground boldly, and prepared to give battle, for he felt that Koma's eyes were upon him, and that he must not run away. But, alas ! his courage would have availed him nothing had his enemy once touched him, for he was large and powerful, and very fierce. From her perch in the tree Koma saw it all, and screamed with all her might, hoping that some one would hear, and come to help. Luckily a servant of the princess to whom the park belonged was walking by, and he drove off the dog, and picking up the trembling Gon in his arms, carried him to his mistress.

So poor little Koma was left alone, while Gon was borne away full of trouble, not in the least knowing what to do. Even the attention paid him by the princess, who was delighted with his beauty and pretty ways, did not console him, but there was no use in fighting against fate, and he could only wait and see what would turn up.

The princess, Gon's new mistress, was so good and

kind that everybody loved her, and she would have led a
happy life, had it not been for a serpent who had fallen
in love with her, and was constantly annoying her by his
presence. Her servants had orders to drive him away as
often as he appeared; but as they were careless, and the
serpent very sly, it sometimes happened that he was
able to slip past them, and to frighten the princess by

HOW GON SLEW THE SNAKE

appearing before her. One day she was seated in her
room, playing on her favourite musical instrument, when
she felt something gliding up her sash, and saw her
enemy making his way to kiss her cheek. She shrieked
and threw herself backwards, and Gon, who had been
curled up on a stool at her feet, understood her terror,
and with one bound seized the snake by his neck. He

The Princess weeps for sympathy.

gave him one bite and one shake, and flung him on the ground, where he lay, never to worry the princess any more. Then she took Gon in her arms, and praised and caressed him, and saw that he had the nicest bits to eat, and the softest mats to lie on ; and he would have had nothing in the world to wish for if only he could have seen Koma again.

Time passed on, and one morning Gon lay before the house door, basking in the sun. He looked lazily at the world stretched out before him, and saw in the distance a big ruffian of a cat teasing and ill-treating quite a little one. He jumped up, full of rage, and chased away the big cat, and then he turned to comfort the little one, when his heart nearly burst with joy to find that it was Koma. At first Koma did not know him again, he had grown so large and stately ; but when it dawned upon her who it was, her happiness knew no bounds. And they rubbed their heads and their noses again and again, while their purring might have been heard a mile off.

Paw in paw they appeared before the princess, and told her the story of their life and its sorrows. The princess wept for sympathy, and promised that they should never more be parted, but should live with her to the end of their days. By-and-bye the princess herself got married, and brought a prince to dwell in the palace in the park. And she told him all about her two cats, and how brave Gon had been, and how he had delivered her from her enemy the serpent.

And when the prince heard, he swore they should never leave them, but should go with the princess wherever she went. So it all fell out as the princess wished ; and Gon and Koma had many children, and so had the princess, and they all played together, and were friends to the end of their lives.

HOW THE DRAGON WAS TRICKED [1]

ONCE upon a time there lived a man who had two sons, but they did not get on at all well together, for the younger was much handsomer than his elder brother, who was very jealous of him. When they grew older, things became worse and worse, and at last one day as they were walking through a wood the elder youth seized hold of the other, tied him to a tree, and went on his way, hoping that the boy might starve to death.

However, it happened that an old and humpbacked shepherd passed the tree with his flock, and seeing the prisoner, he stopped and said to him, 'Tell me, my son, why are you tied to that tree?'

'Because I was so crooked,' answered the young man; 'but it has quite cured me, and now my back is as straight as can be.'

'I wish you would bind me to a tree,' exclaimed the shepherd, 'so that my back would get straight.'

'With all the pleasure in life,' replied the youth. 'If you will loosen these cords I will tie you up with them as firmly as I can.'

This was soon done, and then the young man drove off the sheep, leaving their real shepherd to repent of his folly; and before he had gone very far he met with a horse boy and a driver of oxen, and he persuaded them to turn with him and to seek for adventures.

[1] From *Griechische und Albanesische Märchen*, von J. G. von Hahn. (Leipzig: Engelmann. 1864.)

By these and many other tricks he soon became so celebrated that his fame reached the king's ears, and his majesty was filled with curiosity to see the man who had managed to outwit everybody. So he commanded his guards to capture the young man and bring him before him.

And when the young man stood before the king, the king spoke to him and said, ' By your tricks and the pranks that you have played on other people, you have, in the eye of the law, forfeited your life. But on one condition I will spare you, and that is, if you will bring me the flying horse that belongs to the great dragon. Fail in this, and you shall be hewn in a thousand pieces.'

' If that is all,' said the youth, ' you shall soon have it.'

So he went out and made his way straight to the stable where the flying horse was tethered. He stretched his hand cautiously out to seize the bridle, when the horse suddenly began to neigh as loud as he could. Now the room in which the dragon slept was just above the stable, and at the sound of the neighing he woke and cried to the horse, ' What is the matter, my treasure ? is anything hurting you ? ' After waiting a little while the young man tried again to loose the horse, but a second time it neighed so loudly that the dragon woke up in a hurry and called out to know why the horse was making such a noise. But when the same thing happened the third time, the dragon lost his temper, and went down into the stable and took a whip and gave the horse a good beating. This offended the horse and made him angry, and when the young man stretched out his hand to untie his head, he made no further fuss, but suffered himself to be led quietly away. Once clear of the stable the young man sprang on his back and galloped off, calling over his shoulder, ' Hi ! dragon ! dragon ! if anyone asks you what has become of your horse, you can say that I have got him ! '

But the king said, ' The flying horse is all very

well, but I want something more. You must bring me the covering with the little bells that lies on the bed of the dragon, or I will have you hewn into a thousand pieces.'

'Is that all?' answered the youth. 'That is easily done.'

And when night came he went away to the dragon's house and climbed up on to the roof. Then he opened a little window in the roof and let down the chain from which the kettle usually hung, and tried to hook the bed covering and to draw it up. But the little bells all began to ring, and the dragon woke and said to his wife, 'Wife, you have pulled off all the bed-clothes!' and drew the covering towards him, pulling, as he did so, the young man into the room. Then the dragon flung himself on the youth and bound him fast with cords saying as he tied the last knot, 'To-morrow when I go to church you must stay at home and kill him and cook him, and when I get back we will eat him together.'

So the following morning the dragoness took hold of the young man and reached down from the shelf a sharp knife with which to kill him. But as she untied the cords the better to get hold of him, the prisoner caught her by the legs, threw her to the ground, seized her and speedily cut her throat, just as she had been about to do for him, and put her body in the oven. Then he snatched up the covering and carried it to the king.

The king was seated on his throne when the youth appeared before him and spread out the covering with a deep bow. 'That is not enough,' said his majesty; 'you must bring me the dragon himself, or I will have you hewn into a thousand pieces.'

'It shall be done,' answered the youth; 'but you must give me two years to manage it, for my beard must grow so that he may not know me.'

'So be it,' said the king.

And the first thing the young man did when his beard

THE·DRAGON·OUTWITTED

was grown was to take the road to the dragon's house
and on the way he met a beggar, whom he persuaded to
change clothes with him, and in the beggar's garments
he went fearlessly forth to the dragon.

He found his enemy before his house, very busy
making a box, and addressed him politely, 'Good
morning, your worship. Have you a morsel of bread?'

'You must wait,' replied the dragon, 'till I have
finished my box, and then I will see if I can find
one.'

'What will you do with the box when it is made?'
inquired the beggar.

'It is for the young man who killed my wife, and
stole my flying horse and my bed covering,' said the
dragon.

'He deserves nothing better,' answered the beggar,
'for it was an ill deed. Still that box is too small for
him, for he is a big man.'

'You are wrong,' said the dragon. 'The box is large
enough even for me.'

'Well, the rogue is nearly as tall as you,' replied the
beggar, 'and, of course, if you can get in, he can. But I
am sure you would find it a tight fit.'

'No, there is plenty of room,' said the dragon, tucking
himself carefully inside.

But no sooner was he well in, than the young man
clapped on the lid and called out, 'Now press hard,
just to see if he will be able to get out.'

The dragon pressed as hard as he could, but the lid
never moved.

'It is all right,' he cried; 'now you can open it.'

But instead of opening it, the young man drove in
long nails to make it tighter still; then he took the box on
his back and brought it to the king. And when the king
heard that the dragon was inside, he was so excited that
he would not wait one moment, but broke the lock and
lifted the lid just a little way to make sure he was really

there. He was very careful not to leave enough space for the dragon to jump out, but unluckily there was just room for his great mouth, and with one snap the king vanished down his wide red jaws. Then the young man married the king's daughter and ruled over the land, but what he did with the dragon nobody knows.

THE GOBLIN AND THE GROCER [1]

THERE was once a hard-working student who lived in an attic, and he had nothing in the world of his own. There was also a hard-working grocer who lived on the first floor, and he had the whole house for his own.

The Goblin belonged to him, for every Christmas Eve there was waiting for him at the grocer's a dish of jam with a large lump of butter in the middle.

The grocer could afford this, so the Goblin stayed in the grocer's shop; and this teaches us a good deal. One evening the student came in by the back door to buy a candle and some cheese; he had no one to send, so he came himself.

He got what he wanted, paid for it, and nodded a good evening to the grocer and his wife (she was a woman who could do more than nod; she could talk).

When the student had said good night he suddenly stood still, reading the sheet of paper in which the cheese had been wrapped.

It was a leaf torn out of an old book—a book of poetry.

'There's more of that over there!' said the grocer. 'I gave an old woman some coffee for the book. If you like to give me twopence you can have the rest.'

'Yes,' said the student, 'give me the book instead of the cheese. I can eat my bread without cheese. It would be a shame to leave the book to be torn up. You

---

[1] Translated from the German of Hans Andersen.

are a clever and practical man, but about poetry you understand as much as that old tub over there!'

And that sounded rude as far as the tub was concerned, but the grocer laughed, and so did the student. It was only said in fun.

But the Goblin was angry that anyone should dare to say such a thing to a grocer who owned the house and sold the best butter.

When it was night and the shop was shut, and everyone was in bed except the student, the Goblin went upstairs and took the grocer's wife's tongue. She did not use it when she was asleep, and on whatever object in the room he put it that thing began to speak, and spoke out its thoughts and feelings just as well as the lady to whom it belonged. But only one thing at a time could use it, and that was a good thing, or they would have all spoken together.

The Goblin laid the tongue on the tub in which were the old newspapers.

'Is it true,' he asked, 'that you know nothing about poetry?'

'Certainly not!' answered the tub. 'Poetry is something that is in the papers, and that is frequently cut out. I have a great deal more in me than the student has, and yet I am only a small tub in the grocer's shop.'

And the Goblin put the tongue on the coffee-mill, and how it began to grind! He put it on the butter-cask, and on the till, and all were of the same opinion as the waste-paper tub, and one must believe the majority.

'Now I will tell the student!' and with these words he crept softly up the stairs to the attic where the student lived.

There was a light burning, and the Goblin peeped through the key-hole and saw that he was reading the torn book that he had bought in the shop.

But how bright it was! Out of the book shot a streak of light which grew into a large tree and spread its branches far above the student. Every leaf was alive, and every flower was a beautiful girl's head, some with dark and shining eyes, others with wonderful blue ones. Every fruit was a glittering star, and there was a marvellous music in the student's room. The little Goblin had never even dreamt of such a splendid sight, much less seen it.

He stood on tiptoe gazing and gazing, till the candle in the attic was put out; the student had blown it out and had gone to bed, but the Goblin remained standing outside listening to the music, which very softly and sweetly was now singing the student a lullaby.

'I have never seen anything like this!' said the Goblin. 'I never expected this! I must stay with the student.'

The little fellow thought it over, for he was a sensible Goblin. Then he sighed, 'The student has no jam!'

And on that he went down to the grocer again. And it was a good thing that he did go back, for the tub had nearly worn out the tongue. It had read everything that was inside it, on the one side, and was just going to turn itself round and read from the other side when the Goblin came in and returned the tongue to its owner.

But the whole shop, from the till down to the shavings, from that night changed their opinion of the tub, and they looked up to it, and had such faith in it that they were under the impression that when the grocer read the art and drama critiques out of the paper in the evenings, it all came from the tub.

But the Goblin could no longer sit quietly listening to the wisdom and intellect downstairs. No, as soon as the light shone in the evening from the attic it seemed to him as though its beams were strong ropes dragging him up, and he had to go and peep through the key-hole. There he felt the sort of feeling we have looking at the great rolling sea in a storm, and he burst into tears. He could not himself say why he wept, but in spite of his

What the GOBLIN saw in the Student's room

tears he felt quite happy. How beautiful it must be to sit under that tree with the student, but that he could not do; he had to content himself with the key-hole and be happy there!

There he stood out on the cold landing, the autumn wind blowing through the cracks of the floor. It was cold—very cold, but he first found it out when the light in the attic was put out and the music in the wood died away. Ah! then it froze him, and he crept down again into his warm corner; there it was comfortable and cosy.

When Christmas came, and with it the jam with the large lump of butter, ah! then the grocer was first with him.

But in the middle of the night the Goblin awoke, hearing a great noise and knocking against the shutters —people hammering from outside. The watchman was blowing his horn: a great fire had broken out; the whole town was in flames.

Was it in the house? or was it at a neighbour's? Where was it?

The alarm increased. The grocer's wife was so terrified that she took her gold earrings out of her ears and put them in her pocket in order to save something. The grocer seized his account books, and the maid her black silk dress.

Everyone wanted to save his most valuable possession; so did the Goblin, and in a few leaps he was up the stairs and in the student's room. He was standing quietly by the open window looking at the fire that was burning in the neighbour's house just opposite. The Goblin seized the book lying on the table, put it in his red cap, and clasped it with both hands. The best treasure in the house was saved, and he climbed out on to the roof with it—on to the chimney. There he sat, lighted up by the flames from the burning house opposite, both hands holding tightly on his red cap, in which lay the treasure; and now he knew what his heart really valued most—to whom he really belonged. But when the fire was put out, and the Goblin thought it over—then—

'I will divide myself between the two,' he said. 'I cannot *quite* give up the grocer, because of the jam!'

And it is just the same with us. We also cannot quite give up the grocer—because of the jam.

THE HOUSE IN THE WOOD [1]

A poor woodcutter lived with his wife and three daughters in a little hut on the borders of a great forest.

One morning as he was going to his work, he said to his wife, ' Let our eldest daughter bring me my lunch into the wood ; and so that she shall not lose her way, I will take a bag of millet with me, and sprinkle the seed on the path.'

When the sun had risen high over the forest, the girl set out with a basin of soup. But the field and wood sparrows, the larks and finches, blackbirds and green-finches had picked up the millet long ago, and the girl could not find her way.

She went on and on, till the sun set and night came on. The trees rustled in the darkness, the owls hooted, and she began to be very much frightened. Then she saw in the distance a light that twinkled between the trees. ' There must be people living yonder,' she thought, ' who will take me in for the night,' and she began walking towards it.

Not long afterwards she came to a house with lights in the windows.

She knocked at the door, and a gruff voice called, ' Come in ! '

The girl stepped into the dark entrance, and tapped at the door of the room.

[1] From the German of Grimm.

'Just walk in,' cried the voice, and when she opened the door there sat an old grey-haired man at the table. His face was resting on his hands, and his white beard flowed over the table almost down to the ground.

By the stove lay three beasts, a hen, a cock, and a brindled cow. The girl told the old man her story, and asked for a night's lodging.

The man said :

> Pretty cock,
> Pretty hen,
> And you, pretty brindled cow,
> What do you say now?

'Duks,' answered the beasts ; and that must have meant, 'We are quite willing,' for the old man went on, 'Here is abundance ; go into the back kitchen and cook us a supper.'

The girl found plenty of everything in the kitchen, and cooked a good meal, but she did not think of the beasts.

She placed the full dishes on the table, sat down opposite the grey-haired man, and ate till her hunger was appeased.

When she was satisfied, she said, 'But now I am so tired, where is a bed in which I can sleep?'

The beasts answered :

> You have eaten with him,
> You have drunk with him,
> Of *us* you have not thought,
> Sleep then as you ought !

Then the old man said, 'Go upstairs, and there you will find a bedroom ; shake the bed, and put clean sheets on, and go to sleep.'

The maiden went upstairs, and when she had made the bed, she lay down.

After some time the grey-haired man came, looked at her by the light of his candle, and shook his head. And

when he saw that she was sound asleep, he opened a trap-
door and let her fall into the cellar.

The woodcutter came home late in the evening, and
reproached his wife for leaving him all day without food.

'No, I did not,' she answered; 'the girl went off with
your dinner. She must have lost her way, but will no
doubt come back to-morrow.'

But at daybreak the woodcutter started off into the
wood, and this time asked his second daughter to bring
his food.

'I will take a bag of lentils,' said he; 'they are larger
than millet, and the girl will see them better and be sure
to find her way.'

At midday the maiden took the food, but the lentils
had all gone; as on the previous day, the wood birds had
eaten them all.

The maiden wandered about the wood till nightfall,
when she came in the same way to the old man's house,
and asked for food and a night's lodging.

The man with the white hair again asked the beasts:

> Pretty cock,
> Pretty hen,
> And you, pretty brindled cow,
> What do you say now?

The beasts answered, 'Duks,' and everything happened
as on the former day.

The girl cooked a good meal, ate and drank with the
old man, and did not trouble herself about the animals.

And when she asked for a bed, they replied:

> You have eaten with him,
> You have drunk with him,
> Of *us* you have not thought,
> Now sleep as you ought!

And when she was asleep, the old man shook his head
over her, and let her fall into the cellar.

On the third morning the woodcutter said to his wife,
'Send our youngest child to-day with my dinner. She is
always good and obedient, and will keep to the right path,
and not wander away like her sisters, idle drones!'

But the mother said, 'Must I lose my dearest child
too?'

'Do not fear,' he answered; 'she is too clever and
intelligent to lose her way. I will take plenty of peas
with me and strew them along; they are even larger than
lentils, and will show her the way.'

But when the maiden started off with the basket on
her arm, the wood pigeons had eaten up the peas, and she
did not know which way to go. She was much distressed,
and thought constantly of her poor hungry father and
her anxious mother. At last, when it grew dark, she saw
the little light, and came to the house in the wood. She
asked prettily if she might stay there for the night, and
the man with the white beard asked his beasts again:

> Pretty cock,
> Pretty hen,
> And you, pretty brindled cow,
> What do you say now?

'Duks,' they said. Then the maiden stepped up to
the stove where the animals were lying, and stroked the
cock and the hen, and scratched the brindled cow between
its horns.

And when at the bidding of the old man she had
prepared a good supper, and the dishes were standing on
the table, she said, 'Shall I have plenty while the good
beasts have nothing? There is food to spare outside; I
will attend to them first.'

Then she went out and fetched barley and strewed it
before the cock and hen, and brought the cow an armful
of sweet-smelling hay.

'Eat that, dear beasts,' she said, 'and when you are
thirsty you shall have a good drink.'

Then she fetched a bowl of water, and the cock and hen flew on to the edge, put their beaks in, and then held up their heads as birds do when they drink, and the brindled cow also drank her fill. When the beasts were satisfied, the maiden sat down beside the old man at the table and ate what was left for her. Soon the cock and

THE·MAIDEN·FEEDS·The·THREE·BEASTS·

hen began to tuck their heads under their wings, and the brindled cow blinked its eyes, so the maiden said, 'Shall we not go to rest now?'

> Pretty cock,
> Pretty hen,
> And you, pretty brindled cow,
> What do you say now?

The animals said, ' Duks :

> You have eaten with us
> You have drunk with us,
> You have tended us right,
> So we wish you good night.'

The maiden therefore went upstairs, made the bed and put on clean sheets and fell asleep. She slept peacefully till midnight, when there was such a noise in the house that she awoke. Everything trembled and shook ; the animals sprang up and dashed themselves in terror against the wall ; the beams swayed as if they would be torn from their foundations, it seemed as if the stairs were tumbling down, and then the roof fell in with a crash. Then all became still, and as no harm came to the maiden she lay down again and fell asleep. But when she awoke again in broad daylight, what a sight met her eyes ! She was lying in a splendid room furnished with royal splendour ; the walls were covered with golden flowers on a green ground ; the bed was of ivory and the counter-pane of velvet, and on a stool near by lay a pair of slippers studded with pearls. The maiden thought she must be dreaming, but in came three servants richly dressed, who asked what were her commands. ' Go,' said the maiden, ' I will get up at once and cook the old man's supper for him, and then I will feed the pretty cock and hen and the brindled cow.'

But the door opened and in came a handsome young man, who said, ' I am a king's son, and was condemned by a wicked witch to live as an old man in this wood with no company but that of my three servants, who were transformed into a cock, a hen, and a brindled cow. The spell could only be broken by the arrival of . a maiden who should show herself kind not only to men but to beasts. You are that maiden, and last night at midnight we were freed, and this poor house was again transformed into my royal palace.

As they stood there the king's son told his three servants to go and fetch the maiden's parents to be present at the wedding feast.

'But where are my two sisters?' asked the maid.

'I shut them up in the cellar, but in the morning they shall be led forth into the forest and shall serve a charcoal burner until they have improved, and will never again suffer poor animals to go hungry.'

URASCHIMATARO AND THE TURTLE [1]

THERE was once a worthy old couple who lived on the coast, and supported themselves by fishing. They had only one child, a son, who was their pride and joy, and for his sake they were ready to work hard all day long, and never felt tired or discontented with their lot. This son's name was Uraschimataro, which means in Japanese, 'Son of the island,' and he was a fine well-grown youth and a good fisherman, minding neither wind nor weather. Not the bravest sailor in the whole village dared venture so far out to sea as Uraschimataro, and many a time the neighbours used to shake their heads and say to his parents, ' If your son goes on being so rash, one day he will try his luck once too often, and the waves will end by swallowing him up.' But Uraschimataro paid no heed to these remarks, and as he was really very clever in managing a boat, the old people were very seldom anxious about him.

One beautiful bright morning, as he was hauling his well-filled nets into the boat, he saw lying among the fishes a tiny little turtle. He was delighted with his prize, and threw it into a wooden vessel to keep till he got home, when suddenly the turtle found its voice, and tremblingly begged for its life. 'After all,' it said, ' what good can I do you? I am so young and small, and I would so gladly live a little longer. Be merciful

[1] From the *Japanische Märchen und Sagen*, von David Brauns (Leipzig : Wilhelm Friedrich).

and set me free, and I shall know how to prove my
gratitude.'

Now Uraschimataro was very good-natured, and besides, he could never bear to say no, so he picked up the
turtle, and put it back into the sea.

Years flew by, and every morning Uraschimataro
sailed his boat into the deep sea. But one day as he was
making for a little bay between some rocks, there arose a
fierce whirlwind, which shattered his boat to pieces, and
she was sucked under by the waves. Uraschimataro
himself very nearly shared the same fate. But he was a
powerful swimmer, and struggled hard to reach the
shore. Then he saw a large turtle coming towards him,
and above the howling of the storm he heard what it
said: 'I am the turtle whose life you once saved. I
will now pay my debt and show my gratitude. The land
is still far distant, and without my help you would
never get there. Climb on my back, and I will take you
where you will.' Uraschimataro did not wait to be asked
twice, and thankfully accepted his friend's help. But
scarcely was he seated firmly on the shell, when the
turtle proposed that they should not return to the shore
at once, but go under the sea, and look at some of the
wonders that lay hidden there.

Uraschimataro agreed willingly, and in another moment
they were deep, deep down, with fathoms of blue water
above their heads. Oh, how quickly they darted through
the still, warm sea! The young man held tight, and
marvelled where they were going and how long they
were to travel, but for three days they rushed on, till
at last the turtle stopped before a splendid palace, shining with gold and silver, crystal and precious stones,
and decked here and there with branches of pale pink
coral and glittering pearls. But if Uraschimataro was
astonished at the beauty of the outside, he was struck
dumb at the sight of the hall within, which was lighted
by the blaze of fish scales.

' Where have you brought me ? ' he asked his guide in a low voice.

' To the palace of Ringu, the house of the sea god, whose subjects we all are,' answered the turtle. ' I am

URASCHIMATARO -
Goes-with-the-TURTLE
to-the-SEA-PRINCESS_

the first waiting maid of his daughter, the lovely princess Otohimé, whom you will shortly see.'

Uraschimataro was still so puzzled with the adventures that had befallen him, that he waited in a dazed condition for what would happen next. But the turtle, who had talked so much of him to the princess that she had expressed a wish to see him, went at once to make known his arrival. And directly the princess beheld him her heart was set on him, and she begged him to stay with her, and in return promised that he should never grow old, neither should his beauty fade. 'Is not that reward enough?' she asked, smiling, looking all the while as fair as the sun itself. And Uraschimataro said 'Yes,' and so he stayed there. For how long? That he only knew later.

His life passed by, and each hour seemed happier than the last, when one day there rushed over him a terrible longing to see his parents. He fought against it hard, knowing how it would grieve the princess, but it grew on him stronger and stronger, till at length he became so sad that the princess inquired what was wrong. Then he told her of the longing he had to visit his old home, and that he must see his parents once more. The princess was almost frozen with horror, and implored him to stay with her, or something dreadful would be sure to happen. 'You will never come back, and we shall meet again no more,' she moaned bitterly. But Uraschimataro stood firm and repeated, 'Only this once will I leave you, and then will I return to your side for ever.' Sadly the princess shook her head, but she answered slowly, 'One way there is to bring you safely back, but I fear you will never agree to the conditions of the bargain.'

'I will do anything that will bring me back to you,' exclaimed Uraschimataro, looking at her tenderly, but the princess was silent: she knew too well that when he left her she would see his face no more. Then she took from a shelf a tiny golden box, and gave it to Uraschimataro, praying him to keep it carefully, and above all things never to open it. 'If you can do this,' she said as she bade him farewell, 'your friend the turtle will meet you at the shore, and will carry you back to me.'

HOW URASCHIMATARO MET PRINCESS OTOKIME

Uraschimataro thanked her from his heart, and swore solemnly to do her bidding. He hid the box safely in his garments, seated himself on the back of the turtle, and vanished in the ocean path, waving his hand to the princess. Three days and three nights they swam through the sea, and at length Uraschimataro arrived at the beach which lay before his old home. The turtle bade him farewell, and was gone in a moment.

Uraschimataro drew near to the village with quick and joyful steps. He saw the smoke curling through the roof, and the thatch where green plants had thickly sprouted. He heard the children shouting and calling, and from a window that he passed came the twang of the koto, and everything seemed to cry a welcome for his return. Yet suddenly he felt a pang at his heart as he wandered down the street. After all, everything was changed. Neither men nor houses were those he once knew. Quickly he saw his old home; yes, it was still there, but it had a strange look. Anxiously he knocked at the door, and asked the woman who opened it after his parents. But she did not know their names, and could give him no news of them.

Still more disturbed, he rushed to the burying ground, the only place that could tell him what he wished to know. Here at any rate he would find out what it all meant. And he was right. In a moment he stood before the grave of his parents, and the date written on the stone was almost exactly the date when they had lost their son, and he had forsaken them for the Daughter of the Sea. And so he found that since he had left his home, three hundred years had passed by.

Shuddering with horror at his discovery he turned back into the village street, hoping to meet some one who could tell him of the days of old. But when the man spoke, he knew he was not dreaming, though he felt as if he had lost his senses.

In despair he bethought him of the box which was

the gift of the princess. Perhaps after all this dreadful thing was not true. He might be the victim of some enchanter's spell, and in his hand lay the counter-charm. Almost unconsciously he opened it, and a purple

vapour came pouring out. He held the empty box in his hand, and as he looked he saw that the fresh hand of youth had grown suddenly shrivelled, like the hand of an old, old man. He ran to the brook, which flowed in a clear stream down from the mountain, and saw himself reflected as in a mirror.   It was the face of a mummy which looked back at him.   Wounded to death, he crept back through the village, and no man knew the old, old man to be the strong handsome youth who had run down the street an hour before.   So he toiled wearily back, till he reached the shore, and here he sat sadly on a rock, and called loudly on the turtle.   But she never came back any more, but instead, death came soon, and set him free.   But before that happened, the people who saw him sitting lonely on the shore had heard his story, and when their children were restless they used to tell them of the good son who from love to his parents had given up for their sakes the splendour and wonders of the palace in the sea, and the most beautiful woman in the world besides.

THE SLAYING OF THE TANUKI [1]

NEAR a big river, and between two high mountains, a man and his wife lived in a cottage a long, long time ago. A dense forest lay all round the cottage, and there was hardly a path or a tree in the whole wood that was not familiar to the peasant from his boyhood. In one of his wanderings he had made friends with a hare, and many an hour the two passed together, when the man was resting by the roadside, eating his dinner.

Now this strange friendship was observed by the Tanuki, a wicked, quarrelsome beast, who hated the peasant, and was never tired of doing him an ill turn. Again and again he had crept to the hut, and finding some choice morsel put away for the little hare, had either eaten it if he thought it nice, or trampled it to pieces so that no one else should get it, and at last the peasant lost patience, and made up his mind he would have the Tanuki's blood.

So for many days the man lay hidden, waiting for the Tanuki to come by, and when one morning he marched up the road thinking of nothing but the dinner he was going to steal, the peasant threw himself upon him and bound his four legs tightly, so that he could not move. Then he dragged his enemy joyfully to the house, feeling that at length he had got the better of the mischievous beast which had done him so many ill turns. 'He shall pay for them with his skin,' he said to his wife. We will first kill him, and then cook him.' So saying, he

---

[1] From the *Japanische Märchen und Sagen*.

hanged the Tanuki, head downwards, to a beam, and went out to gather wood for a fire.

Meanwhile the old woman was standing at the mortar pounding the rice that was to serve them for the week with a pestle that made her arms ache with its weight. Suddenly she heard something whining and weeping in the corner, and, stopping her work, she looked round to see what it was. That was all that the rascal wanted, and he put on directly his most humble air, and begged the woman in his softest voice to loosen his bonds, which were hurting him sorely. She was filled with pity for him, but did not dare to set him free, as she knew that her husband would be very angry. The Tanuki, however, did not despair, and seeing that her heart was softened, began his prayers anew. 'He only asked to have his bonds taken from him,' he said. 'He would give his word not to attempt to escape, and if he was once set free he could soon pound her rice for her.' 'Then you can have a little rest,' he went on, 'for rice pounding is very tiring work, and not at all fit for weak women.' These last words melted the good woman completely, and she unfastened the bonds that held him. Poor foolish creature! In one moment the Tanuki had seized her, stripped off all her clothes, and popped her in the mortar. In a few minutes more she was pounded as fine as the rice ; and not content with that, the Tanuki placed a pot on the hearth and made ready to cook the peasant a dinner from the flesh of his own wife !

When everything was complete he looked out of the door, and saw the old man coming from the forest carrying a large bundle of wood. Quick as lightning the Tanuki not only put on the woman's clothes, but, as he was a magician, assumed her form as well. Then he took the wood, kindled the fire, and very soon set a large dinner before the old man, who was very hungry, and had forgotten for the moment all about his enemy. But when the Tanuki saw that he had eaten his fill and would be

THE TANUKI BEGS THE OLD WOMAN
TO RELEASE HIM

thinking about his prisoner, he hastily shook off the clothes behind a door and took his own shape. Then he said to the peasant, 'You are a nice sort of person to seize animals and to talk of killing them! You are caught in your own net. It is your own wife that you have eaten, and if you want to find her bones you have only to look under the floor.' With these words he turned and made for the forest.

The old peasant grew cold with horror as he listened, and seemed frozen to the place where he stood. When he had recovered himself a little, he collected the bones of his dead wife, buried them in the garden, and swore over the grave to be avenged on the Tanuki. After everything was done he sat himself down in his lonely cottage and wept bitterly, and the bitterest thought of all was that he would never be able to forget that he had eaten his own wife.

While he was thus weeping and wailing his friend the hare passed by, and, hearing the noise, pricked up his ears and soon recognised the old man's voice. He wondered what had happened, and put his head in at the door and asked if anything was the matter. With tears and groans the peasant told him the whole dreadful story, and the hare, filled with anger and compassion, comforted him as best he could, and promised to help him in his revenge. 'The false knave shall not go unpunished,' said he.

So the first thing he did was to search the house for materials to make an ointment, which he sprinkled plentifully with pepper and then put in his pocket. Next he took a hatchet, bade farewell to the old man, and departed to the forest. He bent his steps to the dwelling of the Tanuki and knocked at the door. The Tanuki, who had no cause to suspect the hare, was greatly pleased to see him, for he noticed the hatchet at once, and began to lay plots how to get hold of it.

To do this he thought he had better offer to accompany the hare, which was exactly what the hare wished and expected, for he knew all the Tanuki's cunning, and understood his little ways. So he accepted the rascal's company with joy, and made himself very pleasant as they strolled along. When they were wandering in this manner through the forest the hare carelessly raised his

THE HARE SETS LIGHT TO THE WOOD ON THE TANUKI'S BACK

hatchet in passing, and cut down some thick boughs that were hanging over the path, but at length, after cutting down a good big tree, which cost him many hard blows, he declared that it was too heavy for him to carry home, and he must just leave it where it was. This delighted the greedy Tanuki, who said that they would be no weight for him, so they collected the large branches, which the hare bound tightly on his back. Then he trotted gaily to the house, the hare following after with his lighter bundle.

By this time the hare had decided what he would do, and as soon as they arrived, he quietly set on fire the wood on the back of the Tanuki. The Tanuki, who was busy with something else, observed nothing, and only called out to ask what was the meaning of the crackling that he heard. 'It is just the rattle of the stones which are rolling down the side of the mountain,' the hare said ; and the Tanuki was content, and made no further remarks, never noticing that the noise really sprang from the burning boughs on his back, until his fur was in flames, and it was almost too late to put it out. Shrieking with pain, he let fall the burning wood from his back, and stamped and howled with agony. But the hare comforted him, and told him that he always carried with him an excellent plaster in case of need, which would bring him instant relief, and taking out his ointment he spread it on a leaf of bamboo, and laid it on the wound. No sooner did it touch him than the Tanuki leapt yelling into the air, and the hare laughed, and ran to tell his friend the peasant what a trick he had played on their enemy. But the old man shook his head sadly, for he knew that the villain was only crushed for the moment, and that he would shortly be revenging himself upon them. No, the only way ever to get any peace and quiet was to render the Tanuki harmless for ever. Long did the old man and the hare puzzle together how this was to be done, and at last they decided that they would make two boats, a small one of wood and a large one of clay. Then they fell to work at once, and when the boats were ready and properly painted, the hare went to the Tanuki, who was still very ill, and invited him to a great fish-catching. The Tanuki was still feeling angry with the hare about the trick he had played him, but he was weak and very hungry, so he gladly accepted the proposal, and accompanied the hare to the bank of the river, where the two boats were moored, rocked by the waves. They both looked exactly alike, and the Tanuki only saw that one was bigger than the other, and would hold more fish, so he sprang into the large one, while the hare climbed into the one which was made of wood. They loosened their moorings, and made for the middle of the stream, and when they were at some distance from the bank, the hare took his oar, and struck such a heavy blow at the other boat, that it broke in two. The Tanuki fell straight into the water, and was held there by the hare till he was quite dead. Then he put the body in his boat and rowed to land, and told the old man that his enemy was dead at last. And the old man rejoiced that his wife was avenged, and he took the hare into his house, and they lived together all their days in peace and quietness upon the mountain.

THE FLYING TRUNK [1]

THERE was once a merchant who was so rich that he could have paved the whole street, and perhaps even a little side-street besides, with silver. But he did not do that; he knew another way of spending his money. If he spent a shilling he got back a florin—such an excellent merchant he was—till he died.

Now his son inherited all this money. He lived very merrily; he went every night to the theatre, made paper kites out of five-pound notes, and played ducks and drakes with sovereigns instead of stones. In this way the money was likely to come soon to an end, and so it did.

At last he had nothing left but four shillings, and he had no clothes except a pair of slippers and an old dressing-gown.

His friends did not trouble themselves any more about him; they would not even walk down the street with him.

But one of them who was rather good-natured sent him an old trunk with the message, 'Pack up!' That was all very well, but he had nothing to pack up, so he got into the trunk himself.

It was an enchanted trunk, for as soon as the lock was pressed it could fly. He pressed it, and away he flew in it up the chimney, high into the clouds, further and further away. But whenever the bottom gave a

[1] Translated from the German of Hans Andersen.

little creak he was in terror lest the trunk should go to pieces, for then he would have turned a dreadful somersault—just think of it!

In this way he arrived at the land of the Turks. He hid the trunk in a wood under some dry leaves, and then walked into the town. He could do that quite well, for all the Turks were dressed just as he was—in a dressing-gown and slippers.

He met a nurse with a little child.

'Halloa! you Turkish nurse,' said he, 'what is that great castle there close to the town? The one with the windows so high up?'

'The sultan's daughter lives there,' she replied. 'It is prophesied that she will be very unlucky in her husband, and so no one is allowed to see her except when the sultan and sultana are by.'

'Thank you,' said the merchant's son, and he went into the wood, sat himself in his trunk, flew on to the roof, and crept through the window into the princess's room.

She was lying on the sofa asleep, and was so beautiful that the young merchant *had* to kiss her. Then she woke up and was very much frightened, but he said he was a Turkish god who had come through the air to see her, and that pleased her very much.

They sat close to each other, and he told her a story about her eyes. They were beautiful dark lakes in which her thoughts swam about like mermaids. And her forehead was a snowy mountain, grand and shining. These were lovely stories.

Then he asked the princess to marry him, and she said yes at once.

'But you must come here on Saturday,' she said, 'for then the sultan and the sultana are coming to tea with me. They will be indeed proud that I receive the god of the Turks. But mind you have a really good story ready, for my parents like them immensely. My mother

likes something rather moral and high-flown, and my
father likes something merry to make him laugh.'

'Yes, I shall only bring a fairy story for my dowry,'
said he, and so they parted. But the princess gave him
a sabre set with gold pieces which he could use.

HE TOLD HER STORIES ABOUT HER EYES.

Then he flew away, bought himself a new dressing-
gown, and sat down in the wood and began to make up
a story, for it had to be ready by Saturday, and that was
no easy matter.

When he had it ready it was Saturday.

The sultan, the sultana, and the whole court were at tea with the princess.

He was most graciously received.

'Will you tell us a story?' said the sultana; 'one that is thoughtful and instructive?'

'But something that we can laugh at,' said the sultan.

'Oh, certainly,' he replied, and began : 'Now, listen attentively. There was once a box of matches which lay between a tinder-box and an old iron pot, and they told the story of their youth.

'"We used to be on the green fir-boughs. Every morning and evening we had diamond-tea, which was the dew, and the whole day long we had sunshine, and the little birds used to tell us stories. We were very rich, because the other trees only dressed in summer, but we had green dresses in summer and in winter. Then the woodcutter came, and our family was split up. We have now the task of making light for the lowest people. That is why we grand people are in the kitchen."

'"My fate was quite different," said the iron pot, near which the matches lay.

'"Since I came into the world I have been many times scoured, and have cooked much. My only pleasure is to have a good chat with my companions when I am lying nice and clean in my place after dinner."

'"Now you are talking too fast," spluttered the fire.

'"Yes, let us decide who is the grandest!" said the matches.

'"No, I don't like talking about myself," said the pot.

'"Let us arrange an evening's entertainment. I will tell the story of my life.

'"On the Baltic by the Danish shore——"

'"What a beautiful beginning!" said all the plates. "That's a story that will please us all."

'And the end was just as good as the beginning. All the plates clattered for joy.

' " Now I will dance," said the tongs, and she danced. Oh! how high she could kick!

' The old chair-cover in the corner split when he saw her.

' The urn would have sung but shè said she had a cold; she could not sing unless she boiled.

' In the window was an old quill pen. There was nothing remarkable about her except that she had been dipped too deeply into the ink. But she was very proud of that.

' " If the urn will not sing," said she, " outside the door hangs a nightingale in a cage who will sing."

' " *I* don't think it's proper," said the kettle, " that such a foreign bird should be heard."

' " Oh, let us have some acting," said everyone. " Do let us ! "

' Suddenly the door opened and the maid came in. Everyone was quite quiet. There was not a sound. But each pot knew what he might have done, and how grand he was.

' The maid took the matches and lit the fire with them. How they spluttered and flamed, to be sure! " Now everyone can see," they thought, " that we are the grandest! How we sparkle! What a light——"

' But here they were burnt out.'

' That was a delightful story ! ' said the sultana. ' I quite feel myself in the kitchen with the matches. Yes, now you shall marry our daughter.'

' Yes, indeed,' said the sultan, ' you shall marry our daughter on Monday.' And they treated the young man as one of the family.

The wedding was arranged, and the night before the whole town was illuminated.

Biscuits and gingerbreads were thrown among the people, the street boys stood on tiptoe crying hurrahs and whistling through their fingers. It was all splendid.

' Now I must also give them a treat,' thought the

THE PRINCESS WAITED ALL DAY ON THE ROOF

merchant's son. And so he bought rockets, crackers, and
all the kinds of fireworks you can think of, put them in
his trunk, and flew up with them into the air.

Whirr-r-r, how they fizzed and blazed!

All the Turks jumped so high that their slippers flew
above their heads ; such a splendid glitter they had never
seen before.

Now they could quite well understand that it was the
god of the Turks himself who was to marry the princess.

As soon as the young merchant came down again into
the wood with his trunk he thought, ' Now I will just go
into the town to see how the show has taken.'

And it was quite natural that he should want to do
this.

Oh ! what stories the people had to tell !

Each one whom he asked had seen it differently, but
they had all found it beautiful.

' I saw the Turkish god himself,' said one. ' He had
eyes like glittering stars, and a beard like foaming water.'

' He flew away in a cloak of fire,' said another.
They were splendid things that he heard, and the next
day was to be his wedding day.

Then he went back into the wood to sit in his trunk ;
but what had become of it ? The trunk had been burnt.
A spark of the fireworks had set it alight, and the trunk
was in ashes. He could no longer fly, and could never
reach his bride.

She stood the whole day long on the roof and waited ;
perhaps she is waiting there still.

But he wandered through the world and told stories ;
though they are not so merry as the one he told about the
matches.

THE SNOW-MAN [1]

'How astonishingly cold it is! My body is cracking all
over!' said the Snow-man. 'The wind is really cutting
one's very life out! And how that fiery thing up there
glares!' He meant the sun, which was just setting.
'It sha'n't make me blink, though, and I shall keep quite
cool and collected.'

Instead of eyes he had two large three-cornered pieces
of slate in his head; his mouth consisted of an old rake,
so that he had teeth as well.

He was born amidst the shouts and laughter of the
boys, and greeted by the jingling bells and cracking
whips of the sledges.

The sun went down, the full moon rose, large, round,
clear and beautiful, in the dark blue sky.

'There it is again on the other side!' said the Snow-
man, by which he meant the sun was appearing again.
'I have become quite accustomed to its glaring. I hope
it will hang there and shine, so that I may be able to see
myself. I wish I knew, though, how one ought to set
about changing one's position. I should very much like
to move about. If I only could, I would glide up and
down the ice there, as I saw the boys doing; but somehow or other, I don't know how to run.'

'Bow-wow!' barked the old yard-dog; he was rather
hoarse and couldn't bark very well. His hoarseness

[1] Translated from the German of Hans Christian Andersen.

came on when he was a house-dog and used to lie in front of the stove. 'The sun will soon teach you to run! I saw that last winter with your predecessor, and farther back still with *his* predecessors! They have all run away!'

'I don't understand you, my friend,' said the Snow-man. 'That thing up there is to teach me to run?' He meant the moon. 'Well, it certainly did run just now, for I saw it quite plainly over there, and now here it is on this side.'

'You know nothing at all about it,' said the yard-dog. 'Why, you have only just been made. The thing you see there is the moon; the other thing you saw going down the other side was the sun. He will come up again to-morrow morning, and will soon teach you how to run away down the gutter. The weather is going to change; I feel it already by the pain in my left hind-leg; the weather is certainly going to change.'

'I can't understand him,' said the Snow-man; 'but I have an idea that he is speaking of something unpleasant. That thing that glares so, and then disappears, the sun, as he calls it, is not my friend. I know that by instinct.'

'Bow-wow!' barked the yard-dog, and walked three times round himself, and then crept into his kennel to sleep. The weather really did change. Towards morning a dense damp fog lay over the whole neighbourhood; later on came an icy wind, which sent the frost packing. But when the sun rose, it was a glorious sight. The trees and shrubs were covered with rime, and looked like a wood of coral, and every branch was thick with long white blossoms. The most delicate twigs, which are lost among the foliage in summer-time, came now into prominence, and it was like a spider's web of glistening white. The lady-birches waved in the wind; and when the sun shone, everything glittered and sparkled as if it were sprinkled with diamond dust, and great diamonds were lying on the snowy carpet.

"The Sun will soon teach you to run" said the Yard-dog.

'Isn't it wonderful?' exclaimed a girl who was walking with a young man in the garden. They stopped near the Snow-man, and looked at the glistening trees. 'Summer cannot show a more beautiful sight,' she said, with her eyes shining.

'And one can't get a fellow like this in summer either,' said the young man, pointing to the Snow-man. 'He's a beauty!'

The girl laughed, and nodded to the Snow-man, and then they both danced away over the snow.

'Who were those two?' asked the Snow-man of the yard-dog. 'You have been in this yard longer than I have. Do you know who they are?'

'Do I know them indeed?' answered the yard-dog. 'She has often stroked me, and he has given me bones. I don't bite either of them!'

'But what are they?' asked the Snow-man.

'Lovers!' replied the yard-dog. 'They will go into one kennel and gnaw the same bone!'

'Are they the same kind of beings that we are?' asked the Snow-man.

'They are our masters,' answered the yard-dog. 'Really people who have only been in the world one day know very little! That's the conclusion I have come to. Now *I* have age and wisdom; I know everyone in the house, and I can remember a time when I was not lying here in a cold kennel. Bow-wow!'

'The cold is splendid,' said the Snow-man. 'Tell me some more. But don't rattle your chain so, it makes me crack!'

'Bow-wow!' barked the yard-dog. 'They used to say I was a pretty little fellow; then I lay in a velvet-covered chair in my master's house. My mistress used to nurse me, and kiss and fondle me, and call me her dear, sweet little Alice! But by-and-by I grew too big, and I was given to the housekeeper, and I went into the kitchen. You can see into it from where you are standing;

you can look at the room in which I was master, for so I
was when I was with the housekeeper. Of course it was
a smaller place than upstairs, but it was more comfortable,
for I wasn't chased about and teased by the children as I
had been before. My food was just as good, or even
better. I had my own pillow, and there was a stove there,
which at this time of year is the most beautiful thing in
the world. I used to creep right under that stove. Ah
me! I often dream of that stove still! Bow-wow!'

'Is a stove so beautiful?' asked the Snow-man. 'Is
it anything like me?'

'It is just the opposite of you! It is coal-black, and
has a long neck with a brass pipe. It eats firewood, so
that fire spouts out of its mouth. One has to keep close
beside it—quite underneath is the nicest of all. You can
see it through the window from where you are standing.'

And the Snow-man looked in that direction, and saw a
smooth polished object with a brass pipe. The flicker
from the fire reached him across the snow. The Snow-
man felt wonderfully happy, and a feeling came over him
which he could not express ; but all those who are not
snow-men know about it.

'Why did you leave her?' asked the Snow-man. He
had a feeling that such a being must be a lady. 'How
could you leave such a place?'

'I had to!' said the yard-dog. 'They turned me out
of doors, and chained me up here. I had bitten the
youngest boy in the leg, because he took away the bone I
was gnawing ; a bone for a bone, I thought! But they
were very angry, and from that time I have been chained
here, and I have lost my voice. Don't you hear how
hoarse I am? Bow-wow! I can't speak like other dogs.
Bow-wow! That was the end of happiness!'

The Snow-man, however, was not listening to him any
more ; he was looking into the room where the housekeeper lived, where the stove stood on its four iron legs,
and seemed to be just the same size as the Snow-man.

'How something is cracking inside me!' he said.
'Shall I never be able to get in there? It is certainly a
very innocent wish, and our innocent wishes ought to be
fulfilled. I must get there, and lean against the stove, if
I have to break the window first!'

'You will never get inside there!' said the yard-dog;
'and if you were to reach the stove you would disappear.
Bow-wow!'

'I'm as good as gone already!' answered the Snow-
man. 'I believe I'm breaking up!'

The whole day the Snow-man looked through the
window; towards dusk the room grew still more inviting;
the stove gave out a mild light, not at all like the moon or
even the sun; no, as only a stove can shine, when it has
something to feed upon. When the door of the room was
open, it flared up—this was one of its peculiarities; it
flickered quite red upon the Snow-man's white face.

'I can't stand it any longer!' he said. 'How
beautiful it looks with its tongue stretched out like that!'

It was a long night, but the Snow-man did not find it
so; there he stood, wrapt in his pleasant thoughts, and
they froze, so that he cracked.

Next morning the panes of the kitchen window were
covered with ice, and the most beautiful ice-flowers that
even a snow-man could desire, only they blotted out the
stove. The window would not open; he couldn't see the
stove which he thought was such a lovely lady. There
was a cracking and cracking inside him and all around;
there was just such a frost as a snow-man would delight
in. But this Snow-man was different: how could he feel
happy?

'Yours is a bad illness for a Snow-man!' said the
yard-dog. 'I also suffered from it, but I have got over
it. Bow-wow!' he barked. 'The weather is going to
change!' he added.

The weather did change. There came a thaw.

When this set in the Snow-man set off. He did not

say anything, and he did not complain, and those are bad signs.

One morning he broke up altogether. And lo ! where he had stood there remained a broomstick standing upright, round which the boys had built him !

'Ah ! now I understand why he loved the stove,' said the yard-dog. ' That is the raker they use to clean out the stove ! The Snow-man had a stove-raker in his body ! That's what was the matter with him ! And now it's all over with him ! Bow-wow ! '

And before long it was all over with the winter too ! 'Bow-wow ! ' barked the hoarse yard-dog.

But the young girl sang :

> Woods, your bright green garments don !
> Willows, your woolly gloves put on !
> Lark and cuckoo, daily sing—
> February has brought the spring !
> My heart joins in your song so sweet ;
> Come out, dear sun, the world to greet !

And no one thought of the Snow-man.

THE SHIRT-COLLAR [1]

THERE was once a fine gentleman whose entire worldly possessions consisted of a boot-jack and a hair-brush; but he had the most beautiful shirt-collar in the world, and it is about this that we are going to hear a story.

The shirt-collar was so old that he began to think about marrying; and it happened one day that he and a garter came into the wash-tub together.

'Hulloa!' said the shirt-collar, 'never before have I seen anything so slim and delicate, so elegant and pretty! May I be permitted to ask your name?'

'I shan't tell you,' said the garter.

'Where is the place of your abode?' asked the shirt-collar.

But the garter was of a bashful disposition, and did not think it proper to answer.

'Perhaps you are a girdle?' said the shirt-collar—'an under girdle? for I see that you are for use as well as for ornament, my pretty miss!'

'You ought not to speak to me!' said the garter; 'I'm sure I haven't given you any encouragement!'

'When anyone is as beautiful as you,' said the shirt-collar, 'is not that encouragement enough?'

'Go away, don't come so close!' said the garter. 'You seem to be a gentleman!'

'So I am, and a very fine one too!' said the shirt-collar; 'I possess a boot-jack and a hair-brush!'

[1] Translated from the German of Hans Christian Andersen.

That was not true; it was his master who owned
these things; but he was a terrible boaster.

'Don't come so close,' said the garter. 'I'm not
accustomed to such treatment!'

'What affectation!' said the shirt-collar. And then
they were taken out of the wash-tub, starched, and hung
on a chair in the sun to dry, and then laid on the ironing-
board. Then came the glowing iron.

'Mistress widow!' said the shirt-collar, 'dear mistress
widow! I am becoming another man, all my creases
are coming out; you are burning a hole in me! Ugh!
Stop, I implore you!'

'You rag!' said the iron, travelling proudly over the
shirt-collar, for it thought it was a steam-engine and
ought to be at the station drawing trucks.

'Rag!' it said.

The shirt-collar was rather frayed out at the edge, so
the scissors came to cut off the threads.

'Oh!' said the shirt-collar, 'you must be a dancer!
How high you can kick! That is the most beautiful
thing I have ever seen! No man can imitate you!'

'I know that!' said the scissors.

'You ought to be a duchess!' said the shirt-collar.
'My worldly possessions consist of a fine gentleman, a
boot-jack, and a hair-brush. If only I had a duchy!'

'What! He wants to marry me?' said the scissors,
and she was so angry that she gave the collar a sharp
snip, so that it had to be cast aside as good for nothing.

'Well, I shall have to propose to the hair-brush!'
thought the shirt-collar. 'It is really wonderful what
fine hair you have, madam! Have you never thought of
marrying?'

'Yes, that I have!' answered the hair-brush; 'I'm
engaged to the boot-jack!'

'Engaged!' exclaimed the shirt-collar. And now
there was no one he could marry, so he took to despising
matrimony.

Time passed, and the shirt-collar came in a rag-bag to the paper-mill. There was a large assortment of rags, the fine ones in one heap, and the coarse ones in another, as they should be. They had all much to tell, but no one more than the shirt-collar, for he was a hopeless braggart.

'I have had a terrible number of love affairs!' he said. 'They gave me no peace. I was such a fine gentleman, so stiff with starch! I had a boot-jack and a hair-brush, which I never used! You should just have seen me then! Never shall I forget my first love! She was a girdle, so delicate and soft and pretty! She threw herself into a wash-tub for my sake! Then there was a widow, who glowed with love for me. But I left her alone, till she became black. Then there was the dancer, who inflicted the wound which has caused me to be here now; she was very violent! My own hair-brush was in love with me, and lost all her hair in consequence. Yes, I have experienced much in that line; but I grieve most of all for the garter,—I mean, the girdle, who threw herself into a wash-tub. I have much on my conscience; it is high time for me to become white paper!'

And so he did! he became white paper, the very paper on which this story is printed. And that was because he had boasted so terribly about things which were not true. We should take this to heart, so that it may not happen to us, for we cannot indeed tell if we may not some day come to the rag-bag, and be made into white paper, on which will be printed our whole history, even the most secret parts, so that we too go about the world relating it, like the shirt-collar.

THE PRINCESS IN THE CHEST [1]

THERE were once a king and a queen who lived in a beautiful castle, and had a large, and fair, and rich, and happy land to rule over. From the very first they loved each other greatly, and lived very happily together, but they had no heir.

They had been married for seven years, but had neither son nor daughter, and that was a great grief to both of them. More than once it happened that when the king was in a bad temper, he let it out on the poor queen, and said that here they were now, getting old, and neither they nor the kingdom had an heir, and it was all her fault. This was hard to listen to, and she went and cried and vexed herself.

Finally, the king said to her one day, ' This can't be borne any longer. I go about childless, and it's your fault. I am going on a journey and shall be away for a year. If you have a child when I come back again, all will be well, and I shall love you beyond all measure, and never more say an angry word to you. But if the nest is just as empty when I come home, then I must part with you.'

After the king had set out on his journey, the queen went about in her loneliness, and sorrowed and vexed herself more than ever. At last her maid said to her one day, ' I think that some help could be found, if your majesty would seek it.' Then she told about a wise old woman in that country, who had helped many in troubles

[1] Translated from the Danish.

of the same kind, and could no doubt help the queen as
well, if she would send for her. The queen did so, and
the wise woman came, and to her she confided her
sorrow, that she, was childless, and the king and his
kingdom had no heir.

The wise woman knew help for this. ' Out in the
king's garden,' said she, ' under the great oak that stands
on the left hand, just as one goes out from the castle, is a
little bush, rather brown than green, with hairy leaves
and long spikes. On that bush there are just at this
moment three buds. If your majesty goes out there
alone, fasting, before sunrise, and takes the middle one
of the three buds, and eats it, then in six months you
will bring a princess into the world. As soon as she is
born, she must have a nurse, whom I shall provide, and
this nurse must live with the child in a secluded part of
the palace ; no other person must visit the child ; neither
the king nor the queen must see it until it is fourteen
years old, for that would cause great sorrow and misfortune.'

The queen rewarded the old woman richly, and next
morning, before the sun rose, she was down in the
garden, found at once the little bush with the three buds,
plucked the middle one and ate it. It was sweet to
taste, but afterwards was as bitter as gall. Six months
after this, she brought into the world a little girl. There
was a nurse in readiness, whom the wise woman had
provided, and preparations were made for her living with
the child, quite alone, in a secluded wing of the castle,
looking out on the pleasure-park. The queen did as the
wise woman had told her ; she gave up the child immediately, and the nurse took it and lived with it there.

When the king came home and heard that a daughter
had been born to him, he was of course very pleased and
happy, and wanted to see her at once.

The queen had then to tell him this much of the
story, that it had been foretold that it would cause great

sorrow and misfortune if either he or she got a sight of the child until it had completed its fourteenth year.

This was a long time to wait. The king longed so much to get a sight of his daughter, and the queen no less than he, but she knew that it was not like other children, for it could speak immediately after it was born, and was

The Queen eats the Magic bud

as wise as older folk. This the nurse had told her, for with her the queen had a talk now and again, but there was no one else who had ever seen the princess. The queen had also seen what the wise woman could do, so she insisted strongly that her warning should be obeyed. The king often lost his patience, and was determined to see his daughter, but the queen always put him off the

idea, and so things went on, until the very day before
the princess completed her fourteenth year.

The king and the queen were out in the garden then,
and the king said, ' Now I *can't* and I *won't* wait any
longer. I *must* see my daughter *at once.* A few hours,
more or less, can't make any difference.'

The queen begged him to have patience till the
morning. When they had waited so long, they could
surely wait a single day more. But the king was quite
unreasonable. ' No nonsense,' said he ; ' she is just as
much mine as yours, and I *will* see her,' and with that
he went straight up to her room.

He burst the door open, and pushed aside the nurse,
who tried to stop him, and there he saw his daughter.
She was the loveliest young princess, red and white, like
milk and blood, with clear blue eyes and golden hair,
but right in the middle of her forehead there was a little
tuft of brown hair.

The princess went to meet her father, fell on his neck
and kissed him, but with that she said, ' O father, father !
what have you done now ? to-morrow I must die, and
you must choose one of three things : either the land
must be smitten by the black pestilence, or you must
have a long and bloody war, or you must, as soon as I
am dead, lay me in a plain wooden chest, and set it in
the church, and for a whole year place a sentinel beside
it every night.'

The king was frightened indeed, and thought she was
raving, but in order to please her, he said, ' Well, of these
three things I shall choose the last ; if you die, I shall
lay you at once in a plain wooden chest, and have it set
in the church, and every night I shall place a sentinel
beside it. But you shall not die, even if you are ill now.'

He immediately summoned all the best doctors in
the country, and they came with all their prescriptions
and their medicine bottles, but next day the princess was
stiff and cold in death. All the doctors could certify to

that, and they all put their names to this and appended
their seals, and then they had done all they could.

The king kept his promise. The princess's body was
lain the same day in a plain wooden chest, and set in
the chapel of the castle, and on that night and every
night after it, a sentinel was posted in the church, to
keep watch over the chest.

The first morning when they came to let the sentinel
out, there was no sentinel there. They thought he had
just got frightened and run away, and next evening a
new one was posted in the church. In the morning he
was also gone. So it went every night. When they
came in the morning to let the sentinel out, there was no
one there, and it was impossible to discover which way
he had gone if he had run away. And what should they
run away for, every one of them, so that nothing more
was ever heard or seen of them, from the hour that they
were set on guard beside the princess's chest?

It became now a general belief that the princess's
ghost walked, and ate up all those who were to guard
her chest, and very soon there was no one left who
would be placed on this duty, and the king's soldiers
deserted the service, before their turn came to be her
bodyguard. The king then promised a large reward to
the soldier who would volunteer for the post. This did
for some time, as there were found a few reckless fellows,
who wished to earn this good payment. But they never
got it, for in the morning they too had disappeared like
the rest.

So it had gone on for something like a whole year ;
every night a sentinel had been placed beside the chest,
either by compulsion or of his own free will, but not a
single one of the sentinels was to be seen, either on the
following day or any time thereafter. And so it had also
gone with one, on the night before a certain day, when a
merry young smith came wandering to the town where
the king's castle stood. It was the capital of the country,

and people of every kind came to it to get work. This
smith, whose name was Christian, had come for that
same purpose. There was no work for him in the place
he belonged to, and he wanted now to seek a place in the
capital.

There he entered an inn where he sat down in the
public room, and got something to eat. Some under-
officers were sitting there, who were out to try to get
some one enlisted to stand sentry. They had to go in
this way, day after day, and hitherto they had always
succeeded in finding one or other reckless fellow. But
on this day they had, as yet, found no one. It was too
well known how all the sentinels disappeared, who were
set on that post, and all that they had got hold of had
refused with thanks. These sat down beside Christian,
and ordered drinks, and drank along with him. Now
Christian was a merry fellow who liked good company;
he could both drink and sing, and talk and boast as well,
when he got a little drop in his head. He told these
under-officers that he was one of that kind of folk who
never are afraid of anything. Then he was just the kind
of man they liked, said they, and he might easily earn a
good penny, before he was a day older, for the king paid
a hundred dollars to anyone who would stand as sentinel
in the church all night, beside his daughter's chest.

Christian was not afraid of *that*—*he* wasn't afraid of
anything, so they drank another bottle of wine on this,
and Christian went with them up to the colonel, where
he was put into uniform, with musket, and all the rest,
and was then shut up in the church, to stand as sentinel
that night.

It was eight o'clock when he took up his post, and
for the first hour he was quite proud of his courage;
during the second hour he was well pleased with the
large reward that he would get, but in the third hour,
when it was getting near eleven, the effects of the wine
passed off, and he began to get uncomfortable, for he

had heard about this post; that no one had ever escaped alive from it, so far as was known. But neither did anyone know what had become of all the sentinels. The thought of this ran in his head so much, after the wine was out of it, that he searched about everywhere for a way of escape, and finally, at eleven o'clock, he found a little postern in the steeple which was not locked, and out at this he crept, intending to run away.

At the same moment as he put his foot outside the church door, he saw standing before him a little man, who said, ' Good evening, Christian, where are *you* going?'

With that he felt as if he were rooted to the spot and could not move.

' Nowhere,' said he.

' Oh, yes,' said the little man, ' You were just about to run away, but you have taken upon you to stand sentinel in the church to-night, and there you must stay.'

Christian said, very humbly, that he dared not, and therefore wanted to get away, and begged to be let go.

' No,' said the little one, ' you must remain at your post, but I shall give you a piece of good advice ; you shall go up into the pulpit, and remain standing there. You need never mind what you see or hear, it will not be able to do you any harm, if you remain in your place until you hear the lid of the chest slam down again behind the dead : then all danger is past, and you can go about the church, wherever you please.'

The little man then pushed him in at the door again, and locked it after him. Christian made haste to get up into the pulpit, and stood there, without noticing anything, until the clock struck twelve. Then the lid of the princess's chest sprang up, and out of it there came something like the princess, dressed as you see in the picture. It shrieked and howled, ' Sentry, where are you? Sentry, where are you? If you don't come, you shall get the most cruel death anyone has ever got.'

It went all round the church, and when it finally caught sight of the smith, up in the pulpit, it came rushing thither and mounted the steps. But it could not get up the whole way, and for all that it stretched and strained, it could not touch Christian, who meanwhile stood and trembled up in the pulpit. When the clock struck one, the appearance had to go back into the chest again, and Christian heard the lid slam after it. After this there was dead silence in the church. He lay down where he was and fell asleep, and did not awake before it was bright daylight, and he heard steps outside, and the noise of the key being put into the lock. Then he came down from the pulpit, and stood with his musket in front of the princess's chest.

It was the colonel himself who came with the patrol, and he was not a little surprised when he found the recruit safe and sound. He wanted to have a report, but Christian would give him none, so he took him straight up to the king, and announced for the first time that here was the sentinel who had stood guard in the church over-night. The king immediately got out of bed, and laid the hundred dollars for him on the table, and then wanted to question him. 'Have you seen anything?' said he. 'Have you seen my daughter?' 'I have stood at my post,' said the young smith, 'and that is quite enough; I undertook nothing more.' He was not sure whether he dared tell what he had seen and heard, and besides he was also a little conceited because he had done what no other man had been able to do, or had had courage for. The king professed to be quite satisfied, and asked him whether he would engage himself to stand on guard again the following night. 'No, thank you,' said Christian, 'I will have no more of that!'

'As you please,' said the king, 'you have behaved like a brave fellow, and now you shall have your breakfast. You must be needing something to strengthen you after *that* turn.'

The king had breakfast laid for him, and sat down at the table with him in person ; he kept constantly filling his glass for him and praising him, and drinking his health. Christian needed no pressing, but did full justice both to the food and drink, and not least to the latter. Finally he grew bold, and said that if the king would give him two hundred dollars for it, he was his man to stand sentry next night as well.

When this was arranged, Christian bade him ' Good-day,' and went down among the guards, and then out into the town along with other soldiers and under-officers. He had his pocket full of money, and treated them, and drank with them and boasted and made game of the good-for-nothings who were afraid to stand on guard, because they were frightened that the dead princess would eat them. See whether she had eaten *him !* So the day passed in mirth and glee, but when eight o'clock came, Christian was again shut up in the church, all alone.

Before he had been there two hours, he got tired of it, and thought only of getting away. He found a little door behind the altar which was not locked, and at ten o'clock he slipped out at it, and took to his heels and made for the beach. He had got half-way thither, when all at once the same little man stood in front of him and said, ' Good evening, Christian, where are *you* going ? ' ' I've leave to go where I please,' said the smith, but at the same time he noticed that he could not move a foot. ' No, you have undertaken to keep guard to-night as well,' said the little man, ' and you must attend to that.' He then took hold of him, and, however unwilling he was, Christian had to go with him right back to the same little door that he had crept out at. When they got there, the little man said to him, ' Go in front of the altar now, and take in your hand the book that is lying there. There you shall stay till you hear the lid of the chest slam down over the dead. In that way you will come to no harm.'

With that, the little man shoved him in at the door, and locked it. Christian then immediately went in front of the altar, and took the book in his hand, and stood thus until the clock struck twelve, and the appearance sprang out of the chest. ' Sentry, where are you? Sentry, where are you?' it shrieked, and then rushed to the pulpit, and right up into it. But there was no one there that night. Then it howled and shrieked again,

> My father has set no sentry in,
> War and Pest this night begin.

At the same moment, it noticed the smith standing in front of the altar, and came rushing towards him. 'Are you there?' it screamed; 'now I'll catch you.' But it could not come up over the step in front of the altar, and there it continued to howl, and scream, and threaten, until the clock struck one, when it had to go into the chest again, and Christian heard the lid slam above it. That night, however, it had not the same appearance as on the previous one; it was less ugly.

When all was quiet in the church, the smith lay down before the altar and slept calmly till the following morning, when the colonel came to fetch him. He was taken up to the king again, and things went as on the day before. He got his money, but would give no explanation whether he had seen the king's daughter, and he would not take the post again, he said. But after he had got a good breakfast, and tasted well of the king's wines, he undertook to go on guard again the third night, but he would not do it for less than the half of the kingdom, he said, for it was a dangerous post, and the king had to agree, and promise him this.

The remainder of the day went like the previous one. He played the boastful soldier, and the merry smith, and he had comrades and boon-companions in plenty. At eight o'clock he had to put on his uniform again, and was shut up in the church. He had not been there for an hour before he had come to his senses, and thought, 'It's best to stop now, while the game is going well.' The third night, he was sure, would be the worst; he had been drunk when he promised it, and the half of the kingdom, the king could never have been in earnest about *that !* So he decided to leave, without waiting so long as on the previous nights. In that way he would escape the little man who had watched him before. All the doors and posterns were locked, but he finally thought of creeping up to a window, and opening that, and as the clock struck nine, he crept out there. It was fairly high in the wall, but he got to the ground with no bones broken, and started to run. He got down to the shore without meeting anyone, and there he got into a boat, and pushed off from land. He laughed immensely to himself at the thought of how cleverly he had managed and how he had cheated the little man. Just then he heard a voice from the shore, 'Good evening, Christian, where are *you* going?' He gave no answer. 'To-night your legs will be too short,' he thought, and pulled at the oars. But he then felt something lay hold of the boat, and drag it straight in to shore, for all that he sat and struggled with the oars.

The man then laid hold of him, and said, ' You must remain at your post, as you have promised,' and whether he liked it or not, Christian had just to go back with him the whole way to the church.

He could never get in at that window again, Christian said; it was far too high up.

'You *must* go in there, and you *shall* go in there,' said the little man, and with that he lifted him up on to the window-sill. Then he said to him: 'Notice well now what you have to do. This evening you must stretch yourself out on the left-hand side of her chest. The lid opens to the right, and she comes out to the left. When she has got out of the chest and passed over you, you must get into it and lie there, and *that* in a hurry, without her seeing you. There you must remain lying until day dawns, and whether she threatens or entreats you, you must not come out of it, or give her any answer. Then she has no power over you, and both you and she are freed.'

The smith then had to go in at the window, just as he came out, and went and laid himself all his length on the left side of the princess's chest, close up to it, and there he lay as stiff as a rock until the clock struck twelve. Then the lid sprang up to the right, and the princess came out, straight over him, and rushed round the church, howling and shrieking 'Sentry, where are you? Sentry, where are you?' She went towards the altar, and right up to it, but there was no one there; then she screamed again,

> My father has set no sentry in,
> War and Pest will now begin.

Then she went round the whole church, both up and down, sighing and weeping,

> My father has set no sentry in,
> War and Pest will now begin.

Then she went away again, and at the same moment the clock in the tower struck one.

Then the smith heard in the church a soft music, which grew louder and louder, and soon filled the whole building. He heard also a multitude of footsteps, as if the church was being filled with people. He heard the priest go through the service in front of the altar, and there was singing more beautiful than he had ever heard before. Then he also heard the priest offer up a prayer of thanksgiving because the land had been freed from war and pestilence, and from all misfortune, and the king's daughter was delivered from the evil one. Many voices joined in, and a hymn of praise was sung; then he heard the priest again, and heard his own name and that of the princess, and thought that he was being wedded to her. The church was packed full, but he could see nothing. Then he heard again the many footsteps as of folk leaving the church, while the music sounded fainter and fainter, until it altogether died away. When it was silent, the light of day began to break in through the windows.

The smith sprang up out of the chest and fell on his knees and thanked God. The church was empty, but up in front of the altar lay the princess, white and red, like a human being, but sobbing and crying, and shaking with cold in her white shroud. The smith took his sentry coat and wrapped it round her; then she dried her tears, and took his hand and thanked him, and said that he had now freed her from all the sorcery that had been in her from her birth, and which had come over her again when her father broke the command against seeing her until she had completed her fourteenth year.

She said further, that if he who had delivered her would take her in marriage, she would be his. If not, she would go into a nunnery, and he could marry no other as long as she lived, for he was wedded to her with the service of the dead, which he had heard.

She was now the most beautiful young princess that anyone could wish to see, and he was now lord of half the kingdom, which had been promised him for standing on guard the third night. So they agreed that they would have each other, and love each other all their days.

With the first sunbeam the watch came and opened the church, and not only was the colonel there, but the king in person, come to see what had happened to the sentinel. He found them both sitting hand in hand on the step in front of the altar, and immediately knew his daughter again, and took her in his arms, thanking God and her deliverer. He made no objections to what they had arranged, and so Christian the smith held his wedding

HE WRAPT HER IN HIS SOLDIER'S CLOAK.

with the princess, and got half the kingdom at once, and the whole of it when the king died.

As for the other sentries, with so many doors and windows open, no doubt they had run away, and gone into the Prussian service. And as for what Christian said he saw, he had been drinking more wine than was good for him.

THE THREE BROTHERS[1]

THERE was once a man who had three sons, and no other possessions beyond the house in which he lived. Now the father loved his three sons equally, so that he could not make up his mind which of them should have the house after his death, because he did not wish to favour any one more than the others. And he did not want to sell the house, because it had belonged to his family for generations ; otherwise he could have divided the money equally amongst them. At last an idea struck him, and he said to his sons : ' You must all go out into the world, and look about you, and each learn a trade, and then, when you return, whoever can produce the best masterpiece shall have the house.'

The sons were quite satisfied. The eldest wished to be a blacksmith, the second a barber, and the third a fencing-master. They appointed a time when they were to return home, and then they all set out.

It so happened that each found a good master, where he learnt all that was necessary for his trade in the best possible way. The blacksmith had to shoe the king's horses, and thought to himself, ' Without doubt the house will be yours ! ' The barber shaved the best men in the kingdom, and he, too, made sure that the house would be his. The fencing-master received many a blow, but he set his teeth, and would not allow himself to be

Translated from the German of the Brothers Grimm.

troubled by them, for he thought to himself, 'If you are afraid of a blow you will never get the house.'

When the appointed time had come the three brothers met once more, and they sat down and discussed the best opportunity of showing off their skill. Just then a hare came running across the field towards them. 'Look!' said the barber, 'here comes something in the nick of time!' seized basin and soap, made a lather whilst the hare was approaching, and then, as it ran at full tilt, shaved its moustaches, without cutting it or injuring a single hair on its body.

'I like that very much indeed,' said the father. 'Unless the others exert themselves to the utmost, the house will be yours.'

Soon after they saw a man driving a carriage furiously towards them. 'Now, father, you shall see what I can do!' said the blacksmith, and he sprang after the carriage, tore off the four shoes of the horse as it was going at the top of its speed, and shod it with four new ones without checking its pace.

'You are a clever fellow!' said the father, 'and know your trade as well as your brother. I really don't know to which of you I shall give the house.'

Then the third son said, 'Father, let me also show you something;' and, as it was beginning to rain, he drew his sword and swung it in cross cuts above his head, so that not a drop fell on him, and the rain fell heavier and heavier, till at last it was coming down like a waterspout, but he swung his sword faster and faster, and kept as dry as if he were under cover.

When the father saw this he was astonished, and said, 'You have produced the greatest masterpiece: the house is yours.'

Both the other brothers were quite satisfied, and praised him too, and as they were so fond of each other they all three remained at home and plied their trades; and as they were so experienced and skilful they earned a great deal of money. So they lived happily together till they were quite old, and when one was taken ill and died the two others were so deeply grieved that they were also taken ill and died too. And so, because they had all been so clever, and so fond of each other, they were all laid in one grave.

THE SNOW-QUEEN [1]

THERE was once a dreadfully wicked hobgoblin. One
day he was in capital spirits because he had made a
looking-glass which reflected everything that was good
and beautiful in such a way that it dwindled almost to
nothing, but anything that was bad and ugly stood out
very clearly and looked much worse. The most beautiful
landscapes looked like boiled spinach, and the best
people looked repulsive or seemed to stand on their heads
with no bodies ; their faces were so changed that they
could not be recognised, and if anyone had a freckle you
might be sure it would be spread over the nose and
mouth.

That was the best part of it, said the hobgoblin.

But one day the looking-glass was dropped, and it
broke into a million-billion and more pieces.

And now came the greatest misfortune of all, for each
of the pieces was hardly as large as a grain of sand, and
they flew about all over the world, and if anyone had a
bit in his eye there it stayed, and then he would see
everything awry, or else could only see the bad sides of
a case. For every tiny splinter of the glass possessed
the same power that the whole glass had.

Some people got a splinter in their hearts, and that
was dreadful, for then it began to turn into a lump of ice.

The hobgoblin laughed till his sides ached, but still
the tiny bits of glass flew about.

[1] Translated from the German of Hans Andersen by Miss Alma
Alleyne.

And now we will hear all about it.

In a large town, where there were so many people and houses that there was not room enough for everybody to

The Hobgoblin laughed till his sides ached

have gardens, lived two poor children. They were not brother and sister, but they loved each other just as much as if they were. Their parents lived opposite one another in two attics, and out on the leads they had put two boxes filled with flowers. There were sweet peas in it, and two rose trees, which grew beautifully, and in summer the two children were allowed to take their little chairs and sit out under the roses. Then they had splendid games.

In the winter they could not do this, but then they put hot pennies against the frozen window-panes, and made round holes to look at each other through.

His name was Kay, and hers was Gerda.

Outside it was snowing fast.

'Those are the white bees swarming,' said the old grandmother.

'Have they also a queen bee?' asked the little boy, for he knew that the real bees have one.

'To be sure,' said the grandmother. 'She flies wherever they swarm the thickest. She is larger than any of them, and never stays upon the earth, but flies again up into the black clouds. Often at midnight she flies through the streets, and peeps in at all the windows, and then they freeze in such pretty patterns and look like flowers.'

'Yes, we have seen that,' said both children; they knew that it was true.

'Can the Snow-queen come in here?' asked the little girl.

'Just let her!' cried the boy, 'I would put her on the stove, and melt her!'

But the grandmother stroked his hair, and told some more stories.

In the evening, when little Kay was going to bed, he jumped on the chair by the window, and looked through the little hole. A few snow-flakes were falling outside, and one of them, the largest, lay on the edge of one of the window-boxes. The snow-flake grew larger and larger till it took the form of a maiden, dressed in finest white gauze.

THE SNOW QUEEN APPEARS TO LITTLE KAY

She was so beautiful and dainty, but all of ice, hard bright ice.

Still she was alive; her eyes glittered like two clear stars, but there was no rest or peace in them. She nodded at the window, and beckoned with her hand. The little boy was frightened, and sprang down from the chair. It seemed as if a great white bird had flown past the window.

The next day there was a harder frost than before.

Then came the spring, and then the summer, when the roses grew and smelt more beautifully than ever.

Kay and Gerda were looking at one of their picture-books—the clock in the great church-tower had just struck five, when Kay exclaimed, 'Oh! something has stung my heart, and I've got something in my eye!'

The little girl threw her arms round his neck; he winked hard with both his eyes; no, she could see nothing in them.

'I think it is gone now," said he; but it had not gone. It was one of the tiny splinters of the glass of the magic mirror which we have heard about, that turned everything great and good reflected in it small and ugly. And poor Kay had also a splinter in his heart, and it began to change into a lump of ice. It did not hurt him at all, but the splinter was there all the same.

'Why are you crying?' he asked; 'it makes you look so ugly! There's nothing the matter with me. 'Just look! that rose is all slug-eaten, and this one is stunted! What ugly roses they are!'

And he began to pull them to pieces.

'Kay, what *are* you doing?' cried the little girl.

And when he saw how frightened she was, he pulled off another rose, and ran in at his window away from dear little Gerda.

When she came later on with the picture book, he said that it was only fit for babies, and when his grand-mother told them stories, he was always interrupting with, 'But—' and then he would get behind her and put on her spectacles, and speak just as she did. This he did very well, and everybody laughed. Very soon he could imitate the way all the people in the street walked and talked.

His games were now quite different. On a winter's day he would take a burning glass and hold it out on his blue coat and let the snow-flakes fall on it.

'Look in the glass, Gerda! Just see how regular they are! They are much more interesting than real flowers. Each is perfect; they are all made according to rule. If only they did not melt!'

One morning Kay came out with his warm gloves on, and his little sledge hung over his shoulder. He shouted to Gerda, 'I am going to the market-place to play with the other boys,' and away he went.

In the market-place the boldest boys used often to fasten their sledges to the carts of the farmers, and then they got a good ride.

When they were in the middle of their games there drove into the square a large sledge, all white, and in it sat a figure dressed in a rough white fur pelisse with a white fur cap on.

The sledge drove twice round the square, and Kay fastened his little sledge behind it and drove off. It went quicker and quicker into the next street. The driver turned round, and nodded to Kay in a friendly way as if they had known each other before. Every time that Kay tried to unfasten his sledge the driver nodded again, and Kay sat still once more. Then they drove out of the town, and the snow began to fall so thickly that the little boy could not see his hand before him, and on and on they went. He quickly unfastened the cord to get loose from the big sledge, but it was of no use ; his little sledge hung on fast, and it went on like the wind.

Then he cried out, but nobody heard him. He was dreadfully frightened.

The snowflakes grew larger and larger till they looked like great white birds. All at once they flew aside, the large sledge stood still, and the figure who was driving stood up. The fur cloak and cap were all of snow. It was a lady, tall and slim, and glittering. It was the Snow-queen.

'We have come at a good rate,' she said; 'but you are almost frozen. Creep in under my cloak.'

And she set him close to her in the sledge and drew the cloak over him. He felt as though he were sinking into a snow-drift.

'Are you cold now?' she asked, and kissed his forehead. The kiss was cold as ice and reached down to his heart, which was already half a lump of ice.

'My sledge! Don't forget my sledge!' He thought of that first, and it was fastened to one of the white birds who flew behind with the sledge on its back.

The Snow-queen kissed Kay again, and then he forgot all about little Gerda, his grandmother, and everybody at home.

'Now I must not kiss you any more,' she said, 'or else I should kiss you to death.'

Then away they flew over forests and lakes, over sea and land. Round them whistled the cold wind, the wolves howled, and the snow hissed; over them flew the black shrieking crows. But high up the moon shone large and bright, and thus Kay passed the long winter night. In the day he slept at the Snow-queen's feet.

But what happened to little Gerda when Kay did not come back?

What had become of him? Nobody knew. The other boys told how they had seen him fasten his sledge on to a large one which had driven out of the town gate.

Gerda cried a great deal. The winter was long and dark to her.

Then the spring came with warm sunshine. 'I will go and look for Kay,' said Gerda.

· THE · SNOW · QUEEN · TAKES · KAY · IN · HER · SLEDGE ·

So she went down to the river and got into a little boat that was there. Presently the stream began to carry it away.

'Perhaps the river will take me to Kay,' thought Gerda. She glided down, past trees and fields, till she came to a large cherry garden, in which stood a little house with strange red and blue windows and a straw roof. Before the door stood two wooden soldiers, who were shouldering arms.

Gerda called to them, but they naturally did not answer. The river carried the boat on to the land.

Gerda called out still louder, and there came out of the house a very old woman. She leant upon a crutch, and she wore a large sun-hat which was painted with the most beautiful flowers.

'You poor little girl!' said the old woman.

And then she stepped into the water, brought the boat in close with her crutch, and lifted little Gerda out.

'And now come and tell me who you are, and how you came here,' she said.

Then Gerda told her everything, and asked her if she had seen Kay. But she said he had not passed that way yet, but he would soon come.

She told Gerda not to be sad, and that she should stay with her and take of the cherry trees and flowers, which were better than any picture-book, as they could each tell a story.

She then took Gerda's hand and led her into the little house and shut the door.

The windows were very high, and the panes were red, blue, and yellow, so that the light came through in curious colours. On the table were the most delicious cherries, and the old woman let Gerda eat as many as she liked, while she combed her hair with a gold comb as she ate.

The beautiful sunny hair rippled and shone round the dear little face, which was so soft and sweet. 'I have always longed to have a dear little girl just like you, and you shall see how happy we will be together.'

And as she combed Gerda's hair, Gerda thought less and less about Kay, for the old woman was a witch, but not a wicked witch, for she only enchanted now and then to amuse herself, and she did want to keep little Gerda very much.

So she went into the garden and waved her stick over all the rose bushes and blossoms and all; they sank down into the black earth, and no one could see where they had been.

The old woman was afraid that if Gerda saw the roses she would begin to think about her own, and then would remember Kay and run away.

Then she led Gerda out into the garden. How glorious it was, and what lovely scents filled the air ! All the flowers you can think of blossomed there all the year round.

Gerda jumped for joy and played there till the sun set behind the tall cherry trees, and then she slept in a beautiful bed with red silk pillows filled with violets, and she slept soundly and dreamed as a queen does on her wedding day.

The next day she played again with the flowers in the warm sunshine, and so many days passed by. Gerda knew every flower, but although there were so many, it seemed to her as if *one* were not there, though she could not remember which.

She was looking one day at the old woman's sun-hat which had the painted flowers on it, and there she saw a rose.

The witch had forgotten to make that vanish when she had made the other roses disappear under the earth. It is so difficult to think of everything.

' Why, there are no roses here ! ' cried Gerda, and she hunted amongst all the flowers, but not one was to be found. Then she sat down and cried, but her tears fell just on the spot where a rose bush had sunk, and when her warm tears watered the earth, the bush came up in full bloom just as it had been before. Gerda kissed the roses and thought of the lovely roses at home, and with them came the thought of little Kay.

'Oh, what have I been doing!' said the little girl. 'I wanted to look for Kay.'

She ran to the end of the garden. The gate was shut, but she pushed against the rusty lock so that it came open.

She ran out with her little bare feet. No one came after her. At last she could not run any longer, and she sat down on a large stone. When she looked round she saw that the summer was over; it was late autumn. It had not changed in the beautiful garden, where were sunshine and flowers all the year round.

'Oh, dear, how late I have made myself!' said Gerda. 'It's autumn already! I cannot rest!' And she sprang up to run on.

Oh, how tired and sore her little feet grew, and it became colder and colder.

She had to rest again, and there on the snow in front of her was a large crow.

It had been looking at her for some time, and it nodded its head and said, 'Caw! caw! good day.' Then it asked the little girl why she was alone in the world. She told the crow her story, and asked if he had seen Kay.

The crow nodded very thoughtfully and said, 'It might be! It *might* be!'

'What! Do you think you have?' cried the little girl, and she almost squeezed the crow to death as she kissed him.

'Gently, gently!' said the crow. 'I think—I know —I think—it might be little Kay, but now he has forgotten you for the princess!'

'Does he live with a princess?' asked Gerda.

' Yes, listen,' said the crow.

Then he told all he knew.

' In the kingdom in which we are now sitting lives a princess who is dreadfully clever. She has read all the newspapers in the world and has forgotten them again. She is as clever as that. The other day she came to the throne, and that is not so pleasant as people think. Then she began to say, " Why should I not marry ? " But she wanted a husband who could answer when he was spoken to, not one who would stand up stiffly and look respectable—that would be too dull.

' When she told all the Court ladies, they were delighted. You can believe every word I say,' said the crow. ' I have a tame sweetheart in the palace, and she tells me everything.'

Of course his sweetheart was a crow.

' The newspapers came out next morning with a border of hearts round it, and the princess's monogram on it, and inside you could read that every good-looking young man might come into the palace and speak to the princess, and whoever should speak loud enough to be heard would be well fed and looked after, and the one who spoke best should become the princess's husband. Indeed,' said the crow, ' you can quite believe me. It is as true as that I am sitting here.

' Young men came in streams, and there was such a crowding and a mixing together ! But nothing came of it on the first nor on the second day. They could all speak quite well when they were in the street, but as soon as they came inside the palace door, and saw the guards in silver, and upstairs the footmen in gold, and the great hall all lighted up, then their wits left them ! And when they stood in front of the throne where the princess was sitting, then they could not think of anything to say except to repeat the last word she had spoken, and she did not much care to hear that again. It seemed as if they were walking in their sleep until they came out into the street again, when they could speak once more. There was a row stretching from the gate of the town up to the castle.

' They were hungry and thirsty, but in the palace they did not even get a glass of water.

' A few of the cleverest had brought some slices of bread and butter with them, but they did not share them with their neighbour, for they thought, " If he looks hungry, the princess will not take him ! " '

' But what about Kay ? ' asked Gerda. ' When did he come ? Was he in the crowd ? '

' Wait a bit ; we are coming to him ! On the third day a little figure came without horse or carriage and walked jauntily up to the palace. His eyes shone as yours do ; he had lovely curling hair, but quite poor clothes.'

' That was Kay ! ' cried Gerda with delight. ' Oh, then I have found him ! ' and she clapped her hands.

' He had a little bundle on his back,' said the crow.

' No, it must have been his skates, for he went away with his skates ! '

' Very likely,' said the crow, ' I did not see for certain. But I know this from my sweetheart, that when he came to the palace door and saw the royal guards in silver, and on the stairs the footmen in gold, he was not the least bit put out. He nodded to them, saying, " It must be rather dull standing on the stairs ; I would rather go inside ! "

' The halls blazed with lights ; councillors and ambassadors were walking about in noiseless shoes carrying gold dishes. It was enough to make one nervous ! His boots creaked dreadfully loud, but he was not frightened.'

' That *must* be Kay ! ' said Gerda. ' I know he had new boots on ; I have heard them creaking in his grandmother's room ! '

' They *did* creak, certainly ! ' said the crow. ' And, not one bit afraid, up he went to the princess, who was

sitting on a large pearl as round as a spinning wheel.
All the ladies-in-waiting were standing round, each with
their attendants, and the lords-in-waiting with *their*
attendants. The nearer they stood to the door the
prouder they were.'

'HE HAD NOT COME TO WOO' HE SAID ·

'It must have been dreadful!' said little Gerda.
'And Kay did win the princess?'

'I heard from my tame sweetheart that he was
merry and quick-witted; he had not come to woo, he
said, but to listen to the princess's wisdom. And the
end of it was that they fell in love with each other.'

'Oh, yes; that was Kay!' said Gerda. 'He was so clever; he could do sums with fractions. Oh, do lead me to the palace!'

'That's easily said!' answered the crow, 'but how are we to manage that? I must talk it over with my tame sweetheart. She may be able to advise us, for I must tell you that a little girl like you could never get permission to enter it.'

'Yes, I will get it!' said Gerda. 'When Kay hears that I am there he will come out at once and fetch me!'

'Wait for me by the railings,' said the crow, and he nodded his head and flew away.

It was late in the evening when he came back.

'Caw, caw!' he said, 'I am to give you her love, and here is a little roll for you. She took it out of the kitchen; there's plenty there, and you must be hungry. You cannot come into the palace. The guards in silver and the footmen in gold would not allow it. But don't cry! You shall get in all right. My sweetheart knows a little back-stairs which leads to the sleeping-room, and she knows where to find the key.'

They went into the garden, and when the lights in the palace were put out one after the other, the crow led Gerda to a back-door.

Oh, how Gerda's heart beat with anxiety and longing! It seemed as if she were going to do something wrong, but she only wanted to know if it were little Kay. Yes, it must be he! She remembered so well his clever eyes, his curly hair. She could see him smiling as he did when they were at home under the rose trees! He would be so pleased to see her, and to hear how they all were at home.

Now they were on the stairs; a little lamp was burning, and on the landing stood the tame crow. She put her head on one side and looked at Gerda, who bowed as her grandmother had taught her.

'My betrothed has told me many nice things about

you, my dear young lady,' she said. 'Will you take the lamp while I go in front? We go this way so as to meet no one.'

Through beautiful rooms they came to the sleeping-room. In the middle of it, hung on a thick rod of gold, were two beds, shaped like lilies, one all white, in which lay the princess, and the other red, in which Gerda hoped to find Kay. She pushed aside the curtain, and saw a brown neck. Oh, it *was* Kay! She called his name out loud, holding the lamp towards him.

He woke up, turned his head and—it was *not* Kay!

It was only his neck that was like Kay's, but he was young and handsome. The princess sat up in her lily-bed and asked who was there.

Then Gerda cried, and told her story and all that the crows had done.

'You poor child!' said the prince and princess, and they praised the crows, and said that they were not angry with them, but that they must not do it again. Now they should have a reward.

'Would you like to fly away free?' said the princess, 'or will you have a permanent place as court crows with what you can get in the kitchen?'

And both crows bowed and asked for a permanent appointment, for they thought of their old age.

And they put Gerda to bed, and she folded her hands, thinking, as she fell asleep, 'How good people and animals are to me!'

The next day she was dressed from head to foot in silk and satin. They wanted her to stay on in the palace, but she begged for a little carriage and a horse, and a pair of shoes so that she might go out again into the world to look for Kay.

They gave her a muff as well as some shoes; she was warmly dressed, and when she was ready, there in front of the door stood a coach of pure gold, with a coachman, footmen and postilions with gold crowns on.

The prince and princess helped her into the carriage and wished her good luck.

The wild crow who was now married drove with her for the first three miles ; the other crow could not come because she had a bad headache.

' Good-bye, good-bye ! ' called the prince and princess ; and little Gerda cried, and the crow cried.

When he said good-bye, he flew on to a tree and waved with his black wings as long as the carriage, which shone like the sun, was in sight.

They came at last to a dark wood, but the coach lit it up like a torch. When the robbers saw it, they rushed out, exclaiming 'Gold ! gold ! '

They seized the horses, killed the coachman, footmen and postilions, and dragged Gerda out of the carriage.

' She is plump and tender ! I will eat her ! ' said the old robber-queen, and she drew her long knife, which glittered horribly.

' You shall not kill her ! ' cried her little daughter. ' She shall play with me. She shall give me her muff and her beautiful dress, and she shall sleep in my bed.'

The little robber-girl was as big as Gerda, but was stronger, broader, with dark hair and black eyes. She threw her arms round Gerda and said, ' They shall not kill you, so long as you are not naughty. Aren't you a princess ? '

' No,' said Gerda, and she told all that had happened to her, and how dearly she loved little Kay.

The robber-girl looked at her very seriously, and nodded her head, saying, ' They shall not kill you, even if you are naughty, for then I will kill you myself ! '

And she dried Gerda's eyes, and stuck both her hands in the beautiful warm muff.

The little robber-girl took Gerda to a corner of the robbers' camp where she slept.

All round were more than a hundred wood-pigeons

which seemed to be asleep, but they moved a little when the two girls came up.

There was also, near by, a reindeer which the robber-girl teased by tickling it with her long sharp knife. Gerda lay awake for some time.

' Coo, coo! ' said the wood-pigeons. ' We have seen little Kay. A white bird carried his sledge ; he was sitting in the Snow-queen's carriage which drove over the forest when our little ones were in the nest. She breathed on them, and all except we two died. Coo, coo ! '

' What are you saying over there ? ' cried Gerda. ' Where was the Snow-queen going to ? Do you know at all ? '

' She was probably travelling to Lapland, where there is always ice and snow. Ask the reindeer.'

' There is capital ice and snow there ! ' said the reindeer. ' One can jump about there in the great sparkling valleys. There the Snow-queen has her summer palace, but her best palace is up by the North Pole, on the island called Spitzbergen.'

' O Kay, my little Kay ! ' sobbed Gerda.

' You must lie still ! ' said the little robber-girl, ' or else I shall stick my knife into you ! '

In the morning Gerda told her all that the wood-pigeons had said. She nodded. ' Do you know where Lapland is ? ' she asked the reindeer.

' Who should know better than I ? ' said the beast, and his eyes sparkled. ' I was born and bred there on the snow-fields.'

' Listen ! ' said the robber-girl to Gerda ; ' you see that all the robbers have gone ; only my mother is left, and she will fall asleep in the afternoon—then I will do something for you ! '

When her mother had fallen asleep, the robber-girl went up to the reindeer and said, ' I am going to set you free so that you can run to Lapland. But you must go quickly and carry this little girl to the Snow-queen's palace, where her playfellow is. You must have heard all that she told about it, for she spoke loud enough! '

The reindeer sprang high for joy. The robber-girl lifted little Gerda up, and had the foresight to tie her on firmly, and even gave her a little pillow for a saddle. ' You must have your fur boots,' she said, ' for it will be cold; but I shall keep your muff, for it is so cosy! But, so that you may not freeze, here are my mother's great fur gloves; they will come up to your elbows. Creep into them! '

And Gerda cried for joy.

' Don't make such faces! ' said the little robber-girl. ' You must look very happy. And here are two loaves and a sausage; now you won't be hungry! '

They were tied to the reindeer, the little robber-girl opened the door, made all the big dogs come away, cut through the halter with her sharp knife, and said to the reindeer, ' Run now! But take great care of the little girl.'

And Gerda stretched out her hands with the large fur gloves towards the little robber-girl and said, ' Good-bye! '

Then the reindeer flew over the ground, through the great forest, as fast as he could.

The wolves howled, the ravens screamed, the sky seemed on fire.

' Those are my dear old northern lights,' said the reindeer; ' see how they shine! '

And then he ran faster still, day and night.

The loaves were eaten, and the sausage also, and then they came to Lapland.

They stopped by a wretched little house; the roof almost touched the ground, and the door was so low that you had to creep in and out.

There was no one in the house except an old Lapland woman who was cooking fish over an oil-lamp. The reindeer told Gerda's whole history, but first he told his

The Robber-girl sends Gerda off on the Reindeer

own, for that seemed to him much more important, and Gerda was so cold that she could not speak.

'Ah, you poor creatures!' said the Lapland woman; 'you have still further to go! You must go over a hundred miles into Finland, for there the Snow-queen lives, and every night she burns Bengal lights. I will write some words on a dried stock-fish, for I have no paper, and you must give it to the Finland woman, for she can give you better advice than I can.'

And when Gerda was warmed and had had something to eat and drink, the Lapland woman wrote on a dried stock-fish, and begged Gerda to take care of it, tied Gerda securely on the reindeer's back, and away they went again.

The whole night was ablaze with northern lights, and then they came to Finland and knocked at the Finland woman's chimney, for door she had none.

Inside it was so hot that the Finland woman wore very few clothes; she loosened Gerda's clothes and drew off her fur gloves and boots. She laid a piece of ice on the reindeer's head, and then read what was written on the stock-fish. She read it over three times till she knew it by heart, and then put the fish in the saucepan, for she never wasted anything.

Then the reindeer told his story, and afterwards little Gerda's, and the Finland woman blinked her eyes but said nothing.

'You are very clever,' said the reindeer, 'I know. Cannot you give the little girl a drink so that she may have the strength of twelve men and overcome the Snow-queen?'

'The strength of twelve men!' said the Finland woman; '*that* would not help much. Little Kay is with the Snow-queen, and he likes everything there very much and thinks it the best place in the world. But that is because he has a splinter of glass in his heart and a bit in his eye. If these do not come out, he will never be free, and the Snow-queen will keep her power over him.'

'But cannot you give little Gerda something so that she can have power over her?'

'I can give her no greater power than she has already; don't you see how great it is? Don't you see how men and beasts must help her when she wanders into the wide world with her bare feet? She is powerful already, because she is a dear little innocent child. If she cannot by herself conquer the Snow-queen and take away the glass splinters from little Kay, *we* cannot help her! The Snow-queen's garden begins two miles from here. You can carry the little maiden so far; put her down by the large bush with red berries growing in the snow. Then you must come back here as fast as you can.'

Then the Finland woman lifted little Gerda on the reindeer and away he sped.

'Oh, I have left my gloves and boots behind!' cried Gerda. She missed them in the piercing cold, but the reindeer did not dare to stop. On he ran till he came to the bush with red berries. Then he set Gerda down and kissed her mouth, and great big tears ran down his cheeks, and then he ran back. There stood poor Gerda without shoes or gloves in the middle of the bitter cold of Finland.

She ran on as fast as she could. A regiment of gigantic snowflakes came against her, but they melted when they touched her, and she went on with fresh courage.

And now we must see what Kay was doing. He was not thinking of Gerda, and never dreamt that she was standing outside the palace.

The walls of the palace were built of driven snow, and the doors and windows of piercing winds.

There were more than a hundred halls in it all of frozen snow. The largest was several miles long; the bright Northern lights lit them up, and very large and empty and cold and glittering they were ! In the middle of the great hall was a frozen lake which had cracked in a thousand pieces ; each piece was exactly like the other. Here the Snow-queen used to sit when she was at home.

Little Kay was almost blue and black with cold, but he did not feel it, for she had kissed away his feelings and his heart was a lump of ice.

He was pulling about some sharp, flat pieces of ice, and trying to fit one into the other. He thought each was most beautiful, but that was because of the splinter of glass in his eye. He fitted them into a great many shapes, but he wanted to make them spell the word ' Love.' The Snow-queen had said, ' If you can spell out that word you shall be your own master. I will give you the whole world and a new pair of skates.'

But he could not do it.

' Now I must fly to warmer countries,' said the Snow-queen. ' I must go and powder my black kettles ! ' (This was what she called Mount Etna and Mount Vesuvius.) ' It does the lemons and grapes good.'

And off she flew, and Kay sat alone in the great hall trying to do his puzzle.

He sat so still that you would have thought he was frozen.

Then it happened that little Gerda stepped into the hall. The biting cold winds became quiet as if they had fallen asleep when she appeared in the great, empty, freezing hall.

She caught sight of Kay; she recognised him, ran and put her arms round his neck, crying, ' Kay ! dear little Kay ! I have found you at last ! '

But he sat quite still and cold. Then Gerda wept hot tears which fell on his neck and thawed his heart and swept away the bit of the looking-glass. He looked at her and then he burst into tears. He cried so much that the glass splinter swam out of his eye ; then he knew

her, and cried out, 'Gerda! dear little Gerda! Where
have you been so long? and where have I been?'

And he looked round him.

'How cold it is here! How wide and empty!' and
he threw himself on Gerda, and she laughed and wept

for joy It was such a happy time that the pieces of ice
even danced round them for joy, and when they were
tired and lay down again they formed themselves into
the letters that the Snow-queen had said he must spell
in order to become his own master and have the whole
world and a new pair of skates.

And Gerda kissed his cheeks and they grew rosy ; she kissed his eyes and they sparkled like hers ; she kissed his hands and feet and he became warm and glowing. The Snow-queen might come home now ; his release— the word ' Love '—stood written in sparkling ice.

They took each other's hands and wandered out of the great palace ; they talked about the grandmother and the roses on the leads, and wherever they came the winds hushed and the sun came out. When they reached the bush with red berries there stood the reindeer waiting for them.

He carried Kay and Gerda first to the Finland woman, who warmed them in her hot room and gave them advice for their journey home.

Then they went to the Lapland woman, who gave them new clothes and mended their sleigh. The reindeer ran with them till they came to the green fields fresh with the spring green. Here he said good-bye.

They came to the forest, which was bursting into bud, and out of it came a splendid horse which Gerda knew ; it was one which had drawn the gold coach ridden by a young girl with a red cap on and pistols in her belt. It was the little robber girl who was tired of being at home and wanted to go out into the world. She and Gerda knew each other at once.

' You are a nice fellow ! ' she said to Kay. ' I should like to know if you deserve to be run after all over the world ! '

But Gerda patted her cheeks and asked after the prince and princess.

' They are travelling about,' said the robber girl.

' And the crow ? ' asked Gerda.

' Oh, the crow is dead ! ' answered the robber girl. ' His tame sweetheart is a widow and hops about with a bit of black crape round her leg. She makes a great fuss, but it's all nonsense. But tell me what happened to you, and how you caught him.'

And Kay and Gerda told her all.

'Dear, dear!' said the robber girl, shook both their hands, and promised that if she came to their town she would come and see them. Then she rode on.

But Gerda and Kay went home hand in hand. There they found the grandmother and everything just as it had been, but when they went through the doorway they found they were grown-up.

There were the roses on the leads; it was summer, warm, glorious summer.

THE FIR-TREE [1]

THERE was once a pretty little fir-tree in a wood. It was
in a capital position, for it could get sun, and there was
enough air, and all around grew many tall companions,
both pines and firs. The little fir-tree's greatest desire
was to grow up. It did not heed the warm sun and the
fresh air, or notice the little peasant children who ran
about chattering when they came out to gather wild
strawberries and raspberries. Often they found a whole
basketful and strung strawberries on a straw; they
would sit down by the little fir-tree and say, 'What a
pretty little one this is!' The tree did not like that at all.

By the next year it had grown a whole ring taller,
and the year after that another ring more, for you can
always tell a fir-tree's age from its rings.

'Oh! if I were only a great tree like the others!'
sighed the little fir-tree, 'then I could stretch out my
branches far and wide and look out into the great world!
The birds would build their nests in my branches, and
when the wind blew I would bow to it politely just like
the others!' It took no pleasure in the sunshine, nor in
the birds, nor in the rose-coloured clouds that sailed over
it at dawn and at sunset. Then the winter came, and
the snow lay white and sparkling all around, and a hare
would come and spring right over the little fir-tree,
which annoyed it very much. But when two more
winters had passed the fir-tree was so tall that the hare

[1] Translated from the German of Hans Christian Andersen.

had to run round it. 'Ah! to grow and grow, and
become great and old! that is the only pleasure in life,'
thought the tree. In the autumn the woodcutters used
to come and hew some of the tallest trees ; this happened
every year, and the young fir-tree would shiver as the
magnificent trees fell crashing and crackling to the
ground, their branches hewn off, and the great trunks
left bare, so that they were almost unrecognisable. But
then they were laid on waggons and dragged out of the
wood by horses. 'Where are they going? What will
happen to them?'

In spring, when the swallows and storks came, the
fir-tree asked them, 'Do you know where they were
taken? Have you met them?'

The swallows knew nothing of them, but the stork
nodded his head thoughtfully, saying, 'I think I know.
I met many new ships as I flew from Egypt ; there
were splendid masts on the ships. I'll wager those were
they! They had the scent of fir-trees. Ah! those are
grand, grand!'

'Oh! if I were only big enough to sail away over the
sea too! What sort of thing is the sea? what does it
look like?'

'Oh! it would take much too long to tell you all
that,' said the stork, and off he went.

'Rejoice in your youth,' said the sunbeams, 'rejoice
in the sweet growing time, in the young life within you.'

And the wind kissed it and the dew wept tears over it,
but the fir-tree did not understand.

Towards Christmas-time quite little trees were cut
down, some not as big as the young fir-tree, or just the
same age, and now it had no peace or rest for longing to
be away. These little trees, which were chosen for their
beauty, kept all their branches ; they were put in carts
and drawn out of the wood by horses.

'Whither are those going?' asked the fir-tree; 'they
are no bigger than I, and one there was much smaller

even! Why do they keep their branches? Where are they taken to?'

'We know! we know!' twittered the sparrows. 'Down there in the city we have peeped in at the windows, we know where they go! They attain to the greatest splendour and magnificence you can imagine! We have looked in at the windows and seen them planted in the middle of the warm room and adorned with the most beautiful things—golden apples, sweetmeats, toys and hundreds of candles.'

'And then?' asked the fir-tree, trembling in every limb with eagerness, 'and then? what happens then?'

'Oh, we haven't seen anything more than that. That was simply matchless!'

'Am I too destined to the same brilliant career?' wondered the fir-tree excitedly. 'That is even better than sailing over the sea! I am sick with longing. If it were only Christmas! Now I am tall and grown-up like those which were taken away last year. Ah, if I were only in the cart! If I were only in the warm room with all the splendour and magnificence! And then? Then comes something better, something still more beautiful, else why should they dress us up? There must be something greater, something grander to come—but what? Oh! I am pining away! I really don't know what's the matter with me!'

'Rejoice in us,' said the air and sunshine, 'rejoice in your fresh youth in the free air!'

But it took no notice, and just grew and grew; there it stood fresh and green in winter and in summer, and all who saw it said, 'What a beautiful tree!' And at Christmas-time it was the first to be cut down. The axe went deep into the pith; the tree fell to the ground with a groan; it felt bruised and faint. It could not think of happiness, it was sad at leaving its home, the spot where it had sprung up; it knew, too, that it would never see again its dear old companions, or the little shrubs and flowers, perhaps not even the birds. Altogether the parting was not pleasant.

When the tree came to itself again it was packed in a yard with other trees, and a man was saying, 'This is a splendid one, we shall only want this.'

Then came two footmen in livery and carried the fir-tree into a large and beautiful room. There were pictures hanging upon the walls, and near the Dutch stove stood great Chinese vases with lions on their lids; there were armchairs, silk-covered sofas, big tables laden with picture-books and toys, worth hundreds of pounds—at least, so the children said. The fir-tree was placed in a great tub filled with sand, but no one could see that it was a tub, for it was all hung with greenery and stood on a gay carpet. How the tree trembled! What was coming now? The young ladies and the servants decked it out. On its branches they hung little nets cut out of coloured paper, each full of sugarplums; gilt apples and nuts hung down as if they were growing, and over a hundred red, blue, and white tapers were fastened among the branches. Dolls as life-like as human beings—the fir-tree had never seen any before—were suspended among the green, and right up at the top was fixed a gold tinsel star; it was gorgeous, quite unusually gorgeous!

'To-night,' they all said, 'to-night it will be lighted!'

'Ah!' thought the tree, 'if it were only evening! Then the tapers would soon be lighted. What will happen then? I wonder whether the trees will come from the wood to see me, or if the sparrows will fly against the window panes? Am I to stand here decked out thus through winter and summer?'

It was not a bad guess, but the fir-tree had real bark-ache from sheer longing, and bark-ache in trees is just as bad as head-ache in human beings.

Now the tapers were lighted. What a glitter! What splendour! The tree quivered in all its branches so much, that one of the candles caught the green, and singed it. 'Take care!' cried the young ladies, and they extinguished it.

Now the tree did not even dare to quiver. It was really terrible! It was so afraid of losing any of its ornaments, and it was quite bewildered by all the radiance. And then the folding doors were opened, and a crowd of children rushed in, as though they wanted to knock down the whole tree, whilst the older people followed soberly. The children stood quite silent, but only for a moment, and then they shouted again, and danced round the tree, and snatched off one present after another.

'What are they doing?' thought the tree. 'What is going to happen?' And the tapers burnt low on the branches, and were put out one by one, and then the children were given permission to plunder the tree. They rushed at it so that all its boughs creaked; if it had not been fastened by the gold star at the top to the ceiling, it would have been overthrown.

The children danced about with their splendid toys, and no one looked at the tree, except the old nurse, who came and peeped amongst the boughs, just to see if a fig or an apple had been forgotten.

'A story! a story!' cried the children, and dragged a little stout man to the tree; he sat down beneath it, saying, 'Here we are in the greenwood, and the tree will be delighted to listen! But I am only going to tell one story. Shall it be Henny Penny or Humpty Dumpty who fell downstairs, and yet gained great honour and married a princess?'

'Henny Penny!' cried some: 'Humpty Dumpty!' cried others; there was a perfect babel of voices! Only the fir-tree kept silent, and thought, 'Am I not to be in it? Am I to have nothing to do with it?'

But it had already been in it, and played out its part. And the man told them about Humpty Dumpty who fell downstairs and married a princess. The children clapped their hands and cried, 'Another! another!' They wanted

the story of Henny Penny also, but they only got Humpty
Dumpty. The fir-tree stood quite astonished and thoughtful : the birds in the wood had never related anything like
that. 'Humpty Dumpty fell downstairs and yet married
a princess ! yes, that is the way of the world !' thought
the tree, and was sure it must be true, because such a
nice man had told the story. 'Well, who knows? Perhaps I shall fall downstairs and marry a princess.' And
it rejoiced to think that next day it would be decked out
again with candles, toys, glittering ornaments, and fruits.
'To-morrow I shall quiver again with excitement. I
shall enjoy to the full all my splendour. To-morrow I
shall hear Humpty Dumpty again, and perhaps Henny
Penny too.' And the tree stood silent and lost in thought
all through the night.

Next morning the servants came in. 'Now the
dressing up will begin again,' thought the tree. But they
dragged it out of the room, and up the stairs to the
lumber-room, and put it in a dark corner, where no ray
of light could penetrate. 'What does this mean?' thought
the tree. 'What am I to do here? What is there for
me to hear?' And it leant against the wall, and thought
and thought. And there was time enough for that, for
days and nights went by, and no one came ; at last when
some one did come, it was only to put some great boxes
into the corner. Now the tree was quite covered ; it
seemed as if it had been quite forgotten.

'Now it is winter out-doors,' thought the fir-tree.
'The ground is hard and covered with snow, they can't
plant me yet, and that is why I am staying here under
cover till the spring comes. How thoughtful they are !
Only I wish it were not so terribly dark and lonely here ;
not even a little hare ! It was so nice out in the wood,
when the snow lay all around, and the hare leapt past
me ; yes, even when he leapt over me : but I didn't like
it then. It's so dreadfully lonely up here.'

'Squeak, squeak !' said a little mouse, stealing out,

followed by a second. They sniffed at the fir-tree, and
then crept between its boughs. ' It's frightfully cold,'
said the little mice. ' How nice it is to be here ! Don't
you think so too, you old fir-tree ? '

' I'm not at all old,' said the tree ; ' there are many
much older than I am.'

' Where do you come from ? ' asked the mice, ' and
what do you know ? ' They were extremely inquisitive.
' Do tell us about the most beautiful place in the world.
Is that where you come from ? Have you been in the
storeroom, where cheeses lie on the shelves, and hams
hang from the ceiling, where one dances on tallow
candles, and where one goes in thin and comes out fat ? '

' I know nothing about that,' said the tree. ' But I
know the wood, where the sun shines, and the birds sing.'
And then it told them all about its young days, and the
little mice had never heard anything like that before, and
they listened with all their ears, and said : ' Oh, how
much you have seen ! How lucky you have been ! '

' I ? ' said the fir-tree, and then it thought over what
it had told them. ' Yes, on the whole those were very
happy times.' But then it went on to tell them about
Christmas Eve, when it had been adorned with sweetmeats and tapers.

' Oh ! ' said the little mice, ' how lucky you have been,
you old fir-tree ! '

' I'm not at all old,' said the tree. ' I only came from
the wood this winter. I am only a little backward, perhaps, in my growth.'

' How beautifully you tell stories ! ' said the little
mice. And next evening they came with four others,
who wanted to hear the tree's story, and it told still more,
for it remembered everything so clearly and thought :
' Those were happy times ! But they may come again.
Humpty Dumpty fell downstairs, and yet he married a
princess ; perhaps I shall also marry a princess ! ' And
then it thought of a pretty little birch-tree that grew out

in the wood, and seemed to the fir-tree a real princess, and a very beautiful one too.

'Who is Humpty Dumpty?' asked the little mice. And then the tree told the whole story; it could remember every single word, and the little mice were ready to leap on to the topmost branch out of sheer joy! Next night many more mice came, and on Sunday even two rats; but they did not care about the story, and that troubled the little mice, for now they thought less of it too.

'Is that the only story you know?' asked the rats.

'The only one,' answered the tree. 'I heard that on my happiest evening, but I did not realise then how happy I was.'

'That's a very poor story. Don't you know one about bacon or tallow candles? a storeroom story?'

'No,' said the tree.

'Then we are much obliged to you,' said the rats, and they went back to their friends.

At last the little mice went off also, and the tree said, sighing: 'Really it was very pleasant when the lively little mice sat round and listened whilst I told them stories. But now that's over too. But now I will think of the time when I shall be brought out again, to keep up my spirits.'

But when did that happen? Well, it was one morning when they came to tidy up the lumber-room; the boxes were set aside, and the tree brought out; they threw it really rather roughly on the floor, but a servant dragged it off at once downstairs, where there was daylight once more.

'Now life begins again!' thought the tree. It felt the fresh air, the first rays of the sun, and there it was out in the yard! Everything passed so quickly; the tree quite forgot to notice itself, there was so much to look at all around. The yard opened on a garden full of flowers;

the roses were so fresh and sweet, hanging over a little
trellis, the lime-trees were in blossom, and the swallows
flew about, saying: 'Quirre-virre-vit, my husband has
come home;' but it was not the fir-tree they meant.

'Now I shall live,' thought the tree joyfully, stretching
out its branches wide; but, alas! they were all withered
and yellow; and it was lying in a corner among weeds
and nettles. The golden star was still on its highest
bough, and it glittered in the bright sunlight. In the
yard some of the merry children were playing, who had
danced so gaily round the tree at Christmas. One of the
little ones ran up, and tore off the gold star.

'Look what was left on the ugly old fir-tree!' he
cried, and stamped on the boughs so that they cracked
under his feet.

And the tree looked at all the splendour and freshness
of the flowers in the garden, and then looked at itself, and
wished that it had been left lying in the dark corner of
the lumber-room; it thought of its fresh youth in the
wood, of the merry Christmas Eve, and of the little mice
who had listened so happily to the story of Humpty
Dumpty.

'Too late! Too late!' thought the old tree. 'If only
I had enjoyed myself whilst I could. Now all is over
and gone.'

And a servant came and cut the tree into small pieces,
there was quite a bundle of them; they flickered brightly
under the great copper in the brew-house; the tree sighed
deeply, and each sigh was like a pistol-shot; so the
children who were playing there ran up, and sat in front
of the fire, gazing at it, and crying, 'Piff! puff! bang!'
But for each report, which was really a sigh, the tree was
thinking of a summer's day in the wood, or of a winter's
night out there, when the stars were shining; it thought
of Christmas Eve, and of Humpty Dumpty, which was
the only story it had heard, or could tell, and then the
tree had burnt away.

The children played on in the garden, and the youngest had the golden star on his breast, which the tree had worn on the happiest evening of its life ; and now that was past —and the tree had passed away—and the story too, all ended and done with.

And that's the way with all stories !

.　　　.　　　.　　　.　　　.

Here our Danish author ends.　This is what people call *sentiment*, and I hope you enjoy it !

HANS, THE MERMAID'S SON [1]

IN a village there once lived a smith called Basmus, who was in a very poor way. He was still a young man, and a strong handsome fellow to boot, but he had many little children and there was little to be earned by his trade. He was, however, a diligent and hard-working man, and when he had no work in the smithy he was out at sea fishing, or gathering wreckage on the shore.

It happened one time that he had gone out to fish in good weather, all alone in a little boat, but he did not come home that day, nor the following one, so that all believed that he had perished out at sea. On the third day, however, Basmus came to shore again and had his boat full of fish, so big and fat that no one had ever seen their like. There was nothing the matter with him, and he complained neither of hunger nor thirst. He had got into a fog, he said, and could not find land again. What he did not tell, however, was where he had been all the time ; that only came out six years later, when people got to know that he had been caught by a mermaid out on the deep sea, and had been her guest during the three days that he was missing. From that time forth he went out no more to fish ; nor, indeed, did he require to do so, for whenever he went down to the shore it never failed that some wreckage was washed up, and in it all kinds of valuable things. In those days everyone took what they found and got leave to keep it, so that the smith grew more prosperous day by day.

[1] Translated from the Danish.

Basnus & the Mermaid

When seven years had passed since the smith went out to sea, it happened one morning, as he stood in the smithy, mending a plough, that a handsome young lad came in to him and said, 'Good-day, father; my mother the mermaid sends her greetings, and says that *she* has had me for six years now, and *you* can keep me for as long.'

He was a strange enough boy to be six years old, for he looked as if he were eighteen, and was even bigger and stronger than lads commonly are at that age.

'Will you have a bite of bread?' said the smith.

'Oh, yes,' said Hans, for that was his name.

The smith then told his wife to cut a piece of bread for him. She did so, and the boy swallowed it at one mouthful and went out again to the smithy to his father.

'Have you got all you can eat?' said the smith.

'No,' said Hans, 'that was just a little bit.'

The smith went into the house and took a whole loaf, which he cut into two slices and put butter and cheese between them, and this he gave to Hans. In a while the boy came out to the smithy again.

'Well, have you got as much as you can eat?' said the smith.

'No, not nearly,' said Hans; 'I must try to find a better place than this, for I can see that I shall never get my fill here.'

Hans wished to set off at once, as soon as his father would make a staff for him of such a kind as he wanted.

'It must be of iron,' said he, 'and one that can hold out.'

The smith brought him an iron rod as thick as an ordinary staff, but Hans took it and twisted it round his finger, so *that* wouldn't do. Then the smith came dragging one as thick as a waggon-pole, but Hans bent it over his knee and broke it like a straw. The smith then had to collect all the iron he had, and Hans held it while his father forged for him a staff, which was heavier than the anvil. When Hans had got this he said, 'Many thanks, father; now I have got my inheritance.' With this he set off into the country, and the smith was very well pleased to be rid of *that* son, before he ate him out of house and home.

Hans first arrived at a large estate, and it so happened that the squire himself was standing outside the farm-yard.

'Where are you going?' said the squire.

'I am looking for a place,' said Hans, 'where they have need of strong fellows, and can give them plenty to eat.'

'Well,' said the squire, 'I generally have twenty-four men at this time of the year, but I have only twelve just now, so I can easily take you on.'

'Very well,' said Hans, 'I shall easily do twelve men's work, but then I must also have as much to eat as the twelve would.'

All this was agreed to, and the squire took Hans into the kitchen, and told the servant girls that the new man was to have as much food as the other twelve. It was arranged that he should have a pot to himself, and he could then use the ladle to take his food with.

It was in the evening that Hans arrived there, so he did nothing more that day than eat his supper—a big pot of buck-wheat porridge, which he cleaned to the bottom, and was then so far satisfied that he said he could sleep on that, so he went off to bed. He slept both well and long, and all the rest were up and at their work while he was still sleeping soundly. The squire was also on foot, for he was curious to see how the new man would behave who was both to eat and work for twelve.

But as yet there was no Hans to be seen, and the sun was already high in the heavens, so the squire himself went and called on him.

'Get up, Hans,' he cried; 'you are sleeping too long.'

Hans woke up and rubbed his eyes. 'Yes, that's true,' he said, 'I must get up and have my breakfast.'

So he rose and dressed himself, and went into the kitchen, where he got his pot of porridge; he swallowed all of this, and then asked what work he was to have.

He was to thresh that day, said the squire; the other twelve men were already busy at it. There were twelve threshing-floors, and the twelve men were at work on six of them—two on each. Hans must thresh by himself all that was lying upon the other six floors. He went out to the barn and got hold of a flail. Then he looked to see how the others did it and did the same, but at the first stroke he smashed the flail in pieces. There were several flails hanging there, and Hans took the one after the other, but they all went the same way, every one flying in splinters at the first stroke. He then looked round for something else to work with, and found a pair of strong beams lying near. Next he caught sight of a horse-hide nailed up on the barn-door. With the beams he made a flail, using the skin to tie them together. The one beam he used as a handle, and the other to strike with, and now *that* was all right. But the barn was too low, there was no room to swing the flail, and the floors were too small. Hans, however, found a remedy for this —he simply lifted the whole roof off the barn, and set it down in the field beside. He then emptied down all the corn that he could lay his hands on and threshed away. He went through one lot after another, and it was all the same to him what he got hold of, so before midday he had threshed all the squire's grain, his rye and wheat and barley and oats, all mixed through each other. When he was finished with this, he lifted the roof up on the barn again, like setting a lid on a box, and went in and told the squire that that job was done.

The squire opened his eyes at this announcement; and came out to see if it was really true. It was true, sure enough, but he was scarcely delighted with the mixed grain that he had got from all his crops. However, when he saw the flail that Hans had used, and learned how he had made room for himself to swing it, he was so afraid of the strong fellow, that he dared not say anything, except that it was a good thing he had got it threshed; but it had still to be cleaned.

'What does that mean?' asked Hans.

It was explained to him that the corn and the chaff had to be separated; as yet both were lying in one heap, right up to the roof. Hans began to take up a little and sift it in his hands, but he soon saw that this would never do. He soon thought of a plan, however; he opened both barn-doors, and then lay down at one end and blew, so that all the chaff flew out and lay like a sand-bank at the other end of the barn, and the grain was as clean as it could be. Then he reported to the squire that that job also was done. The squire said that that was well; there was nothing more for him to do that day. Off went Hans to the kitchen, and got as much as he could eat; then he went and took a midday nap which lasted till supper-time.

Meanwhile the squire was quite miserable, and made his moan to his wife, saying that she must help him to find some means of getting rid of this strong fellow, for he durst not give him his leave. She sent for the steward, and it was arranged that next day all the men should go to the forest for fire-wood, and that they should make a bargain among them, that the one who came home last with his load should be hanged. They thought they could easily manage that it would be Hans who would lose his life, for the others would be early on the road, while Hans would certainly oversleep himself. In the evening, therefore, the men sat and talked together, saying that next morning they must set out early to the forest, and as they had a hard day's work and a long journey before them, they would, for their amusement, make a compact, that whichever of them came home last with his load should lose his life on the gallows. So Hans had no objections to make.

Long before the sun was up next morning, all the twelve men were on foot. They took all the best horses and carts, and drove off to the forest. Hans, however, lay and slept on, and the squire said, ' Just let him lie.'

At last, Hans thought it was time to have his breakfast, so he got up and put on his clothes. He took plenty of time to his breakfast, and then went out to get his horse and cart ready. The others had taken everything that was any good, so that he had a difficulty in scraping together four wheels of different sizes and fixing them to an old cart, and he could find no other horses than a pair of old hacks. These he harnessed to his cart and drove off to the forest. He did not know where it lay, but he followed the track of the other carts, and in that way came to it all right. On coming to the gate leading into the forest, he was unfortunate enough to break it in pieces, so he took a huge stone that was lying on the field, seven ells long, and seven ells broad, and set this in the gap, then he went on and joined the others. These laughed at him heartily, for they had laboured as hard as they could since daybreak, and had helped each other to fell trees and put them on the carts, so that all of these were now loaded except one.

Hans got hold of a woodman's axe and proceeded to fell a tree, but he destroyed the edge and broke the shaft at the first blow. He therefore laid down the axe, put his arms round the tree, and pulled it up by the roots. This he threw upon his cart, and then another and another, and thus he went on while all the others forgot their work, and stood with open mouths, gazing at this strange woodcraft. All at once they began to hurry; the last cart was loaded, and they whipped up their horses, so as to be the first to arrive home.

When Hans had finished his work, he again put his

old hacks into the cart, but they could not move it from
the spot. He was annoyed at this, and took them out
again, twisted a rope round the cart, and all the trees,
lifted the whole affair on his back, and set off home, leading the horses behind him by the rein. When he reached
the gate, he found the whole row of carts standing there,
unable to get any further for the stone which lay in the
gap.

'What!' said Hans, 'can twelve men not move *that*
stone?' With that he lifted it and threw it out of the
way, and went on with his burden on his back, and the
horses behind him, and arrived at the farm long before
any of the others. The squire was walking about there,
looking and looking, for he was very curious to know
what had happened. Finally, he caught sight of Hans
coming along in this fashion, and was so frightened that
he did not know what to do, but he shut the gate and
put on the bar. When Hans reached the gate of the
courtyard, he laid down the trees and hammered at it,
but no one came to open it. He then took the trees and
tossed them over the barn into the yard, and the cart after
them, so that every wheel flew off in a different direction.

When the squire saw this, he thought to himself,
'The horses will come the same way if I don't open the
door,' so he did this.

'Good day, master,' said Hans, and put the horses
into the stable, and went into the kitchen, to get something to eat. At length the other men came home
with their loads. When they came in, Hans said to them,
'Do you remember the bargain we made last night?
Which of you is it that's going to be hanged?' 'Oh,'
said they, 'that was only a joke; it didn't mean anything.'
'Oh well, it doesn't matter,' said Hans, and there was no
more about it.

The squire, however, and his wife and the steward,
had much to say to each other about the terrible man
they had got, and all were agreed that they must get rid

of him in some way or other.   The steward said that he
would manage this all right.   Next morning they were to
clean the well, and they would make use of that opportunity.   They would get him down into the well, and
then have a big mill-stone ready to throw down on top of
him—that would settle him.   After that they could just
fill in the well, and then escape being at any expense for
his funeral.   Both the squire and his wife thought this
a splendid idea, and went about rejoicing at the thought
that now they would get rid of Hans.

But Hans was hard to kill, as we shall see.   He slept
long next morning, as he always did, and finally, as he
would not waken by himself, the squire had to go and
call him.   'Get up, Hans, you are sleeping too long,' he
cried.   Hans woke up and rubbed his eyes.   'That's so,'
said he, 'I shall rise and have my breakfast.'   He got up
then and dressed himself, while the breakfast stood waiting for him.   When he had finished the whole of this, he
asked what he was to do that day.   He was told to help
the other men to clean out the well.   That was all right,
and he went out and found the other men waiting for him.
To these he said that they could choose whichever task
they liked—either to go down into the well and fill the
buckets while he pulled them up, or pull them up, and
he alone would go down to the bottom of the well.   They
answered that they would rather stay above-ground, as
there would be no room for so many of them down in
the well.

Hans therefore went down alone, and began to clean
out the well, but the men had arranged how they were to
act, and immediately each of them seized a stone from a
heap of huge blocks, that lay in the farmyard just as
big as they could lift, and threw them down above him,
thinking to kill him with these.   Hans, however, gave no
more heed to this than to shout up to them, to keep the
hens away from the well, for they were scraping gravel
down on the top of him

They then saw that they could not kill him with little stones, but they had still the big one left. The whole twelve of them set to work with poles and rollers and rolled the big mill-stone to the brink of the well. It was with the greatest difficulty that they got it thrown down there, and now they had no doubt that he had got all that he wanted. But the stone happened to fall so luckily that his head went right through the hole in the middle of the mill-stone, so that it sat round his neck like a priest's collar. At this, Hans would stay down no longer. He came out of the well, with the mill-stone round his neck, and went straight to the squire and complained that the other men were trying to make a fool of him. He would not be their priest, he said; he had too little learning for that. Saying this, he bent down his head and shook the stone off, so that it crushed one of the squire's big toes.

The squire went limping in to his wife, and the steward was sent for. He was told that he must devise some plan for getting rid of this terrible person. The scheme he had devised before had been of no use, and now good counsel was scarce.

'Oh, no,' said the steward, 'there are good enough ways yet. The squire can send him this evening to fish in Devilmoss Lake: he will never escape alive from there, for no one can go there by night for Old Eric.'

That was a grand idea, both the squire and his wife thought, and so he limped out again to Hans, and said that he would punish his men for having tried to make a fool of him. Meanwhile, Hans could do a little job where he would be free from these rascals. He should go out on the lake and fish there that night, and would then be free from all work on the following day.

'All right,' said Hans; 'I am well content with that, but I must have something with me to eat—a baking of bread, a cask of butter, a barrel of ale, and a keg of brandy. I can't do with less than that.'

The squire said that he could easily get all that, so Hans got all of these tied up together, hung them over his shoulder on his good staff, and tramped away to Devilmoss Lake.

There he got into the boat, rowed out upon the lake, and got everything ready to fish. As he now lay out there in the middle of the lake, and it was pretty late in the evening, he thought he would have something to eat first, before starting to work. Just as he was at his busiest with this, Old Eric rose out of the lake, caught him by the cuff of the neck, whipped him out of the boat, and dragged him down to the bottom. It was a lucky thing that Hans had his walking-stick with him that day, and had just time to catch hold of it when he felt Old Eric's claws in his neck, so when they got down to the bottom he said, 'Stop now, just wait a little ; here is solid ground.' With that he caught Old Eric by the back of the neck with one hand, and hammered away on his back with the staff, till he beat him out as flat as a pancake. Old Eric then began to lament and howl, begging him just to let him go, and he would never come back to the lake again.

'No, my good fellow,' said Hans, 'you won't get off until you promise to bring all the fish in the lake up to the squire's courtyard, before to-morrow morning,'

Old Eric eagerly promised this, if Hans would only let him go ; so Hans rowed ashore, ate up the rest of his provisions, and went home to bed.

Next morning, when the squire rose and opened his front door, the fish came tumbling into the porch, and the whole yard was crammed full of them. He ran in again to his wife, for he could never devise anything himself, and said to her, 'What shall we do with him now ? Old Eric hasn't taken him. I am certain all the fish are out of the lake, for the yard is just filled with them.'

'Yes, that's a bad business,' said she ; 'you must see if you can't get him sent to Purgatory, to demand tribute.' The

squire therefore made his way to the men's quarters, to
speak to Hans, and it took him all his time to push his
way along the walls, under the eaves, on account of the
fish that filled the yard.   He thanked Hans for having

OLD ERIC CATCHES HANS

fished so well, and said that now he had an errand for
him, which he could only give to a trusty servant, and
that was to journey to Purgatory, and demand three
years tribute, which, he said, was owing to him from that
quarter.

'Willingly,' said Hans; 'but what road do I go, to get there?'

The squire stood, and did not know what to say, and had first to go in to his wife to ask her.

'Oh, what a fool you are!' said she, 'can't you direct him straight forward, south through the wood? Whether he gets there or not, *we* shall be quit of him.'

Out goes the squire again to Hans.

'The way lies straight forward, south through the wood,' said he.

Hans then must have his provisions for the journey; two bakings of bread, two casks of butter, two barrels ale, and two kegs of brandy. He tied all these up together, and got them on his shoulder hanging on his good walking-stick, and off he tramped southward.

After he had got through the wood, there was more than one road, and he was in doubt which of them was the right one, so he sat down and opened up his bundle of provisions. He found he had left his knife at home, but by good chance, there was a plough lying close at hand, so he took the coulter of this to cut the bread with. As he sat there and took his bite, a man came riding past him.

'Where are you from?' said Hans.

'From Purgatory,' said the man.

'Then stop and wait a little,' said Hans; but the man was in a hurry, and would not stop, so Hans ran after him and caught the horse by the tail. This brought it down on its hind legs, and the man went flying over its head into a ditch. 'Just wait a little,' said Hans; 'I am going the same way.' He got his provisions tied up again, and laid them on the horse's back; then he took hold of the reins, and said to the man, 'We two can go along together on foot.'

As they went on their way Hans told the stranger both about the errand he had on hand and the fun he had had with Old Eric. The other said but little, but he was well acquainted with the way, and it was no long time before they arrived at the gate. There both horse and rider disappeared, and Hans was left alone outside. ' They will come and let me in presently,' he thought to himself; but no one came. He hammered at the gate ; still no one appeared. Then he got tired of waiting, and smashed at the gate with his staff until he knocked it in pieces and got inside. A whole troop of little demons came down upon him and asked what he wanted. His master's compliments, said Hans, and he wanted three years' tribute. At this they howled at him, and were about to lay hold of him and drag him off; but when they had got some raps from his walking-stick they let go again, howled still louder than before, and ran in to Old Eric, who was still in bed, after his adventure in the lake. They told him that a messenger had come from the squire at Devilmoss to demand three years' tribute. He had knocked the gate in pieces and bruised their arms and legs with his iron staff.

' Give him three years' ! give him ten ! ' shouted Old Eric, ' only don't let him come near me.'

So all the little demons came dragging so much silver and gold that it was something awful. Hans filled his bundle with gold and silver coins, put it on his neck, and tramped back to his master, who was scared beyond all measure at seeing him again.

But Hans was also tired of service now. Of all the gold and silver he brought with him he let the squire keep one half, and *he* was glad enough, both for the money and at getting rid of Hans. The other half he took home to his father the smith in Furreby. To him also he said ' Farewell ; ' he was now tired of living on shore among mortal men, and preferred to go home again to his mother. Since that time no one has ever seen Hans, the Mermaid's Son.

PETER BULL [1]

THERE once lived in Denmark a peasant and his wife
who owned a very good farm, but had no children. They
often lamented to each other that they had no one of
their own to inherit all the wealth that they possessed·
They continued to prosper, and became rich people, but
there was no heir to it all.

One year it happened that they owned a pretty little
bull-calf, which they called Peter. It was the prettiest
little creature they had ever seen—so beautiful and so
wise that it understood everything that was said to it,
and so gentle and so full of play that both the man and
his wife came to be as fond of it as if it had been their
own child.

One day the man said to his wife, 'I wonder, now,
whether our parish clerk could teach Peter to talk; in
that case we could not do better than adopt him as our
son, and let him inherit all that we possess.'

'Well, I don't know,' said his wife, 'our clerk is tre-
mendously learned, and knows much more than his
Paternoster, and I could almost believe that he might be
able to teach Peter to talk, for Peter has a wonderfully
good head too. You might at least ask him about it.'

Off went the man to the clerk, and asked him whether
he thought he could teach a bull-calf that they had to
speak, for they wished so much to have it as their heir.

[1] From the Danish.

The clerk was no fool ; he looked round about to see that no one could overhear them, and said, ' Oh, yes, I can easily do that, but you must not speak to anyone about it. It must be done in all secrecy, and the priest must not know of it, otherwise I shall get into trouble, as it is forbidden. It will also cost you something, as some very expensive books are required.'

That did not matter at all, the man said ; they would not care so very much what it cost. The clerk could have a hundred dollars to begin with to buy the books. He also promised to tell no one about it, and to bring the calf round in the evening.

He gave the clerk the hundred dollars on the spot, and in the evening took the calf round to him, and the clerk promised to do his best with it. In a week's time he came back to the clerk to hear about the calf and see how it was thriving. The clerk, however, said that he could not get a sight of it, for then Peter would long after him and forget all that he had already learned. He was getting on well with his learning, but another hundred dollars were needed, as they must have more books. The peasant had the money with him, so he gave it to the clerk, and went home again with high hopes.

In another week the man came again to learn what progress Peter had made now.

' He is getting on very well,' said the clerk.

' I suppose he can't say anything yet ? ' said the man.

' Oh, yes,' said the clerk, ' he can say " Moo" now.'

'Do you think he will get on with his learning? ' asked the peasant.

' Oh, yes,' said the clerk, ' but I shall want another hundred dollars for books. Peter can't learn well out of the ones that he has got.'

' Well, well,' said the man, ' what must be spent *shall* be spent.'

So he gave the clerk the third hundred dollars for books, and a cask of good old ale for Peter. The clerk drank the ale himself, and gave the calf milk, which he thought would be better for it.

Some weeks passed, during which the peasant did not come round to ask after the calf, being frightened lest it should cost him another hundred dollars, for he had begun to squirm a bit at having to part with so much money. Meanwhile the clerk decided that the calf was as fat as it could be, so he killed it. After he had got all the beef out of the way he went inside, put on his black clothes, and made his way to the peasant's house.

As soon as he had said 'Good-day' he asked, 'Has Peter come home here?'

'No, indeed, he hasn't,' said the man; 'surely he hasn't run away?'

'I hope,' said the clerk, 'that he would not behave so contemptibly after all the trouble I have had to teach him, and all that I have spent upon him. I have had to spend at least a hundred dollars of my own money to buy books for him before I got him so far on. He could say anything he liked now, so he said to-day that he longed to see his parents again. I was willing to give him that pleasure, but I was afraid that he wouldn't be able to find the way here by himself, so I made myself ready to go with him. When we had got outside the house I remembered that I had left my stick inside, and went in again to get it. When I came out again Peter had gone off on his own account. I thought he would be here, and if he isn't I don't know where he is.'

The peasant and his wife began to lament bitterly that Peter had run away in this fashion just when they were to have so much joy of him, and after they had spent so much on his education. The worst of it was that now they had no heir after all. The clerk comforted them as best he could; he also was greatly distressed that Peter should have behaved in such a way just when he should have gained honour from his pupil. Perhaps he had only gone astray, and he would advertise him at church next Sunday, and find out whether anyone had seen him. Then he bade them 'Good-bye,' and went home and dined on a good fat veal roast.

Now it so happened that the clerk took in a newspaper, and one day he chanced to read in its columns of a new merchant who had settled in a town at some distance, and whose name was 'Peter Bull.' He put the newspaper in his pocket, and went round to the sorrowing couple who had lost their heir. He read the paragraph to them, and added, ' I wonder, now, whether that could be your bull-calf Peter ? '

' Yes, of course it is,' said the man ; 'who else would it be ? '

His wife then spoke up and said, ' You must set out, good man, and see about him, for it *is* him, I am perfectly certain. Take a good sum of money with you, too ; for who knows but what he may want some cash now that he has turned a merchant ! '

Next day the man got a bag of money on his back and a sandwich in his pocket, and his pipe in his mouth, and set out for the town where the new merchant lived. It was no short way, and he travelled for many days before he finally arrived there. He reached it one morning, just at daybreak, found out the right place, and asked if the merchant was at home. Yes, he was, said the people, but he was not up yet.

'That doesn't matter,' said the peasant, ' for I am his father. Just show me up to his bedroom.'

He was shown up to the room, and as soon as he entered it, and caught sight of the merchant, he recognised him at once. He had the same broad forehead, the same thick neck, and same red hair, but in other respects he was now like a human being. The peasant rushed straight up to him and took a firm hold of him. ' O Peter,' said he, 'what a sorrow you have caused us, both myself and your mother, by running off like this just as we had got you well educated ! Get up, now,

so that I can see you properly, and have a talk with
you.'

The merchant thought that it was a lunatic who had
made his way in to him, and thought it best to take
things quietly.

'All right,' said he, 'I shall do so at once.' He got
out of bed and made haste to dress himself.

'Ay,' said the peasant, 'now I can see how clever our
clerk is. He has done well by you, for now you look
just like a human being. If one didn't know it, one
would never think that it was you we got from the red
cow; will you come home with me now?'

'No,' said the merchant, 'I can't find time just now.
I have a big business to look after.'

'You could have the farm at once, you know,' said
the peasant, 'and we old people would retire. But if
you would rather stay in business, of course you may do
so. Are you in want of anything?'

'Oh, yes,' said the merchant; 'I want nothing so much
as money. A merchant has always a use for that.'

'I can well believe that,' said the peasant, 'for you
had nothing at all to start with. I have brought some
with me for that very end.' With that he emptied his
bag of money out upon the table, so that it was all
covered with bright dollars.

When the merchant saw what kind of man he had
before him he began to speak him fair, and invited him
to stay with him for some days, so that they might have
some more talk together.

'Very well,' said the peasant, 'but you must call me
" Father." '

'I have neither father nor mother alive,' said Peter Bull.

'I know that,' said the man; 'your real father was
sold at Hamburg last Michaelmas, and your real mother
died while calving in spring; but my wife and I have
adopted you as our own, and you are our only heir, so
you must call me " Father." '

Peter Bull was quite willing to do so, and it was settled that he should keep the money, while the peasant made his will and left to him all that he had, before he went home to his wife, and told her the whole story.

She was delighted to hear that it was true enough about Peter Bull—that he was no other than their own bull· calf.

' You must go at once and tell the clerk,' said she, ' and pay him the hundred dollars of his own money that he spent upon our son. He has earned them well, and more besides, for all the joy he has given us in having such a son and heir.'

The man agreed with this, and thanked the clerk for all he had done, and gave him two hundred dollars. Then he sold the farm, and removed with his wife to the town where their dear son and heir was living. To him they gave all their wealth, and lived with him till their dying day.

THE BIRD 'GRIP'[1]

IT happened once that a king, who had a great kingdom and three sons, became blind, and no human skill or art could restore to him his sight. At last there came to the palace an old woman, who told him that in the whole world there was only one thing that could give him back his sight, and that was to get the bird Grip; his song would open the king's eyes.

When the king's eldest son heard this he offered to bring the bird Grip, which was kept in a cage by a king in another country, and carefully guarded as his greatest treasure. The blind king was greatly rejoiced at his son's resolve, fitted him out in the best way he could, and let him go. When the prince had ridden some distance he came to an inn, in which there were many guests, all of whom were merry, and drank and sang and played at dice. This joyous life pleased the prince so well that he stayed in the inn, took part in the playing and drinking, and forgot both his blind father and the bird Grip.

Meanwhile the king waited with both hope and anxiety for his son's return, but as time went on and nothing was heard of him, the second prince asked leave to go in search of his brother, as well as to bring the bird Grip. The king granted his request, and fitted him out in the finest fashion. But when the prince came to the inn and found his brother among his merry companions,

---

[1] Translated from the Swedish.

he also remained there, and forgot both the bird Grip and his blind father.

When the king noticed that neither of his sons returned, although a long time had passed since the second one set out, he was greatly distressed, for not only had he lost all hope of getting back his sight, but he had also lost his two eldest sons. The youngest now came to him, and offered to go in search of his brothers and to bring the bird Grip ; he was quite certain that he would succeed in this. The king was unwilling to risk his third son on such an errand, but he begged so long that his father had at last to consent. This prince also was fitted out in the finest manner, like his brothers, and so rode away.

He also turned into the same inn as his brothers, and when these saw him they assailed him with many entreaties to remain with them and share their merry life. But he answered that now, when he had found them, his next task was to get the bird Grip, for which his blind father was longing, and so he had not a single hour to spare with them in the inn. He then said farewell to his brothers, and rode on to find another inn in which to pass the night. When he had ridden a long way, and it began to grow dark, he came to a house which lay deep in the forest. Here he was received in a very friendly manner by the host, who put his horse into the stable, and led the prince himself into the guest-chamber, where he ordered a maid-servant to lay the cloth and set down the supper. It was now dark, and while the girl was laying the cloth and setting down the dishes, and the prince had begun to appease his hunger, he heard the most piteous shrieks and cries from the next room. He sprang up from the table and asked the girl what these cries were, and whether he had fallen into a den of robbers. The girl answered that these shrieks were heard every night,.but it was no living being who uttered them ; it was a dead man, whose life the host had taken because he could not pay for the meals he had had in the inn. The host further refused to bury the dead man, as he had left nothing to pay the expenses of the funeral, and every night he went and scourged the dead body of his victim.

When she had said this she lifted the cover off one of the dishes, and the prince saw that there lay on it a knife and an axe. He understood then that the host meant to ask him by this what kind of death he preferred to die, unless he was willing to ransom his life with his money. He then summoned the host, gave him a large sum for his own life, and paid the dead man's debt as well, besides paying him for burying the body, which the murderer now promised to attend to.

The prince, however, felt that his life was not safe in this murderer's den, and asked the maid to help him to escape that night. She replied that the attempt to do so might cost her her own life, as the key of the stable in which the prince's horse stood lay under the host's pillow ; but, as she herself was a prisoner there, she would help him to escape if he would take her along with him. He promised to do so, and they succeeded in getting away from the inn, and rode on until they came to another far away from it, where the prince got a good place for the girl before proceeding on his journey.

As he now rode all alone through a forest there met him a fox, who greeted him in a friendly fashion, and asked him where he was going, and on what errand he was bent. The prince answered that his errand was too important to be confided to everyone that he met.

' You are right in that,' said the fox, ' for it relates to the bird Grip, which you want to take and bring home to your blind father ; I could help you in this, but in that case you must follow my counsel.'

The prince thought that this was a good offer, especially as the fox was ready to go with him and show him the way to the castle, where the bird Grip sat in his cage, and so he promised to obey the fox's instructions. When they had traversed the forest together they saw the castle at some distance. Then the fox gave the prince three grains of gold, one of which he was to throw into the guard-room, another into the room where the bird Grip sat, and the third into its cage. He could then take the bird, but he must beware of stroking it; otherwise it would go ill with him.

The prince took the grains of gold, and promised to follow the fox's directions faithfully. When he came to the guard-room of the castle he threw one of the grains in there, and the guards at once fell asleep. The same thing happened with those who kept watch in the room beside the bird Grip, and when he threw the third grain into its cage the bird also fell asleep. When the prince got the beautiful bird into his hand he could not resist the temptation to stroke it, whereupon it awoke and began to scream. At this the whole castle woke up, and the prince was taken prisoner.

As he now sat in his prison, and bitterly lamented that his own disobedience had brought himself into trouble, and deprived his father of the chance of recovering his sight, the fox suddenly stood in front of him. The prince was very pleased to see it again, and received with great meekness all its reproaches, as well as promised to be more obedient in the future, if the fox would only help him out of his fix. The fox said that he had come to assist him, but he could do no more than advise the prince, when he was brought up for trial, to answer 'yes' to all the judge's questions, and everything would go well. The prince faithfully followed his instructions, so that when the judge asked him whether he had meant to steal the bird Grip he said 'Yes,' and when the judge asked him if he was a master-thief he again answered 'Yes.'

When the king heard that he admitted being a master-thief, he said that he would forgive him the attempt to steal the bird if he would go to the next kingdom and carry off the world's most beautiful princess, and bring her to him. To this also the prince said 'Yes.'

When he left the castle he met the fox, who went along with him to the next kingdom, and, when they came near the castle there, gave him three grains of gold—one to throw into the guard-room, another into the princess's chamber, and the third into her bed. At the same time he strictly warned him not to kiss the princess. The prince went to the castle, and did with the grains of gold as the fox had told him, so that sleep fell upon everyone there ; but when he had taken the princess into his arms he forgot the fox's warning, at the sight of her beauty, and kissed her. Then both she and all the others in the castle woke ; the prince was taken prisoner, and put into a strong dungeon.

Here the fox again came to him and reproached him with his disobedience, but promised to help him out of this trouble also if he would answer ' yes ' to everything they asked him at his trial. The prince willingly agreed to this, and admitted to the judge that he had meant to steal the princess, and that he was a master-thief.

When the king learned this he said he would forgive his offence if he would go to the next kingdom and steal the horse with the four golden shoes. To this also the prince said ' Yes.'

When he had gone a little way from the castle he met the fox, and they continued on their journey together. When they reached the end of it the prince for the third time received three grains of gold from the fox, with directions to throw one into the guard-chamber, another into the stable, and the third into the horse's stall. But the fox told him that above the horse's stall hung a beautiful golden saddle, which he must not touch, if he did not want to bring himself into new troubles worse than those he had escaped from, for then the fox could help him no longer.

THE · PRINCE · FORGOT · THE · FOX'S · WARNING · & · KISSED · THE · PRINCESS
THEN · BOTH · SHE · AND · ALL · THE · OTHERS · IN · THE · CASTLE · AWOKE ·

The prince promised to be firm this time. He threw the grains of gold in the proper places, and untied the horse, but with that he caught sight of the golden saddle, and thought that none but it could suit so beautiful a horse, especially as it had golden shoes. But just as he stretched out his hand to take it he received from some invisible being so hard a blow on the arm that it was made quite numb. This recalled to him his promise and his danger, so he led out the horse without looking at the golden saddle again.

The fox was waiting for him outside the castle, and the prince confessed to him that he had very nearly given way to temptation this time as well. ' I know that,' said the fox, 'for it was I who struck you over the arm.'

As they now went on together the prince said that he could not forget the beautiful princess, and asked the fox whether he did not think that she ought to ride home to his father's palace on this horse with the golden shoes. The fox agreed that this would be excellent ; if the prince would now go and carry her off he would give him three grains of gold for that purpose. The prince was quite ready, and promised to keep better command of himself this time, and not kiss her.

He got the grains of gold and entered the castle, where he carried off the princess, set her on the beautiful horse, and held on his way. When they came near to the castle where the bird Grip sat in his cage he again asked the fox for three grains of gold. These he got, and with them he was successful in carrying off the bird.

He was now full of joy, for his blind father would now recover his sight, while he himself owned the world's most beautiful princess and the horse with the golden shoes.

The prince and the princess travelled on together with mirth and happiness, and the fox followed them until they came to the forest where the prince first met with him

'Here our ways part,' said the fox. ' You have now got
all that your heart desired, and you will have a prosperous journey to your father's palace if only you do not
ransom anyone's life with money.'

The prince thanked the fox for all his help, promised
to give heed to his warning, said farewell to him, and rode
on, with the princess by his side and the bird Grip on his
wrist.

They soon arrived at the inn where the two eldest
brothers had stayed, forgetting their errand. But now no
merry song or noise of mirth was heard from it. When
the prince came nearer he saw two gallows erected, and
when he entered the inn along with the princess he saw
that all the rooms were hung with black, and that everything inside foreboded sorrow and death. He asked the
reason of this, and was told that two princes were to be
hanged that day for debt ; they had spent all their money
in feasting and playing, and were now deeply in debt to
the host, and as no one could be found to ransom their
lives they were about to be hanged according to the law.

The prince knew that it was his two brothers who had
thus forfeited their lives, and it cut him to the heart to
think that two princes should suffer such a shameful
death ; and, as he had sufficient money with him, he paid
their debts, and so ransomed their lives.

At first the brothers were grateful for their liberty,
but when they saw the youngest brother's treasures they
became jealous of his good fortune, and planned how to
bring him to destruction, and then take the bird Grip,
the princess, and the horse with the golden shoes, and
convey them to their blind father. After they had agreed
on how to carry out their treachery they enticed the prince
to a den of lions and threw him down among them. Then
they set the princess on horseback, took the bird Grip,
and rode homeward. The princess wept bitterly, but they
told her that it would cost her her life if she did not say
that the two brothers had won all the treasures.

When they arrived at their father's palace there was great rejoicing, and everyone praised the two princes for their courage and bravery.

When the king inquired after the youngest brother they answered that he had led such a life in the inn that he had been hanged for debt. The king sorrowed bitterly over this, because the youngest prince was his dearest son, and the joy over the treasures soon died away, for the bird Grip would not sing so that the king might recover his sight, the princess wept night and day, and no one dared to venture so close to the horse as to have a look at his golden shoes.

Now when the youngest prince was thrown down into the lions' den he found the fox sitting there, and the lions, instead of tearing him to pieces, showed him the greatest friendliness. Nor was the fox angry with him for having forgot his last warning. He only said that sons who could so forget their old father and disgrace their royal birth as these had done would not hesitate to betray their brother either. Then he took the prince up out of the lions' den and gave him directions what to do now so as to come by his rights again.

The prince thanked the fox with all his heart for his true friendship, but the fox answered that if he had been of any use to him he would now for his own part ask a service of him. The prince replied that he would do him any service that was in his power.

'I have only one thing to ask of you,' said the fox, ' and that is, that you should cut off my head with your sword.'

The prince was astonished, and said that he could not bring himself to cut the head off his truest friend, and to this he stuck in spite of all the fox's declarations that it was the greatest service he could do him. At this the fox became very sorrowful, and declared that the prince's refusal to grant his request now compelled him to do a deed which he was very unwilling to do—if the prince would not cut off his head, then he must kill the prince himself. Then at last the prince drew his good sword and cut off the fox's head, and the next moment a youth stood before him.

'Thanks,' said he, 'for this service, which has freed me from a spell that not even death itself could loosen. I am the dead man who lay unburied in the robber's inn, where you ransomed me and gave me honourable burial, and therefore I have helped you in your journey.'

With this they parted, and the prince, disguising himself as a horse-shoer, went up to his father's palace and offered his services there.

The king's men told him that a horse-shoer was indeed wanted at the palace, but he must be one who could lift up the feet of the horse with the golden shoes, and such a one they had not yet been able to find. The prince asked to see the horse, and as soon as he entered the stable the steed began to neigh in a friendly fashion, and stood as quiet and still as a lamb while the prince lifted up his hoofs, one after the other, and showed the king's men the famous golden shoes.

After this the king's men began to talk about the bird Grip, and how strange it was that he would not sing, however well he was attended to. The horse-shoer then said that he knew the bird very well ; he had seen it when it sat in its cage in another king's palace, and if it did not sing now it must be because it did not have all that it wanted. He himself knew so much about the bird's ways that if he only got to see it he could tell at once what it lacked.

The king's men now took counsel whether they ought to take the stranger in before the king, for in his chamber sat the bird Grip along with the weeping princess. It was decided to risk doing so, and the horse-shoer was led into the king's chamber, where he had no sooner called the bird by its name than it began to sing and the princess to smile. Then the darkness cleared away from the king's eyes, and the more the bird sang the more clearly did he see, till at last in the strange horse-shoer he recognised his youngest son. Then the princess told the king how treacherously his eldest sons had acted, and he had them banished from his kingdom ;

but the youngest prince married the princess, and got the horse with the golden shoes and half the kingdom from his father, who kept for himself so long as he lived the bird Grip, which now sang with all its heart to the king and all his court.

SNOWFLAKE [1]

ONCE upon a time there lived a peasant called Ivan, and he had a wife whose name was Marie. They would have been quite happy except for one thing : they had no children to play with, and as they were now old people they did not find that watching the children of their neighbours at all made up to them for having none of their own.

One winter, which nobody living will ever forget, the snow lay so deep that it came up to the knees of even the tallest man. When it had all fallen, and the sun was shining again, the children ran out into the street to play, and the old man and his wife sat at their window and gazed at them. The children first made a sort of little terrace, and stamped it hard and firm, and then they began to make a snow woman. Ivan and Marie watched them, the while thinking about many things.

Suddenly Ivan's face brightened, and, looking at his wife, he said, 'Wife, why shouldn't *we* make a snow woman too ? '

' Why not ? ' replied Marie, who happened to be in a very good temper ; ' it might amuse us a little. But there is no use making a woman. Let us make a little snow child, and pretend it is a living one.'

' Yes, let us do that,' said Ivan, and he took down his cap and went into the garden with his old wife.

---

[1] Slavonic story. *Contes Populaires Slaves,* traduits par Louis Léger. Paris : Leroux, Editeur.

Then the two set to work with all their might to make a doll out of the snow. They shaped a little body and two little hands and two little feet. On top of all they placed a ball of snow, out of which the head was to be.

' What in the world are you doing? ' asked a passer-by.

' Can't you guess? ' returned Ivan.

' Making a snow-child,' replied Marie.

They had finished the nose and the chin. Two holes were left for the eyes, and Ivan carefully shaped out the mouth. No sooner had he done so than he felt a warm breath upon his cheek. He started back in surprise and looked—and behold! the eyes of the child met his, and its lips, which were as red as raspberries, smiled at him!

' What is it? ' cried Ivan, crossing himself. ' Am I mad, or is the thing bewitched? '

The snow-child bent its head as if it had been really alive. It moved its little arms and its little legs in the snow that lay about it just as the living children did theirs.

' Ah! Ivan, Ivan,' exclaimed Marie, trembling with joy, ' heaven has sent us a child at last! ' And she threw herself upon Snowflake (for that was the snow-child's name) and covered her with kisses. And the loose snow fell away from Snowflake as an egg shell does from an egg, and it was a little girl whom Marie held in her arms.

' Oh! my darling Snowflake! ' cried the old woman, and led her into the cottage.

And Snowflake grew fast ; each hour as well as each day made a difference, and every day she became more and more beautiful. The old couple hardly knew how to contain themselves for joy, and thought of nothing else. The cottage was always full of village children, for they amused Snowflake, and there was nothing in the world they would not have done to amuse her. She was their doll, and they were continually inventing new dresses for her, and teaching her songs or playing with her. Nobody knew how clever she was! She noticed everything, and could learn a lesson in a moment. Anyone would have taken her for thirteen at least! And, besides all that, she was so good and obedient; and so pretty, too! Her skin was as white as snow, her eyes were as blue as forget-me-nots, and her hair was long and golden. Only her cheeks had no colour in them, but were as fair as her forehead.

So the winter went on, till at last the spring sun mounted higher in the heavens and began to warm the earth. The grass grew green in the fields, and high in the air the larks were heard singing. The village girls met and danced in a ring, singing, ' Beautiful spring, how came you here? How came you here? Did you come on a plough, or was it a harrow?' Only Snowflake sat quite still by the window of the cottage.

' What is the matter, dear child?' asked Marie. ' Why are you so sad? Are you ill? or have they treated you unkindly?'

' No,' replied Snowflake, ' it is nothing, mother; no one has hurt me : I am well.'

The spring sun had chased away the last snow from its hiding place under the hedges; the fields were full of flowers; nightingales sang in the trees, and all the world was gay. But the gayer grew the birds and the flowers the sadder became Snowflake. She hid herself from her playmates, and curled herself up where the shadows were deepest, like a lily amongst its leaves. Her only pleasure was to lie amid the green willows near some sparkling stream. At the dawn and at twilight only she seemed happy. When a great storm broke, and the earth was white with hail, she became bright and joyous as the Snowflake of old; but when the clouds passed, and the hail melted beneath the sun, Snowflake would burst into tears and weep as a sister would weep over her brother.

The spring passed, and it was the eve of St. John, or Midsummer Day. This was the greatest holiday of the year, when the young girls met in the woods to dance and play. They went to fetch Snowflake, and said to Marie : ' Let her come and dance with us.'

But Marie was afraid : she could not tell why, only she could not bear the child to go. Snowflake did not wish to go either, but they had no excuse ready. So Marie kissed the girl and said : ' Go, my Snowflake, and be happy with your friends, and you, dear children, be careful of her. You know she is the light of my eyes to me.'

' Oh, we will take care of her,' cried the girls gaily, and they ran off to the woods. There they wore wreaths, gathered nosegays, and sang songs—some sad, some merry. And whatever they did Snowflake did too.

When the sun set they lit a fire of dry grass, and placed themselves in a row, Snowflake being the last of all. ' Now watch us,' they said, ' and run just as we do.' And they all began to sing and to jump one after another across the fire.

Suddenly, close behind them, they heard a sigh, then a groan. ' Ah ! ' They turned hastily and looked at each other. There was nothing. They looked again. Where was Snowflake ? She has hidden herself for fun, they thought, and searched for her everywhere. ' Snowflake ! Snowflake ! ' But there was no answer. ' Where can she be ? Oh, she must have gone home.' They returned to the village, but there was no Snowflake.

For days after that they sought her high and low. They examined every bush and every hedge, but there was no Snowflake. And long after everyone else had given up hope Ivan and Marie would wander through the woods crying ' Snowflake, my dove, come back, come back ! ' And sometimes they thought they heard a call, but it was never the voice of Snowflake.

And what *had* become of her ? Had a fierce wild beast seized her and dragged her into his lair in the

forest ? Had some bird carried her off across the wide
blue sea ?

No, no beast had touched her, no bird had borne her
away. With the first breath of flame that swept over
her when she ran with her friends Snowflake had melted
away, and a little soft haze floating upwards was all that
remained of her.

I KNOW WHAT I HAVE LEARNED [1]

THERE was once a man who had three daughters, and
they were all married to trolls, who lived underground.
One day the man thought that he would pay them a visit,
and his wife gave him some dry bread to eat by the way.
After he had walked some distance he grew both tired
and hungry, so he sat down on the east side of a mound
and began to eat his dry bread. The mound then opened,
and his youngest daughter came out of it, and said,
'Why, father! why are you not coming in to see me?'

'Oh,' said he, 'if I had known that you lived here,
and had seen any entrance, I would have come in.'

Then he entered the mound along with her.

The troll came home soon after this, and his wife told
him that her father was come, and asked him to go and
buy some beef to make broth with.

'We can get it easier than that!' said the troll.

He fixed an iron spike into one of the beams of the
roof, and ran his head against this till he had knocked
several large pieces off his head. He was just as well as
ever after doing this, and they got their broth without
further trouble.

The troll then gave the old man a sackful of money,
and laden with this he betook himself homewards. When
he came near his home he remembered that he had a
cow about to calve, so he laid down the money on the
ground, ran home as fast as he could, and asked his wife
whether the cow had calved yet.

[1] From the Danish.

'What kind of a hurry is this to come home in?'
said she. 'No, the cow has not calved yet.'

'Then you must come out and help me in with a
sackful of money,' said the man.

'A sackful of money?' cried his wife.

'Yes, a sackful of money,' said he. 'Is that so very
wonderful?'

His wife did not believe very much what he told her,
but she humoured him, and went out with him.

When they came to the spot where he had left it
there was no money there; a thief had come along and
stolen it. His wife then grew angry and scolded him
heartily.

'Well, well!' said he, 'hang the money! I know
what I have learned.'

'What have you learned?' said she.

'Ah! *I* know that,' said the man.

After some time had passed the man had a mind to visit his second eldest daughter. His wife again gave him some dry bread to eat, and when he grew tired and hungry he sat down on the east side of a mound and began to eat it. As he sat there his daughter came up out of the mound, and invited him to come inside, which he did very willingly.

Soon after this the troll came home. It was dark by that time, and his wife bade him go and buy some candles.

THE TROLL GIVES A LIGHT

'Oh, we shall soon get a light,' said the troll. With that he dipped his fingers into the fire, and they then gave light without being burned in the least.

The old man got two sacks of money here, and plodded away homewards with these. When he was very nearly home he again thought of the cow that was with calf, so he laid down the money, ran home, and asked his wife whether the cow had calved yet.

'Whatever is the matter with you?' said she. 'You

come hurrying as if the whole house was about to fall. You may set your mind at rest : the cow has not calved yet.'

The man now asked her to come and help him home with the two sacks of money. She did not believe him very much, but he continued to assure her that it was quite true, till at last she gave in and went with him. When they came to the spot there had again been a

THE TROLL LADLES UP THE FISHES

thief there and taken the money. It was no wonder that the woman was angry about this, but the man only said, ' Ah, if you only knew what I have learned.'

A third time the man set out—to visit his eldest daughter. When he came to a mound he sat down on the east side of it and ate the dry bread which his wife had given him to take with him. The daughter then came out of the mound and invited her father to come inside.

In a little the troll came home, and his wife asked him to go and buy some fish.

'We can get them much more easily than that,' said the troll. 'Give me your dough trough and your ladle.'

They seated themselves in the trough, and rowed out on the lake which was beside the mound. When they had got out a little way the troll said to his wife, ' Are my eyes green ? '

' No, not yet,' said she.

He rowed on a little further and asked again, ' Are my eyes not green yet ? '

' Yes,' said his wife, ' they are green now.'

Then the troll sprang into the water and ladled up so many fish that in a short time the trough could hold no more. They then rowed home again, and had a good meal off the fish.

The old man now got three sacks full of money, and set off home with them. When he was almost home the cow again came into his head, and he laid down the money. This time, however, he took his wooden shoes and laid them above the money, thinking that no one would take it after that. Then he ran home and asked his wife whether the cow had calved. It had not, and she scolded him again for behaving in this way, but in the end he persuaded her to go with him to help him with the three sacks of money.

When they came to the spot they found only the wooden shoes, for a thief had come along in the meantime and taken all the money. The woman was very angry, and broke out upon her husband ; but he took it all very quietly, and only said, ' Hang the money ! I know what I have learned.'

' What have you learned I should like to know ? ' said his wife.

' You will see that yet,' said the man.

One day his wife took a fancy for broth, and said to him, ' Oh, go to the village, and buy a piece of beef to make broth.'

'There's no need of that,' said he; 'we can get it an easier way.' With that he drove a spike into a beam, and ran his head against it, and in consequence had to lie in bed for a long time afterwards.

After he had recovered from this his wife asked him one day to go and buy candles, as they had none.

'No,' he said, 'there's no need for that;' and he stuck his hand into the fire. This also made him take to bed for a good while.

When he had got better again his wife one day wanted fish, and asked him to go and buy some. The man, however, wished again to show what he had learned, so he asked her to come along with him and bring her dough trough and a ladle. They both seated themselves in this, and rowed upon the lake. When they had got out a little way the man said, 'Are my eyes green?'

'No,' said his wife; 'why should they be?'

They rowed a little further out, and he asked again, 'Are my eyes not green yet?'

'What nonsense is this?' said she; 'why should they be green?'

'Oh, my dear,' said he, 'can't you just say that they are green?'

'Very well,' said she, 'they *are* green.'

As soon as he heard this he sprang out into the water with the ladle for the fishes, but he just got leave to stay there with them!

THE CUNNING SHOEMAKER [1]

ONCE upon a time there lived a shoemaker who could get no work to do, and was so poor that he and his wife nearly died of hunger. At last he said to her, 'It is no use waiting on here—I can find nothing; so I shall go down to Mascalucia, and perhaps there I shall be more lucky.'

So down he went to Mascalucia, and walked through the streets crying, ' Who wants some shoes?' And very soon a window was pushed up, and a woman's head was thrust out of it.

'Here are a pair for you to patch,' she said. And he sat down on her doorstep and set about patching them.

'How much do I owe you?' she asked when they were done.

'A shilling.'

'Here is eighteenpence, and good luck to you.' And he went his way. He turned into the next street and set up his cry again, and it was not long before another window was pushed up and another head appeared.

'Here are some shoes for you to patch.'

And the shoemaker sat down on the doorstep and patched them.

'How much do I owe you?' asked the woman when the shoes were finished.

'A florin.'

'Here is a crown piece, and good luck to you.' And she shut the window.

[1] *Sicilianische Mährchen.*

' Well,' thought the shoemaker, ' I have done finely. But I will not go back to my wife just yet, as, if I only go on at this rate, I shall soon have enough money to buy a donkey.'

Having made up his mind what was best to do, he stayed in the town a few days longer—till he had four gold pieces safe in his purse. Then he went to the market and for two of them he bought a good strong donkey, and, mounting on its back, he rode home to Catania. But as he entered a thick wood he saw in the distance a band of robbers who were coming quickly towards him.

' I am lost,' thought he ; ' they are sure to take from me all the money that I have earned, and I shall be as poor as ever I was. What can I do? ' However, being a clever little man and full of spirit, he did not lose heart, but, taking five florins, he fastened them out of sight under the donkey's thick mane. Then he rode on.

Directly the robbers came up to him they seized him exactly as he had foretold and took away all his money.

' Oh, dear friends ! ' he cried, wringing his hands, ' I am only a poor shoemaker, and have nothing but this donkey left in the world.'

As he spoke the donkey gave himself a shake, and down fell the five florins.

' Where did that come from ? ' asked the robbers.

' Ah,' replied the shoemaker, ' you have guessed my secret. The donkey is a golden donkey, and supplies me with all my money.'

' Sell him to us,' said the robbers. ' We will give you any price you like.'

The shoemaker at first declared that nothing would induce him to sell him, but at last he agreed to hand him over to the robbers for fifty gold pieces. ' But listen to what I tell you,' said he. ' You must each take it in turn to own him for a night and a day, or else you will all be fighting over the money.'

With these words they parted, the robbers driving
the donkey to their cave in the forest and the shoemaker
returning home, very pleased with the success of his
trick. He just stopped on the way to pick up a good
dinner, and the next day spent most of his gains in buying
a small vineyard.

Meanwhile the robbers had arrived at the cave where
they lived, and the captain, calling them all round him,
announced that it was his right to have the donkey for
the first night. His companions agreed, and then he
told his wife to put a mattress in the stable. She asked
if he had gone out of his mind, but he answered crossly,
' What is that to you? Do as you are bid, and to-morrow
I will bring you some treasures.'

Very early the captain awoke and searched the stable,
but could find nothing, and guessed that Master Joseph
had been making fun of them. ' Well,' he said to
himself, ' if *I* have been taken in, the others shall not
come off any better.'

So, when one of his men arrived and asked him
eagerly how much money he had got, he answered gaily,
' Oh, comrade, if you only knew! But I shall say
nothing about it till everyone has had his turn! '

One after another they all took the donkey, but no
money was forthcoming for anybody. At length, when
all the band had been tricked, they held a council, and
resolved to march to the shoemaker's house and punish
him well for his cunning. Just as before, the shoemaker
saw them a long way off, and began to think how he
could outwit them again. When he had hit upon a plan
he called his wife, and said to her, ' Take a bladder and
fill it with blood, and bind it round your neck. When
the robbers come and demand the money they gave me
for the donkey I shall shout to you and tell you to get
it quickly. You must argue with me, and decline to
obey me, and then I shall plunge my knife into the
bladder, and you must fall to the ground as if you were

dead. There you must lie till I play on my guitar; then get up and begin to dance.'

The wife made haste to do as she was bid, and there was no time to lose, for the robbers were drawing very near the house. They entered with a great noise, and overwhelmed the shoemaker with reproaches for having deceived them about the donkey.

'The poor beast must have lost its power owing to the change of masters,' said he; 'but we will not quarrel about it. You shall have back the fifty gold pieces that you gave for him. Aite,' he cried to his wife, 'go quickly to the chest upstairs, and bring down the money for these gentlemen.'

'Wait a little,' answered she; 'I must first bake this fish. It will be spoilt if I leave it now.'

'Go this instant, as you are bid,' shouted the shoemaker, stamping as if he was in a great passion; but, as she did not stir, he drew his knife, and stabbed her in the neck. The blood spurted out freely, and she fell to the ground as if she was dead.

'What have you done?' asked the robbers, looking at him in dismay. 'The poor woman was doing nothing.'

'Perhaps I was hasty, but it is easily set right,' replied the shoemaker, taking down his guitar and beginning to play. Hardly had he struck the first notes than his wife sat up; then got on her feet and danced.

The robbers stared with open mouths, and at last they said, 'Master Joseph, you may keep the fifty gold pieces. But tell us what you will take for your guitar, for you must sell it to us?'

'Oh, that is impossible!' replied the shoemaker, 'for every time I have a quarrel with my wife I just strike her dead, and so give vent to my anger. This has become such a habit with me that I don't think I could break myself of it; and, of course, if I got rid of the guitar I could never bring her back to life again.'

However, the robbers would not listen to him, and

at last he consented to take forty gold pieces for the guitar.

Then they all returned to their cave in the forest, delighted with their new purchase, and longing for a chance of trying its powers. But the captain declared that the first trial belonged to him, and after that the others might have their turn.

That evening he called to his wife and said, ' What have you got for supper? '

' Macaroni,' answered she.

' Why have you not boiled a fish? ' he cried, and stabbed her in the neck so that she fell dead. The captain, who was not in the least angry, seized the guitar and began to play; but, let him play as loud as he would, the dead woman never stirred. ' Oh, lying shoemaker! Oh, abominable knave! Twice has he got the better of me. But I will pay him out! '

So he raged and swore, but it did him no good. The fact remained that he had killed his wife and could not bring her back again.

The next morning came one of the robbers to fetch the guitar, and to hear what had happened.

' Well, how have you got on? '

' Oh, splendidly! I stabbed my wife, and then began to play, and now she is as well as ever.'

' Did you really? Then this evening I will try for myself.'

Of course the same thing happened over again, till all the wives had been killed secretly, and when there were no more left they whispered to each other the dreadful tale, and swore to be avenged on the shoemaker.

The band lost no time in setting out for his house, and, as before, the shoemaker saw them coming from afar. He called to his wife, who was washing in the kitchen : ' Listen, Aita : when the robbers come and ask for me say I have gone to the vineyard. Then tell the dog to call me, and chase him from the house.'

When he had given these directions he ran out of the back door and hid behind a barrel. A few minutes later the robbers arrived, and called loudly for the shoemaker.

'Alas! good gentlemen, he is up in the vineyard, but I will send the dog after him at once. Here! now quickly to the vineyard, and tell your master some gentlemen are here who wish to speak to him. Go as fast as you can.' And she opened the door and let the dog out.

'You can really trust the dog to call your husband?' asked the robbers.

'Dear me, yes! He understands everything, and will always carry any message I give him.'

By-and-bye the shoemaker came in and said, 'Good morning, gentlemen; the dog tells me you wish to speak to me.'

'Yes, we do,' replied the robber; 'we have come to speak to you about that guitar. It is your fault that we have murdered all our wives; and, though we played as you told us, none of them ever came back to life.'

'You could not have played properly,' said the shoemaker. 'It was your own fault.'

'Well, we will forget all about it,' answered the robbers, 'if you will only sell us your dog.'

'Oh, that is impossible! I should never get on without him.'

But the robbers offered him forty gold pieces, and at last he agreed to let them have the dog.

So they departed, taking the dog with them, and when they got back to their cave the captain declared that it was his right to have the first trial.

He then called his daughter, and said to her, 'I am going to the inn; if anybody wants me, loose the dog, and send him to call me.'

About an hour after some one arrived on business, and the girl untied the dog and said, 'Go to the inn and call my father!' The dog bounded off, but ran straight to the shoemaker.

When the robber got home and found no dog he thought ' He must have gone back to his old master,' and, though night had already fallen, he went off after him.

' Master Joseph, is the dog here ? ' asked he.

' Ah ! yes, the poor beast is so fond of me ! You must give him time to get accustomed to new ways.'

So the captain brought the dog back, and the following morning handed him over to another of the band, just saying that the animal really could do what the shoe-maker had said.

The second robber carefully kept his own counsel, and fetched the dog secretly back from the shoemaker, and so on through the whole band. At length, when everybody had suffered, they met and told the whole story, and next day they all marched off in fury to the man who had made game of them. After reproaching him with having deceived them, they tied him up in a sack, and told him they were going to throw him into the sea. The shoe-maker lay quite still, and let them do as they would.

They went on till they came to a church, and the robbers said, ' The sun is hot and the sack is heavy ; let us leave it here and go in and rest.' So they put the sack down by the roadside, and went into the church.

Now, on a hill near by there was a swineherd looking after a great herd of pigs and whistling merrily.

When Master Joseph heard him he cried out as loud as he could, ' I won't ; I won't, I say.'

' What won't you do ? ' asked the swineherd.

' Oh,' replied the shoemaker. ' They want me to marry the king's daughter, and I won't do it.'

' How lucky you are ! ' sighed the swineherd. ' Now, if it were only me ! '

' Oh, if that's all ! ' replied the cunning shoemaker, ' get you into this sack, and let me out.'

Then the swineherd opened the sack and took the place of the shoemaker, who went gaily off, driving the pigs before him.

When the robbers were rested they came out of the church, took up the sack, and carried it to the sea, where they threw it in, and it sank directly. As they came back they met the shoemaker, and stared at him with open mouths.

'Oh, if you only knew how many pigs live in the sea,' he cried. 'And the deeper you go the more there are. I have just brought up these, and mean to return for some more.'

'There are still some left there?'

'Oh, more than I could count,' replied the shoemaker. 'I will show you what you must do.' Then he led the robbers back to the shore. 'Now,' said he, 'you must each of you tie a stone to your necks, so that you may be sure to go deep enough, for I found the pigs that you saw very deep down indeed.'

Then the robbers all tied stones round their necks, and jumped in, and were drowned, and Master Joseph drove his pigs home, and was a rich man to the end of his days.

THE KING WHO WOULD HAVE A
BEAUTIFUL WIFE [1]

FIFTY years ago there lived a king who was very anxious to get married; but, as he was quite determined that his wife should be as beautiful as the sun, the thing was not so easy as it seemed, for no maiden came up to his standard. Then he commanded a trusty servant to search through the length and breadth of the land till he found a girl fair enough to be queen, and if he had the good luck to discover one he was to bring her back with him.

The servant set out at once on his journey, and sought high and low—in castles and cottages; but though pretty maidens were plentiful as blackberries, he felt sure that none of them would please the king.

One day he had wandered far and wide, and was feeling very tired and thirsty. By the roadside stood a tiny little house, and here he knocked and asked for a cup of water. Now in this house dwelt two sisters, and one was eighty and the other ninety years old. They were very poor, and earned their living by spinning. This had kept their hands very soft and white, like the hands of a girl, and when the water was passed through the lattice, and the servant saw the small, delicate fingers, he said to himself : ' A maiden must indeed be lovely if she has a hand like that.' And he made haste back, and told the king.

[1] *Sicilianische Mährchen.*

' Go back at once,' said his majesty, ' and try to get a sight of her.'

The faithful servant departed on his errand without losing any time, and again he knocked at the door of the little house and begged for some water. As before, the old woman did not open the door, but passed the water through the lattice.

' Do you live here alone?' asked the man.

' No,' replied she, ' my sister lives with me. We are poor girls, and have to work for our bread.'

' How old are you?'

' I am fifteen, and she is twenty.'

Then the servant went back to the king, and told him all he knew. And his majesty answered: ' I will have the fifteen-year-old one. Go and bring her here.'

The servant returned a third time to the little house, and knocked at the door. In reply to his knock the lattice window was pushed open, and a voice inquired what it was he wanted.

' The king has desired me to bring back the youngest of you to become his queen,' he replied.

' Tell his majesty I am ready to do his bidding, but since my birth no ray of light has fallen upon my face. If it should ever do so I shall instantly grow black. Therefore beg, I pray you, his most gracious majesty to send this evening a shut carriage, and I will return in it to the castle.

When the king heard this he ordered his great golden carriage to be prepared, and in it to be placed some magnificent robes; and the old woman wrapped herself in a thick veil, and was driven to the castle.

The king was eagerly awaiting her, and when she arrived he begged her politely to raise her veil and let him see her face.

But she answered : ' Here the tapers are too bright and the light too strong. Would you have me turn black under your very eyes?'

And the king believed her words, and the marriage took place without the veil being once lifted. Afterwards, when they were alone, he raised the corner, and knew for the first time that he had wedded a wrinkled old woman. And, in a furious burst of anger, he dashed open the window and flung her out. But, luckily for her, her clothes caught on a nail in the wall, and kept her hanging between heaven and earth.

While she was thus suspended, expecting every moment to be dashed to the ground, four fairies happened to pass by.

'Look, sisters,' cried one, 'surely that is the old woman that the king sent for. Shall we wish that her clothes may give way, and that she should be dashed to the ground?'

'Oh no! no!' exclaimed another. 'Let us wish her something good. I myself will wish her youth.'

'And I beauty.'

'And I wisdom.'

'And I a tender heart.'

So spake the fairies, and went their way, leaving the most beautiful maiden in the world behind them.

The next morning when the king looked from his window he saw this lovely creature hanging on the nail. 'Ah! what have I done? Surely I must have been blind last night!'

And he ordered long ladders to be brought and the maiden to be rescued. Then he fell on his knees before her, and prayed her to forgive him, and a great feast was made in her honour.

Some days after came the ninety-year-old sister to the palace and asked for the queen.

'Who is that hideous old witch?' said the king.

'Oh, an old neighbour of mine, who is half silly,' she replied.

But the old woman looked at her steadily, and knew her again, and said : 'How have you managed to grow

so young and beautiful ?   I should like to be young and beautiful too.'

This question she repeated the whole day long, till at length the queen lost patience and said : ' I had my old head cut off, and this new head grew in its place.'

Then the old woman went to a barber, and spoke to him, saying, ' I will give you all you ask if you will only cut off my head, so that I may become young and lovely.'

' But, my good woman, if I do that you will die ! '

But the old woman would listen to nothing ; and at last the barber took out his knife and struck the first blow at her neck.

' Ah ! ' she shrieked as she felt the pain.

' Il faut souffrir pour être belle,' said the barber, who had been in France.

And at the second blow her head rolled off, and the old woman was dead for good and all.

CATHERINE AND HER DESTINY [1]

LONG ago there lived a rich merchant who, besides possessing more treasures than any king in the world, had in his great hall three chairs, one of silver, one of gold, and one of diamonds. But his greatest treasure of all was his only daughter, who was called Catherine.

One day Catherine was sitting in her own room when suddenly the door flew open, and in came a tall and beautiful woman holding in her hands a little wheel.

'Catherine,' she said, going up to the girl, 'which would you rather have—a happy youth or a happy old age?'

Catherine was so taken by surprise that she did not know what to answer, and the lady repeated again, 'Which would you rather have—a happy youth or a happy old age?'

Then Catherine thought to herself, 'If I say a happy youth, then I shall have to suffer all the rest of my life. No, I would bear trouble now, and have something better to look forward to.' So she looked up and replied, 'Give me a happy old age.'

'So be it,' said the lady, and turned her wheel as she spoke, vanishing the next moment as suddenly as she had come.

Now this beautiful lady was the Destiny of poor Catherine.

---

[1] *Sicilianische Mährchen*, von Laura Gonzenbach. Leipzig, Engelmann, 1870.

Only a few days after this the merchant heard the news that all his finest ships, laden with the richest merchandise, had been sunk in a storm, and he was left a beggar. The shock was too much for him. He took to his bed, and in a short time he was dead of his disappointment.

So poor Catherine was left alone in the world without a penny or a creature to help her. But she was a brave girl and full of spirit, and soon made up her mind that the best thing she could do was to go to the nearest town and become a servant. She lost no time in getting herself ready, and did not take long over her journey; and as she was passing down the chief street of the town a noble lady saw her out of the window, and, struck by her sad face, said to her : 'Where are you going all alone, my pretty girl?'

'Ah, my lady, I am very poor, and must go to service to earn my bread.'

'I will take you into my service,' said she; and Catherine served her well.

Some time after her mistress said to Catherine, 'I am obliged to go out for a long while, and must lock the house door, so that no thieves shall get in.'

So she went away, and Catherine took her work and sat down at the window. Suddenly the door burst open, and in came her Destiny.

'Oh! so here you are, Catherine! Did you really think I was going to leave you in peace?' And as she spoke she walked to the linen press where Catherine's mistress kept all her finest sheets and underclothes, tore everything in pieces, and flung them on the floor. Poor Catherine wrung her hands and wept, for she thought to herself, 'When my lady comes back and sees all this ruin she will think it is my fault,' and, starting up, she fled through the open door. Then Destiny took all the pieces and made them whole again, and put them back in the press, and when everything was tidy she too left the house.

CATHERINE & HER DESTINY.

When the mistress reached home she called Catherine, but no Catherine was there. ' Can she have robbed me ? ' thought the old lady, and looked hastily round the house ; but nothing was missing. She wondered why Catherine should have disappeared like this, but she heard no more of her, and in a few days she filled her place.

Meanwhile Catherine wandered on and on, without knowing very well where she was going, till at last she came to another town. Just as before, a noble lady happened to see her passing her window, and called out to her, ' Where are you going all alone, my pretty girl ? '

And Catherine answered, ' Ah, my lady, I am very poor, and must go to service to earn my bread.'

' I will take you into my service,' said the lady ; and Catherine served her well, and hoped she might now be left in peace. But, exactly as before, one day that Catherine was left in the house alone her Destiny came again and spoke to her with hard words : ' What ! are you here now ? ' And in a passion she tore up everything she saw, till in sheer misery poor Catherine rushed out of the house. And so it befell for seven years, and directly Catherine found a fresh place her Destiny came and forced her to leave it.

After seven years, however, Destiny seemed to get tired of persecuting her, and a time of peace set in for Catherine. When she had been chased away from her last house by Destiny's wicked pranks she had taken service with another lady, who told her that it would be part of her daily work to walk to a mountain that over-shadowed the town, and, climbing up to the top, she was to lay on the ground some loaves of freshly baked bread, and cry with a loud voice, ' O Destiny, my mistress,' three times. Then her lady's Destiny would come and take away the offering. ' That will I gladly do,' said Catherine.

So the years went by, and Catherine was still there, and every day she climbed the mountain with her basket of bread on her arm. She was happier than she had been, but sometimes, when no one saw her, she would weep as she thought over her old life, and how different it was to the one she was now leading. One day her lady saw her, and said, ' Catherine, what is it ? Why are you always weeping ? ' And then Catherine told her story.

' I have got an idea,' exclaimed the lady. ' To-morrow, when you take the bread to the mountain, you shall pray my Destiny to speak to yours, and entreat her to leave you in peace. Perhaps something may come of it ! '

At these words Catherine dried her eyes, and next morning, when she climbed the mountain, she told all she had suffered, and cried, ' O Destiny, my mistress, pray, I entreat you, of my Destiny that she may leave me in peace.'

And Destiny answered, ' Oh, my poor girl, know you not your Destiny lies buried under seven coverlids, and can hear nothing? But if you will come to-morrow I will bring her with me.'

And after Catherine had gone her way her lady's Destiny went to find her sister, and said to her, ' Dear sister, has not Catherine suffered enough? It is surely time for her good days to begin ? '

And the sister answered, ' To-morrow you shall bring her to me, and I will give her something that may help her out of her need.'

The next morning Catherine set out earlier than usual for the mountain, and her lady's Destiny took the girl by the hand and led her to her sister, who lay under the seven coverlids. And her Destiny held out to Catherine a ball of silk, saying, ' Keep this—it may be useful some day ; ' then pulled the coverings over her head again.

But Catherine walked sadly down the hill, and went straight to her lady and showed her the silken ball, which was the end of all her high hopes.

' What shall I do with it ? ' she asked. ' It is not worth sixpence, and it is no good to me ! '

'Take care of it,' replied her mistress. 'Who can tell how useful it may be?'

A little while after this grand preparations were made for the king's marriage, and all the tailors in the town were busy embroidering fine clothes. The wedding garment was so beautiful nothing like it had ever been seen before, but when it was almost finished the tailor found that he had no more silk. The colour was very rare, and none could be found like it, and the king made a proclamation that if anyone happened to possess any they should bring it to the court, and he would give them a large sum.

'Catherine!' exclaimed the lady, who had been to the tailors and seen the wedding garment, 'your ball of silk is exactly the right colour. Bring it to the king, and you can ask what you like for it.'

Then Catherine put on her best clothes and went to the court, and looked more beautiful than any woman there.

'May it please your majesty,' she said, 'I have brought you a ball of silk of the colour you asked for, as no one else has any in the town.'

'Your majesty,' asked one of the courtiers, 'shall I give the maiden its weight in gold?'

The king agreed, and a pair of scales were brought; and a handful of gold was placed in one scale and the silken ball in the other. But lo! let the king lay in the scales as many gold pieces as he would, the silk was always heavier still. Then the king took some larger scales, and heaped up all his treasures on the one side, but the silk on the other outweighed them all. At last there was only one thing left that had not been put in, and that was his golden crown. And he took it from his head and set it on top of all, and at last the scale moved and the ball had found its balance.

'Where got you this silk?' asked the king.

'It was given me, royal majesty, by my mistress,' replied Catherine.

'That is not true,' said the king, 'and if you do not tell me the truth I will have your head cut off this instant.'

So Catherine told him the whole story, and how she had once been as rich as he.

Now there lived at the court a wise woman, and she said to Catherine, 'You have suffered much, my poor girl, but at length your luck has turned, and I know by

the weighing of the scales through the crown that you will die a queen.'

'So she shall,' cried the king, who overheard these words; 'she shall die my queen, for she is more beautiful than all the ladies of the court, and I will marry no one else.'

And so it fell out. The king sent back the bride he had promised to wed to her own country, and the same Catherine was queen at the marriage feast instead, and lived happy and contented to the end of her life.

HOW THE HERMIT HELPED TO WIN
THE KING'S DAUGHTER [1]

LONG ago there lived a very rich man who had three
sons. When he felt himself to be dying he divided his
property between them, making them share alike, both in
money and lands. Soon after he died the king set forth
a proclamation through the whole country that whoever
could build a ship that should float both on land and sea
should have his daughter to wife.

The eldest brother, when he heard it, said to the other,
'I think I will spend some of my money in trying to
build that ship, as I should like to have the king for my
father-in-law.' So he called together all the shipbuilders
in the land, and gave them orders to begin the ship without delay. And trees were cut down, and great preparations made, and in a few days everybody knew what it
was all for; and there was a crowd of old people pressing
round the gates of the yard, where the young man spent
the most of his day.

'Ah, master, give us work,' they said, 'so that we may
earn our bread.'

But he only gave them hard words, and spoke roughly
to them. 'You are old, and have lost your strength; of
what use are you?' And he drove them away. Then
came some boys and prayed him, 'Master, give us work,'
but he answered them, 'Of what use can you be, weak-
lings as you are! Get you gone!' And if any presented

[1] *Sicilianische Mährchen.*

themselves that were not skilled workmen he would have none of them.

At last there knocked at the gate a little old man with a long white beard, and said, ' Will you give me work, so that I may earn my bread?' But he was only driven away like the rest.

The ship took a long while to build, and cost a great deal of money, and when it was launched a sudden squall rose, and it fell to pieces, and with it all the young man's hopes of winning the princess. By this time he had not a penny left, so he went back to his two brothers and told his tale. And the second brother said to himself as he listened, ' Certainly he has managed very badly, but I should like to see if I can't do better, and win the princess for my own self.' So he called together all the shipbuilders throughout the country, and gave them orders to build a ship which should float on the land as well as on the sea. But his heart was no softer than his brother's, and every man that was not a skilled workman was chased away with hard words. Last came the white-bearded man, but he fared no better than the rest.

When the ship was finished the launch took place, and everything seemed going smoothly when a gale sprang up, and the vessel was dashed to pieces on the rocks. The young man had spent his whole fortune on it, and now it was all swallowed up, was forced to beg shelter from his youngest brother. When he told his story the youngest said to himself, ' I am not rich enough to support us all three. I had better take my turn, and if I manage to win the princess there will be her fortune as well as my own for us to live on.' So he called together all the shipbuilders in the kingdom, and gave orders that a new ship should be built. Then all the old people came and asked for work, and he answered cheerfully, ' Oh, yes, there is plenty for everybody;' and when the boys begged to be allowed to help he found something that they could do. And when the old man with the long white beard stood before him, praying that he might earn his bread, he replied, ' Oh, father, I could not suffer you to work, but you shall be overseer, and look after the rest.'

Now the old man was a holy hermit, and when he saw how kind-hearted the youth was he determined to do all he could for him to gain the wish of his heart.

By-and-bye, when the ship was finished, the hermit said to his young friend, ' Now you can go and claim the king's daughter, for the ship will float both by land and sea.'

' Oh, good father,' cried the young man, ' you will not forsake me? Stay with me, I pray you, and lead me to the king!'

' If you wish it, I will,' said the hermit, ' on condition that you will give me half of anything you get.'

' Oh, if that is all,' answered he, ' it is easily promised!' And they set out together on the ship.

After they had gone some distance they saw a man standing in a thick fog, which he was trying to put into a sack.

' Oh, good father,' exclaimed the youth, ' what can he be doing?'

' Ask him,' said the old man.

' What are you doing, my fine fellow?'

' I am putting the fog into my sack. That is my business.'

' Ask him if he will come with us,' whispered the hermit.

And the man answered: ' If you will give me enough to eat and drink I will gladly stay with you.'

So they took him on their ship, and the youth said, as they started off again, ' Good father, before we were two, and now we are three!'

After they had travelled a little further they met a man who had torn up half the forest, and was carrying all the trees on his shoulders.

HOW THEY MET THE ARCHER IN THE STREAM

'Good father,' exclaimed the youth, 'only look! What can he have done that for?'

'Ask him why he has torn up all those trees.'

And the man replied, 'Why, I've merely been gathering a handful of brushwood.'

'Beg him to come with us,' whispered the hermit.

And the strong man answered: 'Willingly, as long as you give me enough to eat and drink.' And he came on the ship.

And the youth said to the hermit, 'Good father, before we were three, and now we are four.'

The ship travelled on again, and some miles further on they saw a man drinking out of a stream till he had nearly drunk it dry.

'Good father,' said the youth, 'just look at that man! Did you ever see anybody drink like that?'

'Ask him why he does it,' answered the hermit.

'Why, there is nothing very odd in taking a mouthful of water!' replied the man, standing up.

'Beg him to come with us.' And the youth did so.

'With pleasure, as long as you give me enough to eat and drink.'

And the youth whispered to the hermit, 'Good father, before we were four, and now we are five.'

A little way along they noticed another man in the middle of a stream, who was shooting into the water.

'Good father,' said the youth, 'what can he be shooting at?'

'Ask him,' answered the hermit.

'Hush, hush!' cried the man; 'now you have frightened it away. In the Underworld sits a quail on a tree, and I wanted to shoot it. That is my business. I hit everything I aim at.'

'Ask him if he will come with us.'

And the man replied, 'With all my heart, as long as I get enough to eat and drink.'

So they took him into the ship, and the young man

whispered, 'Good father, before we were five, and now we are six.'

Off they went again, and before they had gone far they met a man striding towards them whose steps were so long that while one foot was on the north of the island the other was right down in the south.

'Good father, look at him! What long steps he takes!'

'Ask him why he does it,' replied the hermit.

'Oh, I am only going out for a little walk,' answered he.

'Ask him if he will come with us.'

'Gladly, if you will give me as much as I want to eat and drink,' said he, climbing up into the ship.

And the young man whispered, 'Good father, before we were six, and now we are seven.' But the hermit knew what he was about, and why he gathered these strange people into the ship.

After many days, at last they reached the town where lived the king and his daughter. They stopped the vessel right in front of the palace, and the young man went in and bowed low before the king.

'O Majesty, I have done your bidding, and now is the ship built that can travel over land and sea. Give me my reward, and let me have your daughter to wife.'

But the king said to himself, 'What! am I to wed my daughter to a man of whom I know nothing? Not even whether he be rich or poor—a knight or a beggar.'

And aloud he spake : 'It is not enough that you have managed to build the ship. You must find a runner who shall take this letter to the ruler of the Underworld, and bring me the answer back in an hour.'

'That is not in the bond,' answered the young man.

'Well, do as you like,' replied the king, 'only you will not get my daughter.'

The young man went out, sorely troubled, to tell his old friend what had happened.

'Silly boy!' cried the hermit. 'Accept his terms at

once. And send off the long-legged man with the letter. He will take it in no time at all.'

So the youth's heart leapt for joy, and he returned to the king. 'Majesty, I accept your terms. Here is the messenger who will do what you wish.'

The king had no choice but to give the man the letter, and he strode off, making short work of the distance that lay between the palace and the Underworld. He soon found the ruler, who looked at the letter, and said to him, ' Wait a little while I write the answer ; ' but the man was so tired with his quick walk that he went sound asleep, and forgot all about his errand.

All this time the youth was anxiously counting the minutes till he could get back, and stood with his eyes fixed on the road down which his messenger must come.

' What can be keeping him ? ' he said to the hermit when the hour was nearly up.

Then the hermit sent for the man who could hit every thing he aimed at, and said to him, ' Just see why the messenger stays so long.'

' Oh, he is sound asleep in the palace of the Underworld. However, I can soon wake him.'

Then he drew his bow, and shot an arrow straight into the man's knee. The messenger awoke with a start, and when he saw that the hour had almost run out he snatched up the answer and rushed back with such speed that the clock had not yet struck when he entered the palace.

Now the young man thought he was sure of his bride, but the king said, ' Still you have not done enough. Before I give you my daughter you must find a man who can drink half the contents of my cellar in one day.'

' That is not in the bond,' complained the poor youth.

' Well, do as you like, only you will not get my daughter.'

The young man went sadly out, and asked the hermit what he was to do.

'Silly boy!' said he. 'Why, tell the man to do it who drinks up everything.'

So they sent for the man and said, 'Do you think you are able to drink half the royal cellar in one day?'

'Dear me, yes, and as much more as you want,' answered he. 'I am never satisfied.'

The king was not pleased at the young man agreeing so readily, but he had no choice, and ordered the servant to be taken downstairs. Oh, how he enjoyed himself! All day long he drank, and drank, and drank, till, instead of half the cellar, he had drunk the whole, and there was not a cask but what stood empty. And when the king saw this he said to the youth, 'You have conquered, and I can no longer withhold my daughter. But, as her dowry, I shall only give so much as one man can carry away.'

'But,' answered he, 'let a man be ever so strong, he cannot carry more than a hundredweight, and what is that for a king's daughter?'

'Well, do as you like; I have said my say. It is your affair—not mine.'

The young man was puzzled, and did not know what to reply, for, though he would gladly have married the princess without a sixpence, he had spent all his money in building the ship, and knew he could not give her all she wanted. So he went to the hermit and said to him, 'The king will only give for her dowry as much as a man can carry. I have no money of my own left, and my brothers have none either.'

'Silly boy! Why, you have only got to fetch the man who carried half the forest on his shoulders.'

And the youth was glad, and called the strong man, and told him what he must do. 'Take everything you can, till you are bent double. Never mind if you leave the palace bare.'

The strong man promised, and nobly kept his word. He piled all he could see on his back—chairs, tables,

wardrobes, chests of gold and silver—till there was
nothing left to pile. At last he took the king's crown,
and put it on the top. He carried his burden to the
ship and stowed his treasures away, and the youth
followed, leading the king's daughter. But the king was
left raging in his empty palace, and he called together
his army, and got ready his ships of war, in order that he

might go after the vessel and bring back what had been
taken away.

And the king's ships sailed very fast, and soon caught
up the little vessel, and the sailors all shouted for joy.
Then the hermit looked out and saw how near they were,
and he said to the youth, ' Do you see that ? '

The youth shrieked and cried, ' Ah, good father, it is
a fleet of ships, and they are chasing us, and in a few
moments they will be upon us.'

But the hermit bade him call the man who had the fog in his sack, and the sack was opened and the fog flew out, and hung right round the king's ships, so that they could see nothing. So they sailed back to the palace, and told the king what strange things had happened. Meanwhile the young man's vessel reached home in safety.

' Well, here you are once more,' said the hermit ; ' and now you can fulfil the promise you made me to give me the half of all you had.'

' That will I do with all my heart,' answered the youth, and began to divide all his treasures, putting part on one side for himself and setting aside the other for his friend. ' Good father, it is finished,' said he at length ; ' there is nothing more left to divide.'

' Nothing more left ! ' cried the hermit. ' Why, you have forgotten the best thing of all ! '

' What can that be ? ' asked he. ' We have divided everything.'

' And the king's daughter ? ' said the hermit.

Then the young man's heart stood still, for he loved her dearly. But he answered, ' It is well ; I have sworn, and I will keep my word,' and drew his sword to cut her in pieces. When the hermit saw that he held his honour dearer than his wife he lifted his hand and cried ' Hold ! she is yours, and all the treasures too. I gave you my help because you had pity on those that were in need. And when you are in need yourself, call upon me, and I will come to you.'

As he spoke he softly touched their heads and vanished.

The next day the wedding took place, and the two brothers came to the house, and they all lived happily together, but they never forgot the holy man who had been such a good friend.

THE WATER OF LIFE[1]

THREE brothers and one sister lived together in a small
cottage, and they loved one another dearly. One day the
eldest brother, who had never done anything but amuse
himself from sunrise to sunset, said to the rest, 'Let us
all work hard, and perhaps we shall grow rich, and be
able to build ourselves a palace.'

And his brothers and sister answered joyfully, 'Yes,
we will all work!'

So they fell to working with all their might, till at last
they became rich, and were able to build themselves a
beautiful palace; and everyone came from miles round
to see its wonders, and to say how splendid it was. No
one thought of finding any faults, till at length an old
woman, who had been walking through the rooms with a
crowd of people, suddenly exclaimed, 'Yes, it is a
splendid palace, but there is still something it needs!'

'And what may that be?'

'A church.'

When they heard this the brothers set to work again
to earn some more money, and when they had got
enough they set about building a church, which should
be as large and beautiful as the palace itself.

And after the church was finished greater numbers
of people than ever flocked to see the palace and the
church and vast gardens and magnificent halls.

[1] *Cuentos Populars Catalans*, per lo Dr. D. Francisco de S.
Maspous y Labros. Barcelona, 1885.

But one day, as the brothers were as usual doing the honours to their guests, an old man turned to them and said, 'Yes, it is all most beautiful, but there is still something it needs!'

'And what may that be?'

'A pitcher of the water of life, a branch of the tree the smell of whose flowers gives eternal beauty, and the talking bird.'

And where am I to find all those?'

'Go to the mountain that is far off yonder, and you will find what you seek.'

After the old man had bowed politely and taken farewell of them the eldest brother said to the rest, 'I will go in search of the water of life, and the talking bird, and the tree of beauty.'

'But suppose some evil thing befalls you?' asked his sister. 'How shall we know?'

'You are right,' he replied; 'I had not thought of that!'

Then they followed the old man, and said to him, 'My eldest brother wishes to seek for the water of life, and the tree of beauty, and the talking bird, that you tell him are needful to make our palace perfect. But how shall we know if any evil thing befall him?'

So the old man took them a knife, and gave it to them, saying, 'Keep this carefully, and as long as the blade is bright all is well; but if the blade is bloody, then know that evil has befallen him.'

The brothers thanked him, and departed, and went straight to the palace, where they found the young man making ready to set out for the mountain where the treasures he longed for lay hid.

And he walked, and he walked, and he walked, till he had gone a great way, and there he met a giant.

'Can you tell me how much further I have still to go before I reach that mountain yonder?'

'And why do you wish to go there?'

' I am seeking the water of life, the talking bird, and a branch of the tree of beauty.'

' Many have passed by seeking those treasures, but none have ever come back ; and you will never come back either, unless you mark my words. Follow this path, and when you reach the mountain you will find it covered with stones. Do not stop to look at them, but keep on your way. As you go you will hear scoffs and laughs behind you ; it will be the stones that mock. Do not heed them ; above all, do not turn round. If you do you will become as one of them. Walk straight on till you get to the top, and then take all you wish for.'

The young man thanked him for his counsel, and walked, and walked, and walked, till he reached the mountain. And as he climbed he heard behind him scoffs and jeers, but he kept his ears steadily closed to them. At last the noise grew so loud that he lost patience, and he stooped to pick up a stone to hurl into the midst of the clamour, when suddenly his arm seemed to stiffen, and the next moment he was a stone himself !

That day his sister, who thought her brother's steps were long in returning, took out the knife and found the blade was red as blood. Then she cried out to her brothers that something terrible had come to pass.

' I will go and find him,' said the second. And he went.

And he walked, and he walked, and he walked, till he met the giant, and asked him if he had seen a young man travelling towards the mountain.

And the giant answered, ' Yes, I have seen him pass, but I have not seen him come back. The spell must have worked upon him.'

' Then what can I do to disenchant him, and find the water of life, the talking bird, and a branch of the tree of beauty ? '

' Follow this path, and when you reach the mountain you will find it covered with stones. Do not stop to look

at them, but climb steadily on. Above all, heed not the
laughs and scoffs that will arise on all sides, and never
turn round. And when you reach the top you can then
take all you desire.'

The young man thanked him for his counsel, and set
out for the mountain. But no sooner did he reach it
than loud jests and gibes broke out on every side, and
almost deafened him. For some time he let them rail,
and pushed boldly on, till he had passed the place which
his brother had gained; then suddenly he thought that
among the scoffing sounds he heard his brother's voice.
He stopped and looked back; and another stone was
added to the number.

Meanwhile the sister left at home was counting the
days when her two brothers should return to her. The
time seemed long, and it would be hard to say how often
she took out the knife and looked at its polished blade
to make sure that this one at least was still safe. The
blade was always bright and clear; each time she looked
she had the happiness of knowing that all was well, till
one evening, tired and anxious, as she frequently was
at the end of the day, she took it from its drawer, and
behold! the blade was red with blood. Her cry of horror
brought her youngest brother to her, and, unable to speak,
she held out the knife!

' I will go,' he said.

So he walked, and he walked, and he walked, until he
met the giant, and he asked, 'Have two young men,
making for yonder mountain, passed this way?'

And the giant answered, ' Yes, they have passed by,
but they never came back, and by this I know that the
spell has fallen upon them.'

' Then what must I do to free them, and to get the
water of life, and the talking bird, and the branch of the
tree of beauty?'

' Go to the mountain, which you will find so thickly
covered with stones that you will hardly be able to place

your feet, and walk straight forward, turning neither to the right hand nor to the left, and paying no heed to the laughs and scoffs which will follow you, till you reach the top, and then you may take all that you desire.'

The young man thanked the giant for his counsel, and set forth to the mountain. And when he began to climb there burst forth all around him a storm of scoffs and jeers; but he thought of the giant's words, and looked neither to the right hand nor to the left, till the mountain top lay straight before him. A moment now and he would have gained it, when, through the groans and yells, he heard his brothers' voices. He turned, and there was one stone the more.

And all this while his sister was pacing up and down the palace, hardly letting the knife out of her hand, and dreading what she knew she would see, and what she *did* see. The blade grew red before her eyes, and she said, 'Now it is my turn.'

So she walked, and she walked, and she walked till she came to the giant, and prayed him to tell her if he had seen three young men pass that way seeking the distant mountain.

'I have seen them pass, but they have never returned, and by this I know that the spell has fallen upon them.'

'And what must I do to set them free, and to find the water of life, and the talking bird, and a branch of the tree of beauty?'

'You must go to that mountain, which is so full of stones that your feet will hardly find a place to tread, and as you climb you will hear a noise as if all the stones in the world were mocking you; but pay no heed to anything you may hear, and, once you gain the top, you have gained everything.'

The girl thanked him for his counsel, and set out for the mountain; and scarcely had she gone a few steps upwards when cries and screams broke forth around her, and she felt as if each stone she trod on was a living thing. But she remembered the words of the giant, and knew not what had befallen her brothers, and kept her face steadily towards the mountain top, which grew nearer and nearer every moment. But as she mounted the clamour increased sevenfold: high above them all rang the voices of her three brothers. But the girl took no heed, and at last her feet stood upon the top.

HOW THE SISTER FETCHED THE WATER OF LIFE

Then she looked round, and saw, lying in a hollow, the pool of the water of life. And she took the brazen pitcher that she had brought with her, and filled it to the brim. By the side of the pool stood the tree of beauty, with the talking bird on one of its boughs; and she caught the bird, and placed it in a cage, and broke off one of the branches.

After that she turned, and went joyfully down the hill again, carrying her treasures, but her long climb had tired her out, and the brazen pitcher was very heavy, and as she walked a few drops of the water spilt on the stones, and as it touched them they changed into young men and maidens, crowding about her to give thanks for their deliverance.

So she learnt by this how the evil spell might be broken, and she carefully sprinkled every stone till there was not one left—only a great company of youths and girls who followed her down the mountain.

When they arrived at the palace she did not lose a moment in planting the branch of the tree of beauty and watering it with the water of life. And the branch shot up into a tree, and was heavy with flowers, and the talking bird nestled in its branches.

Now the fame of these wonders was noised abroad, and the people flocked in great numbers to see the three marvels, and the maiden who had won them; and among the sightseers came the king's son, who would not go till everything was shown him, and till he had heard how it had all happened. And the prince admired the strangeness and beauty of the treasures in the palace, but more than all he admired the beauty and courage of the maiden who had brought them there. So he went home and told his parents, and gained their consent to wed her for his wife.

Then the marriage was celebrated in the church adjoining the palace. Then the bridegroom took her to his own home, where they lived happy for ever after.

THE WOUNDED LION [1]

THERE was once a girl so poor that she had nothing to live on, and wandered about the world asking for charity. One day she arrived at a thatched cottage, and inquired if they could give her any work. The farmer said he wanted a cowherd, as his own had left him, and if the girl liked the place she might take it. So she became a cowherd.

One morning she was driving her cows through the meadows when she heard near by a loud groan that almost sounded human. She hastened to the spot from which the noise came, and found it proceeded from a lion who lay stretched upon the ground.

You can guess how frightened she was! But the lion seemed in such pain that she was sorry for him, and drew nearer and nearer till she saw he had a large thorn in one foot. She pulled out the thorn and bound up the place, and the lion was grateful, and licked her hand by way of thanks with his big rough tongue.

When the girl had finished she went back to find the cows, but they had gone, and though she hunted everywhere she never found them ; and she had to return home and confess to her master, who scolded her bitterly, and afterwards beat her. Then he said, ' Now you will have to look after the asses.'

So every day she had to take the asses to the woods to feed, until one morning, exactly a year after she had

---

[1] *Cuentos Populars Catalans.*

found the lion, she heard a groan which sounded quite human. She went straight to the place from which the noise came, and, to her great surprise, beheld the same lion stretched on the ground with a deep wound across his face.

This time she was not afraid at all, and ran towards him, washing the wound and laying soothing herbs upon it ; and when she had bound it up the lion thanked her in the same manner as before.

After that she returned to her flock, but they were nowhere to be seen. She searched here and she searched there, but they had vanished completely !

Then she had to go home and confess to her master, who first scolded her and afterwards beat her. ' Now go,' he ended, ' and look after the pigs ! '

So the next day she took out the pigs, and found them such good feeding grounds that they grew fatter every day.

Another year passed by, and one morning when the maiden was out with her pigs she heard a groan which sounded quite human. She ran to see what it was, and found her old friend the lion, wounded through and through, fast dying under a tree.

She fell on her knees before him and washed his wounds one by one, and laid healing herbs upon them. And the lion licked her hands and thanked her, and asked if she would not stay and sit by him. But the girl said she had her pigs to watch, and she must go and see after them.

So she ran to the place where she had left them, but they had vanished as if the earth had swallowed them up. She whistled and called, but only the birds answered her.

Then she sank down on the ground and wept bitterly, not daring to return home until some hours had passed away.

And when she had had her cry out she got up and

THE WOUNDED LION.

searched all up and down the wood.   But it was no use ;
there was not a sign of the pigs.

At last she thought that perhaps if she climbed a tree
she might see further.   But no sooner was she seated on
the highest branch than something happened which put
the pigs quite out of her head.   This was a handsome
young man who was coming down the path ; and when
he had almost reached the tree he pulled aside a rock and
disappeared behind it.

The maiden rubbed her eyes and wondered if she had
been dreaming.   Next she thought, ' I will not stir from
here till I see him come out, and discover who he is.'
Accordingly she waited, and at dawn the next morning
the rock moved to one side and a lion came out.

When he had gone quite out of sight the girl climbed
down from the tree and went to the rock, which she pushed
aside, and entered the opening before her.   The path led
to a beautiful house.   She went in, swept and dusted the
furniture, and put everything tidy.   Then she ate a very
good dinner, which was on a shelf in the corner, and once
more clambered up to the top of her tree.

As the sun set she saw the same young man walking
gaily down the path, and, as before, he pushed aside the
rock and disappeared behind it.

Next morning out came the lion.   He looked sharply
about him on all sides, but saw no one, and then
vanished into the forest.

The maiden then came down from the tree and did
exactly as she had done the day before.   Thus three
days went by, and every day she went and tidied up
the palace.   At length, when the girl found she was no
nearer to discovering the secret, she resolved to ask
him, and in the evening when she caught sight of him
coming through the wood she came down from the tree
and begged him to tell her his name.

The young man looked very pleased to see her, and
said he thought it must be she who had secretly kept

his house for so many days. And he added that he was
a prince enchanted by a powerful giant, but was only
allowed to take his own shape at night, for all day he was
forced to appear as the lion whom she had so often helped ;
and, more than this, it was the giant who had stolen the
oxen and the asses and the pigs in revenge for her
kindness.

And the girl asked him, ' What can I do to disenchant
you ? '

But he said he was afraid it was very difficult, because
the only way was to get a lock of hair from the head of a
king's daughter, to spin it, and to make from it a cloak
for the giant, who lived up on the top of a high mountain.

' Very well,' answered the girl, ' I will go to the city,
and knock at the door of the king's palace, and ask
the princess to take me as a servant.'

So they parted, and when she arrived at the city she
walked about the streets crying, ' Who will hire me for a
servant ? Who will hire me for a servant ? ' But, though
many people liked her looks, for she was clean and neat,
the maiden would listen to none, and still continued
crying, ' Who will hire me for a servant ? Who will hire
me for a servant ? '

At last there came the waiting-maid of the princess.

' What can you do ? ' she said ; and the girl was forced
to confess that she could do very little.

' Then you will have to do scullion's work, and wash
up dishes,' said she ; and they went straight back to the
palace.

Then the maiden dressed her hair afresh, and made
herself look very neat and smart, and everyone admired
and praised her, till by-and-bye it came to the ears of the
princess. And she sent for the girl, and when she saw
her, and how beautifully she had dressed her hair, the
princess told her she was to come and comb out hers.

Now the hair of the princess was very thick and
long, and shone like the sun. And the girl combed it and

combed it till it was brighter than ever. And the princess was pleased, and bade her come every day and comb her hair, till at length the girl took courage, and begged leave to cut off one of the long, thick locks.

The princess, who was very proud of her hair, did not like the idea of parting with any of it, so she said no. But the girl could not give up hope, and each day she entreated to be allowed to cut off just one tress. At length the princess lost patience, and exclaimed, 'You may have it, then, on condition that you shall find the handsomest prince in the world to be my bridegroom!'

And the girl answered that she would, and cut off the lock, and wove it into a coat that glittered like silk, and brought it to the young man, who told her to carry it straight to the giant. But that she must be careful to cry out a long way off what she had with her, or else he would spring upon her and run her through with his sword.

So the maiden departed and climbed up the mountain, but before she reached the top the giant heard her foot-steps, and rushed out breathing fire and flame, having a sword in one hand and a club in the other. But she cried loudly that she had brought him the coat, and then he grew quiet, and invited her to come into his house.

He tried on the coat, but it was too short, and he threw it off, and declared it was no use. And the girl picked it up sadly, and returned quite in despair to the king's palace.

The next morning, when she was combing the princess's hair, she begged leave to cut off another lock. At first the princess said no, but the girl begged so hard that at length she gave in on condition that she should find her a prince as bridegroom.

The maiden told her that she had already found him, and spun the lock into shining stuff, and fastened it on to the end of the coat. And when it was finished she carried it to the giant.

THE MAIDEN BRINGS THE COAT OF HAIR TO THE GIANT

This time it fitted him, and he was quite pleased, and asked her what he could give her in return. And she said that the only reward he could give her was to take the spell off the lion and bring him back to his own shape.

For a long time the giant would not hear of it, but in the end he gave in, and told her exactly how it must all be done. She was to kill the lion herself and cut him up very small; then she must burn him, and cast his ashes into the water, and out of the water the prince would come free from enchantment for ever.

But the maiden went away weeping, lest the giant should have deceived her, and that after she had killed the lion she would find she had also slain the prince.

Weeping she came down the mountain, and weeping she joined the prince, who was awaiting her at the bottom ; and when he had heard her story he comforted her, and bade her be of good courage, and to do the bidding of the giant.

And the maiden believed what the prince told her ; and in the morning when he put on his lion's form she took a knife and slew him, and cut him up very small, and burnt him, and cast his ashes into the water, and out of the water came the prince, beautiful as the day, and as glad to look upon as the sun himself.

Then the young man thanked the maiden for all she had done for him, and said she should be his wife and none other. But the maiden only wept sore, and answered that that she could never be, for she had given her promise to the princess when she cut off her hair that the prince should wed her and her only.

But the prince replied, ' If it is the princess, we must go quickly. Come with me.'

So they went together to the king's palace. And when the king and queen and princess saw the young man a great joy filled their hearts, for they knew him for the eldest son, who had long ago been enchanted by a giant and lost to them.

And he asked his parents' consent that he might marry the girl who had saved him, and a great feast was made, and the maiden became a princess, and in due time a queen, and she richly deserved all the honours showered upon her.

THE MAN WITHOUT A HEART

ONCE upon a time there were seven brothers, who were orphans, and had no sister. Therefore they were obliged to do all their own housework. This they did not like at all ; so after much deliberation they decided to get married. There were, unfortunately, no young girls to be found in the place where they lived ; but the elder brothers agreed to go out into the world and seek for brides, promising to bring back a very pretty wife for the youngest also if he would meanwhile stay at home and take care of the house. He consented willingly, and the six young men set off in good spirits.

On their way they came to a small cottage standing quite by itself in a wood ; and before the door stood an old, old man, who accosted the brothers, saying, ' Hullo, you young fellows ! Whither away so fast and cheerily ? '

' We are going to find bonny brides for ourselves, and one for our youngest brother at home,' they replied.

' Oh ! dear youths,' said the old man, ' I am *terribly* lonely here ; pray bring a bride for me also ; only remember, she must be young and pretty.'

' What does a shrivelled old grey thing like that want with a pretty young bride ? ' thought the brothers, and went on their way.

Presently they came to a town where were seven sisters, as young and as lovely as anyone could wish. Each brother chose one, and the youngest they kept for their brother at home. Then the whole party set out on

The Man without a Heart

THE SIX BROTHERS AND THEIR BRIDES
TURNED INTO STONES BY THE OLD MAN.

the return journey, and again their path led through the wood and past the old man's cottage.

There he stood before the door, and cried: 'Oh! you fine fellows, what a charming bride you have brought me!'

'She is not for you,' said the young men. 'She is for our youngest brother, as we promised.'

'What!' said the old man, 'promised! I'll make you eat your promises!' And with that he took his magic wand, and, murmuring a charm, he touched both brothers and brides, and immediately they were turned into grey stones.

Only the youngest sister he had not bewitched. He took her into the cottage, and from that time she was obliged to keep house for him. She was not very unhappy, but one thought troubled her. What if the old man should die and leave her here alone in the solitary cottage deep in the heart of the wood! She would be as 'terribly lonely' as he had formerly been.

One day she told him of her fear.

'Don't be anxious,' he said. 'You need neither fear my death nor desire it, for I have no heart in my breast! However, if I *should* die, you will find my wand above the door, and with it you can set free your sisters and their lovers. Then you will surely have company enough.'

'Where in all the world do you keep your heart, if not in your breast?' asked the girl.

'Do you want to know everything?' her husband said. 'Well, if you *must* know, my heart is in the bed-cover.'

When the old man had gone out about his business his bride passed her time in embroidering beautiful flowers on the bed quilt to make his heart happy. The old man was much amused. He laughed, and said to her: 'You are a good child, but I was only joking. My heart is really in—in——'

'Now where is it, dear husband?'

'It is in the doorway,' he replied.

Next day, while he was out, the girl decorated the door with gay feathers and fresh flowers, and hung garlands upon it. And on his return the old fellow asked what it all meant.

'I did it to show my love for your heart,' said the girl.

And again the old man smiled, saying, 'You are a dear child, but my heart is not in the doorway.'

Then the poor young bride was very vexed, and said, 'Ah, my dear! you really *have* a heart somewhere, so you may die and leave me all alone.'

The old man did his best to comfort her by repeating all he had said before, but she begged him afresh to tell her truly where his heart was, and at last he told her.

'Far, far from here,' said he, 'in a lonely spot, stands a great church, as old as old can be. Its doors are of iron, and round it runs a deep moat, spanned by no bridge. Within that church is a bird which flies up and down; it never eats, and never drinks, and never dies. No one can catch it, and while that bird lives so shall I, for in it is my heart.'

It made the little bride quite sad to think she could do nothing to show her love for the old man's heart. She used to think about it as she sat all alone during the long days, for her husband was almost always out.

One day a young traveller came past the house, and seeing such a pretty girl he wished her 'Good day.'

She returned his greeting, and as he drew near she asked him whence he came and where he was going.

'Alas!' sighed the youth, 'I am very sorrowful. I had six brothers, who went away to find brides for themselves and one for me; but they have never come home, so now I am going to look for them.'

'Oh, good friend,' said the girl, 'you need go no farther. Come, sit down, eat and drink, and afterwards I'll tell you all about it.'

She gave him food, and when he had finished his meal she told him how his brothers had come to the town where she lived with her sisters, how they had each chosen a bride, and, taking herself with them, had started for home. She wept as she told how the others were turned to stone, and how she was kept as the old man's bride. She left out nothing, even telling him the story of her husband's heart.

When the young man heard this he said : ' I shall go in search of the bird. It may be that God will help me to find and catch it.'

' Yes, *do* go,' she said ; ' it will be a good deed, for then you can set your brothers and my sisters free.' Then she hid the young man, for it was now late, and her husband would soon be home.

Next morning, when the old man had gone out, she prepared a supply of provisions for her guest, and sent him off on his travels, wishing him good luck and success.

He walked on and on till he thought it must be time for breakfast; so he opened his knapsack, and was delighted to find such a store of good things. ' What a feast ! ' he exclaimed ; ' will anyone come and share it ? '

' Moo-oo,' sounded close behind him, and looking round he saw a great red ox, which said, ' I have much pleasure in accepting your kind invitation.'

' I'm delighted to see you. Pray help yourself. All I have is at your service,' said the hospitable youth. And the ox lay down comfortably, licking his lips, and made a hearty meal.

' Many thanks to you,' said the animal as it rose up. ' When you are in danger or necessity call me, even if only by a thought,' and it disappeared among the bushes.

The young man packed up all the food that was left, and wandered on till the shortening shadows and his own hunger warned him that it was midday. He laid the cloth on the ground and spread out his provisions,

The Griffin is made welcome

saying at the same time : ' Dinner is ready, and anyone who wishes to share it is welcome.'

Then there was a great rustling in the undergrowth, and out ran a wild boar, grunting, ' Umph, umph, umph ; someone said dinner was ready. Was it you ? and did you mean me to come ? '

' By all means. Help yourself to what I have,' said the young traveller. And the two enjoyed their meal together.

Afterwards the boar got up, saying, ' Thank you ; when in need you be you must quickly call for me,' and he rolled off.

For a long time the youth walked on. By evening he was miles away. He felt hungry again, and, having still some provisions left, thought he had better make ready his supper. When it was all spread out he cried as before, ' Anyone who cares to share my meal is welcome.'

He heard a sound overhead like the flapping of wings, and a shadow was cast upon the ground. Then a huge griffin appeared, saying : ' I heard someone giving an invitation to eat ; is there anything for me ? '

' Why not ? ' said the youth. ' Come down and take all you want. There won't be much left after this.'

So the griffin alighted and ate his fill, saying, as he flew away, ' Call me if you need me.'

' What a hurry he was in ! ' the youth said to himself. ' He might have been able to direct me to the church, for I shall never find it alone.'

He gathered up his things, and started to walk a little farther before resting. He had not gone far when all of a sudden he saw the church !

He soon came to it, or rather to the wide and deep moat which surrounded it without a single bridge by which to cross.

It was too late to attempt anything now ; and, besides,

the poor youth was very tired, so he lay down on the ground and fell fast asleep.

Next morning, when he awoke, he began to wish himself over the moat; and the thought occurred to him that if only the red ox were there, and thirsty enough to drink up all the water in the moat, he might walk across it dry shod.

Scarcely had the thought crossed his brain before the ox appeared and began to drink up the water.

The grateful youth hastened across as soon as the moat was dry, but found it impossible to penetrate the thick walls and strong iron doors of the church.

' I believe that big boar would be of more use here than I am,' he thought, and lo ! at the wish the wild boar came and began to push hard against the wall. He managed to loosen one stone with his tusks, and, having made a beginning, stone after stone was poked out till he had made quite a large hole, big enough to let a man go through.

The young man quickly entered the church, and saw a bird flying about, but he could not catch it.

' Oh ! ' he exclaimed, ' if only the griffin were here, he would soon catch it.'

At these words the griffin appeared, and, seizing the bird, gave it to the youth, who carried it off carefully, while the griffin flew away.

The young man hurried home as fast as possible, and reached the cottage before evening. He told his story to the little bride, who, after giving him some food and drink, hid him with his bird beneath the bed.

Presently the old man came home, and complained of feeling ill. Nothing, he said, would go well with him any more : his ' heart bird ' was caught.

The youth under the bed heard this, and thought, ' This old fellow has done me no particular harm, but then he has bewitched my brothers and their brides, and has kept *my* bride for himself, and that is certainly bad enough.'

So he pinched the bird, and the old man cried, ' Ah! I feel death gripping me! Child, I am dying!'

With these words he fell fainting from his chair, and as the youth, before he knew what he was doing, had squeezed the bird to death, the old man died also.

Out crept the young man from under the bed, and the girl took the magic wand (which she found where the old man had told her), and, touching the twelve grey stones, transformed them at once into the six brothers and their brides.

Then there was great joy, and kissing and embracing. And there lay the old man, quite dead, and no magic wand could restore him to life, even had they wished it.

After that they all went away and were married, and lived many years happily together.

THE TWO BROTHERS [1]

LONG ago there lived two brothers, both of them very handsome, and both so very poor that they seldom had anything to eat but the fish which they caught. One day they had been out in their boat since sunrise without a single bite, and were just thinking of putting up their lines and going home to bed when they felt a little feeble tug, and, drawing in hastily, they found a tiny fish at the end of the hook.

'What a wretched little creature!' cried one brother. 'However, it is better than nothing, and I will bake him with bread crumbs and have him for supper.'

'Oh, do not kill me yet!' begged the fish ; 'I will bring you good luck—indeed I will!'

'You silly thing!' said the young man ; 'I've caught you, and I shall eat you.'

But his brother was sorry for the fish, and put in a word for him.

'Let the poor little fellow live. He would hardly make one bite, and, after all, how do we know we are not throwing away our luck! Put him back into the sea. It will be much better.'

'If you will let me live,' said the fish, 'you will find on the sands to-morrow morning two beautiful horses splendidly saddled and bridled, and on them you can go through the world as knights seeking adventures.'

---

[1] *Sicilianische Mährchen.* L. Gonzenbach.

' Oh dear, what nonsense ! ' exclaimed the elder ; ' and, besides, what proof have we that you are speaking the truth ? '

But again the younger brother interposed : ' Oh, do let him live ! You know if he is lying to us we can always catch him again. It is quite worth while trying.'

At last the young man gave in, and threw the fish back into the sea ; and both brothers went supperless to bed, and wondered what fortune the next day would bring.

At the first streaks of dawn they were both up, and in a very few minutes were running down to the shore. And there, just as the fish had said, stood two magnificent horses, saddled and bridled, and on their backs lay suits of armour and under-dresses, two swords, and two purses of gold.

' There ! ' said the younger brother. ' Are you not thankful you did not eat that fish ? He has brought us good luck, and there is no knowing how great we may become ! Now, we will each seek our own adventures. If you will take one road I will go the other.'

' Very well,' replied the elder ; ' but how shall we let each other know if we are both living ? '

' Do you see this fig-tree ? ' said the younger. ' Well, whenever we want news of each other we have only to come here and make a slit with our swords in the back. If milk flows, it is a sign that we are well and prosperous ; but if, instead of milk, there is blood, then we are either dead or in great danger.'

Then the two brothers put on their armour, buckled their swords, and pocketed their purses ; and, after taking a tender farewell of each other, they mounted their horses and went their various ways.

The elder brother rode straight on till he reached the borders of a strange kingdom. He crossed the frontier, and soon found himself on the banks of a river ; and before him, in the middle of the stream, a beautiful girl sat chained to a rock and weeping bitterly. For in this river dwelt a

serpent with seven heads, who threatened to lay waste
the whole land by breathing fire and flame from his
nostrils unless the king sent him every morning a man
for his breakfast. This had gone on so long that now
there were no men left, and he had been obliged to send
his own daughter instead, and the poor girl was waiting
till the monster got hungry and felt inclined to eat her.

When the young man saw the maiden weeping bitterly
he said to her, ' What is the matter, my poor girl? '

' Oh! ' she answered, ' I am chained here till a
horrible serpent with seven heads comes to eat me. Oh,
sir, do not linger here, or he will eat you too.'

' I shall stay,' replied the young man, ' for I mean to
set you free.'

' That is impossible. You do not know what a fearful
monster the serpent is ; you can do nothing against him.'

' That is my affair, beautiful captive,' answered he ;
' only tell me, which way will the serpent come? '

' Well, if you are resolved to free me, listen to my
advice. Stand a little on one side, and then, when the
serpent rises to the surface, I will say to him, " O serpent,
to-day you can eat two people. But you had better
begin first with the young man, for I am chained and
cannot run away." When he hears this most likely he
will attack you.'

So the young man stood carefully on one side, and by-
and-bye he heard a great rushing in the water ; and a
horrible monster came up to the surface and looked out
for the rock where the king's daughter was chained, for
it was getting late and he was hungry.

But she cried out, ' O serpent, to-day you can eat
two people. And you had better begin with the young
man, for I am chained and cannot run away.'

Then the serpent made a rush at the youth with wide-
open jaws to swallow him at one gulp, but the young
man leaped aside and drew his sword, and fought till he
had cut off all the seven heads. And when the great

serpent lay dead at his feet he loosed the bonds of the king's daughter, and she flung herself into his arms and said, 'You have saved me from that monster, and now you shall be my husband, for my father has made a proclamation that whoever could slay the serpent should have his daughter to wife.'

But he answered, 'I cannot become your husband yet, for I have still far to travel. But wait for me seven years and seven months. Then, if I do not return, you are free to marry whom you will. And in case you should have forgotten, I will take these seven tongues with me, so that when I bring them forth you may know that I am really he who slew the serpent.'

So saying he cut out the seven tongues, and the princess gave him a thick cloth to wrap them in ; and he mounted his horse and rode away.

Not long after he had gone there arrived at the river a slave who had been sent by the king to learn the fate of his beloved daughter. And when the slave saw the princess standing free and safe before him, with the body of the monster lying at her feet, a wicked plan came into his head, and he said, ' Unless you promise to tell your father it was I who slew the serpent, I will kill you and bury you in this place, and no one will ever know what befell.'

What could the poor girl do ? This time there was no knight to come to her aid. So she promised to do as the slave wished, and he took up the seven heads and brought the princess to her father.

Oh, how enchanted the king was to see her again, and the whole town shared his joy !

And the slave was called upon to tell how he had slain the monster, and when he had ended the king declared that he should have the princess to wife.

But she flung herself at her father's feet, and prayed him to delay. 'You have passed your royal word, and cannot go back from it. Yet grant me this grace, and let

THE·FIGHT·WITH·THE·SEVEN·HEADED·SERPENT·

seven years and seven months go by before you wed me.
When they are over, then I will marry the slave.' And
the king listened to her, and seven years and seven
months she looked for her bridegroom, and wept for him
night and day.

All this time the young man was riding through the
world, and when the seven years and seven months were
over he came back to the town where the princess lived—
only a few days before the wedding. And he stood before
the king, and said to him: 'Give me your daughter,
O king, for I slew the seven-headed serpent. And as
a sign that my words are true, look on these seven
tongues, which I cut from his seven heads, and on this
embroidered cloth, which was given me by your daughter.'

Then the princess lifted up her voice and said, ' Yes,
dear father, he has spoken the truth, and it is he who is
my real bridegroom. Yet pardon the slave, for he was
sorely tempted.'

But the king answered, ' Such treachery can no man
pardon. Quick, away with him, and off with his head!'

So the false slave was put to death, that none might
follow in his footsteps, and the wedding feast was held,
and the hearts of all rejoiced that the true bridegroom
had come at last.

These two lived happy and contentedly for a long while,
when one evening, as the young man was looking from
the window, he saw on a mountain that lay out beyond
the town a great bright light.

' What can it be?' he said to his wife.

' Ah! do not look at it,' she answered, 'for it comes
from the house of a wicked witch whom no man can
manage to kill.' But the princess had better have kept
silence, for her words made her husband's heart burn
within him, and he longed to try his strength against the
witch's cunning. And all day long the feeling grew
stronger, till the next morning he mounted his horse, and,
in spite of his wife's tears, he rode off to the mountain.

The distance was greater than he thought, and it was dark before he reached the foot of the mountain ; indeed, he could not have found the road at all had it not been for the bright light, which shone like the moon on his path. At length he came to the door of a fine castle, which had a blaze streaming from every window. He

The Witch casts a Spell
on the Elder Brother.

mounted a flight of steps and entered a hall where a hideous old woman was sitting on a golden chair.

She scowled at the young man and said, 'With a single one of the hairs of my head I can turn you into stone.'

' Oh, what nonsense ! ' cried he. ' Be quiet, old woman. What could you do with one hair ? ' But the witch pulled out a hair and laid it on his shoulder, and his limbs grew cold and heavy, and he could not stir.

Now at this very moment the younger brother was thinking of him, and wondering how he had got on during all the years since they had parted. 'I will go to the fig-tree,' he said to himself, 'to see whether he is alive or dead.' So he rode through the forest till he came where the fig-tree stood, and cut a slit in the bark, and waited. In a moment a little gurgling noise was heard, and out came a stream of blood, running fast. 'Ah, woe is me!' he cried bitterly. 'My brother is dead or dying! Shall I ever reach him in time to save his life?' Then, leaping on his horse, he shouted, 'Now, my steed, fly like the wind!' and they rode right through the world, till one day they came to the town where the young man and his wife lived. Here the princess had been sitting every day since the morning that her husband had left her, weeping bitter tears, and listening for his footsteps. And when she saw his brother ride under the balcony she mistook him for her own husband, for they were so alike that no man might tell the difference, and her heart bounded, and, leaning down, she called to him, 'At last! at last! how long have I waited for thee!' When the younger brother heard these words he said to himself, 'So it was here that my brother lived, and this beautiful woman is my sister-in-law,' but he kept silence, and let her believe he was indeed her husband. Full of joy, the princess led him to the old king, who welcomed him as his own son, and ordered a feast to be made for him. And the princess was beside herself with gladness, but when she would have put her arms round him and kissed him he held up his hand to stop her, saying, 'Touch me not,' at which she marvelled greatly.

In this manner several days went by. And one evening, as the young man leaned from the balcony, he saw a bright light shining on the mountain.

'What can that be?' he said to the princess.

'Oh, come away,' she cried ; 'has not that light already proved your bane? Do you wish to fight a second time with that old witch?'

He marked her words, though she knew it not, and they taught him where his brother was, and what had befallen him. So before sunrise he stole out early, saddled his horse, and rode off to the mountain. But the way was further than he thought, and on the road he met a little old man who asked him whither he was going.

Then the young man told him his story, and added, 'Somehow or other I must free my brother, who has fallen into the power of an old witch.'

'I will tell you what you must do,' said the old man. 'The witch's power lies in her hair ; so when you see her spring on her and seize her by the hair, and then she cannot harm you. Be very careful never to let her hair go, bid her lead you to your brother, and force her to bring him back to life. For she has an ointment that will heal all wounds, and even wake the dead. And when your brother stands safe and well before you, then cut off her head, for she is a wicked woman.'

The young man was grateful for these words, and promised to obey them. Then he rode on, and soon reached the castle. He walked boldly up the steps and entered the hall, where the hideous old witch came to meet him. She grinned horribly at him, and cried out, 'With one hair of my head I can change you into stone.'

'Can you, indeed?' said the young man, seizing her by the hair. 'You old wretch! tell me what you have done with my brother, or I will cut your head off this very instant.' Now the witch's strength was all gone from her, and she had to obey.

'I will take you to your brother,' she said, hoping to get the better of him by cunning, 'but leave me alone. You hold me so tight that I cannot walk.'

'You must manage somehow,' he answered, and held her tighter than ever. She led him into a large hall filled with stone statues, which once had been men, and, pointing out one, she said, 'There is your brother.'

The young man looked at them all and shook his head. 'My brother is not here. Take me to him, or it will be the worse for you.' But she tried to put him off with other statues, though it was no good, and it was not until they had reached the last hall of all that he saw his brother lying on the ground.

'*That* is my brother,' said he. 'Now give me the ointment that will restore him to life.'

Very unwillingly the old witch opened a cupboard close by filled with bottles and jars, and took down one and held it out to the young man. But he was on the watch for trickery, and examined it carefully, and saw that it had no power to heal. This happened many times, till at length she found it was no use, and gave him the one he wanted. And when he had it safe he made her stoop down and smear it over his brother's face, taking care all the while never to loose her hair, and when the dead man opened his eyes the youth drew his sword and cut off her head with a single blow. Then the elder brother got up and stretched himself, and said, 'Oh, how long I have slept! And where am I?'

'The old witch had enchanted you, but now she is dead and you are free. We will wake up the other knights that she laid under her spells, and then we will go.'

This they did, and, after sharing amongst them the jewels and gold they found in the castle, each man went his way. The two brothers remained together, the elder tightly grasping the ointment which had brought him back to life.

They had much to tell each other as they rode along, and at last the younger man exclaimed, 'O fool, to leave such a beautiful wife to go and fight a witch! She took me for her husband, and I did not say her nay.'

When the elder brother heard this a great rage filled

his heart, and, without saying one word, he drew his sword and slew his brother, and his body rolled in the dust. Then he rode on till he reached his home, where his wife was still sitting, weeping bitterly. When she saw him she sprang up with a cry, and threw herself into his arms. ' Oh, how long have I waited for thee ! Never, never must you leave me any more ! '

When the old king heard the news he welcomed him as a son, and made ready a feast, and all the court sat down. And in the evening, when the young man was alone with his wife, she said to him, ' Why would you not let me touch you when you came back, but always thrust me away when I tried to put my arms round you or kiss you ? '

Then the young man understood how true his brother had been to him, and he sat down and wept and wrung his hands because of the wicked murder that he had done. Suddenly he sprang to his feet, for he remembered the ointment which lay hidden in his garments, and he rushed to the place where his brother still lay. He fell on his knees beside the body, and, taking out the salve, he rubbed it over the neck where the wound was gaping wide, and the skin healed and the sinews grew strong, and the dead man sat up and looked round him. And the two brothers embraced each other, and the elder asked forgiveness for his wicked blow ; and they went back to the palace together, and were never parted any more.

MASTER AND PUPIL [1]

THERE was once a man who had a son who was very clever at reading, and took great delight in it. He went out into the world to seek service somewhere, and as he was walking between some mounds he met a man, who asked him where he was going.

'I am going about seeking for service,' said the boy.

'Will you serve me?' asked the man.

'Oh, yes; just as readily you as anyone else,' said the boy.

'But can you read?' asked the man.

'As well as the priest,' said the boy.

'Then I can't have you,' said the man. 'In fact, I was just wanting a boy who couldn't read. His only work would be to dust my old books.'

The man then went on his way, and left the boy looking after him.

'It was a pity I didn't get that place,' thought he 'That was just the very thing for me.'

Making up his mind to get the situation if possible, he hid himself behind one of the mounds, and turned his jacket outside in, so that the man would not know him again so easily. Then he ran along behind the mounds, and met the man at the other end of them.

'Where are you going, my little boy?' said the man, who did not notice that it was the same one he had met before.

[1] From the Danish.

' I am going about seeking for service ? ' said the boy.

' Will you serve me ? ' asked the man.

' Oh, yes ; just as readily you as anyone else,' said the boy.

' But can you read ? ' said the man.

' No, I don't know a single letter,' said the boy.

The man then took him into his service, and all the work he had to do was to dust his master's books. But as he did this he had plenty of time to read them as well, and he read away at them until at last he was just as wise as his master—who was a great wizard—and could perform all kinds of magic. Among other feats, he could change himself into the shape of any animal, or any other thing that he pleased.

When he had learned all this he did not think it worth while staying there any longer, so he ran away home to his parents again. Soon after this there was a market in the next village, and the boy told his mother that he had learned how to change himself into the shape of any animal he chose.

' Now,' said he, ' I shall change myself to a horse, and father can take me to market and sell me. I shall come home again all right.'

His mother was frightened at the idea, but the boy told her that she need not be alarmed ; all would be well. So he changed himself to a horse, such a fine horse, too, that his father got a high price for it at the market ; but after the bargain was made, and the money paid, the boy changed again to his own shape, when no one was looking, and went home.

The story spread all over the country about the fine horse that had been sold and then had disappeared, and at last the news came to the ears of the wizard.

' Aha ! ' said he, ' this is that boy of mine, who befooled me and ran away ; but I shall have him yet.'

The next time that there was a market the boy again changed himself to a horse, and was taken thither by his father. The horse soon found a purchaser, and while the two were inside drinking the luck-penny the wizard came along and saw the horse. He knew at once that it was not an ordinary one, so he also went inside, and offered the purchaser far more than he had paid for it, so the latter sold it to him.

The first thing the wizard now did was to lead the horse away to a smith to get a red-hot nail driven into its mouth, because after that it could not change its shape again. When the horse saw this it changed itself to a dove, and flew up into the air. The wizard at once changed himself into a hawk, and flew up after it. The dove now turned into a gold ring, and fell into a girl's lap. The hawk now turned into a man, and offered the girl a great sum of money for the gold ring, but she would not part with it, seeing that it had fallen down to her, as it were, from Heaven. However, the wizard kept on offering her more and more for it, until at last the gold ring grew frightened, and changed itself into a grain of barley, which fell on the ground. The man then turned into a hen, and began to search for the grain of barley, but this again changed itself to a pole-cat, and took off the hen's head with a single snap.

The wizard was now dead, the pole-cat put on human shape, and the youth afterwards married the girl, and from that time forward let all his magic arts alone.

THE GOLDEN LION

THERE was once a rich merchant who had three sons, and when they were grown up the eldest said to him, 'Father, I wish to travel and see the world. I pray you let me.'

So the father ordered a beautiful ship to be fitted up, and the young man sailed away in it. After some weeks the vessel cast anchor before a large town, and the merchant's son went on shore.

The first thing he saw was a large notice written on a board saying that if any man could find the king's daughter within eight days he should have her to wife, but that if he tried and failed his head must be the forfeit.

'Well,' thought the youth as he read this proclamation, 'that ought not to be a very difficult matter;' and he asked an audience of the king, and told him that he wished to seek for the princess.

'Certainly,' replied the king. 'You have the whole palace to search in; but remember, if you fail it will cost you your head.'

So saying, he commanded the doors to be thrown open, and food and drink to be set before the young man, who, after he had eaten, began to look for the princess. But though he visited every corner and chest and cupboard, she was not in any of them, and after eight days he gave it up and his head was cut off.

¹ *Sicilianische Mährchen.* L. Gonzenbach.

All this time his father and brothers had had no news of him, and were very anxious. At last the second son could bear it no longer, and said, ' Dear father, give me, I pray you, a large ship and some money, and let me go and seek for my brother.'

So another ship was fitted out, and the young man sailed away, and was blown by the wind into the same harbour where his brother had landed.

Now when he saw the first ship lying at anchor his heart beat high, and he said to himself, ' My brother cannot surely be far off,' and he ordered a boat and was put on shore.

As he jumped on to the pier his eye caught the notice about the princess, and he thought, ' He has undertaken to find her, and has certainly lost his head. I must try myself, and seek him as well as her. It cannot be such a very difficult matter.' But he fared no better than his brother, and in eight days his head was cut off.

So now there was only the youngest at home, and when the other two never came he also begged for a ship that he might go in search of his lost brothers. And when the vessel started a high wind arose, and blew him straight to the harbour where the notice was set.

' Oho ! ' said he, as he read, ' whoever can find the king's daughter shall have her to wife. It is quite clear now what has befallen my brothers. But in spite of that I think I must try my luck,' and he took the road to the castle.

On the way he met an old woman, who stopped and begged.

' Leave me in peace, old woman,' replied he.

' Oh, do not send me away empty,' she said. ' You are such a handsome young man you will surely not refuse an old woman a few pence.'

' I tell you, old woman, leave me alone.'

' You are in some trouble ? ' she asked. ' Tell me what it is, and perhaps I can help you.'

Then he told her how he had set his heart on finding the king's daughter.

'I can easily manage that for you as long as you have enough money.'

'Oh, as to that, I have plenty,' answered he.

Whoever can find the King's daughter within eight days have her to wife try & fail forfeit. rex

The Merchant's son reads the notice.

'Well, you must take it to a goldsmith and get him to make it into a golden lion, with eyes of crystal; and inside it must have something that will enable it to play tunes. When it is ready bring it to me.'

The young man did as he was bid, and when the lion

was made the old woman hid the youth in it, and brought it to the king, who was so delighted with it that he wanted to buy it. But she replied, 'It does not belong to me, and my master will not part from it at any price.'

'At any rate, leave it with me for a few days,' said he; 'I should like to show it to my daughter.'

'Yes, I can do that,' answered the old woman; 'but to-morrow I must have it back again. And she went away.

The king watched her till she was quite out of sight, so as to make sure that she was not spying upon him; then he took the golden lion into his room and lifted some loose boards from the floor. Below the floor there was a staircase, which he went down till he reached a door at the foot. This he unlocked, and found himself in a narrow passage closed by another door, which he also opened. The young man, hidden in the golden lion, kept count of everything, and marked that there were in all seven doors. After they had all been unlocked the king entered a lovely hall, where the princess was amusing herself with eleven friends. All twelve girls wore the same clothes, and were as like each other as two peas.

'What bad luck!' thought the youth. 'Even supposing that I managed to find my way here again, I don't see how I could ever tell which was the princess.'

And he stared hard at the princess as she clapped her hands with joy and ran up to them, crying, 'Oh, do let us keep that delicious beast for to-night; it will make such a nice plaything.'

The king did not stay long, and when he left he handed over the lion to the maidens, who amused themselves with it for some time, till they got sleepy, and thought it was time to go to bed. But the princess took the lion into her own room and laid it on the floor.

She was just beginning to doze when she heard a voice quite close to her, which made her jump. 'O lovely princess, if you only knew what I have gone

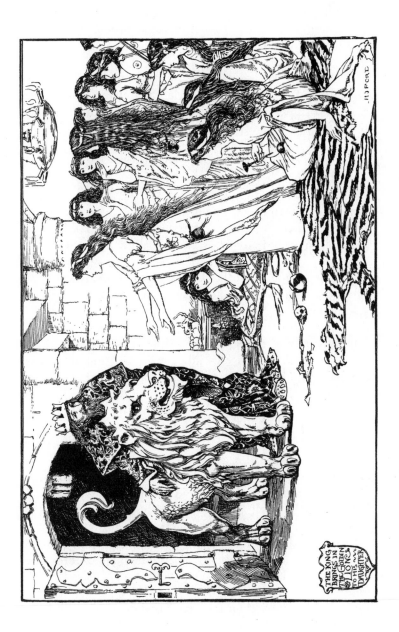

THE KING
BRINGS IN
THE GOLDEN
LION
TO HIS
DAUGHTER

through to find you!' The princess jumped out of bed
screaming, 'The lion! the lion!' but her friends thought
it was a nightmare, and did not trouble themselves to get
up.

'O lovely • princess!' continued the voice, 'fear
nothing! I am the son of a rich merchant, and desire
above all things to have you for my wife. And in order
to get to you I have hidden myself in this golden lion.'

'What use is that?' she asked. 'For if you cannot
pick me out from among my companions you will still
lose your head.'   .

'I look to you to help me,' he said. 'I have done so
much for you that you might do this one thing for me.'

'Then listen to me. On the eighth day I will tie a
white sash round my waist, and by that you will know
me.'

The next morning the king came very early to fetch
the lion, as the old woman was already at the palace
asking for it. When they were safe from view she let
the young man out, and he returned to the king and told
him that he wished to find the princess.

'Very good,' said the king, who by this time was
almost tired of repeating the same words; ' but if you fail
your head will be the forfeit.'

So the youth remained quietly in the castle, eating
and looking at all the beautiful things around him, and
every now and then pretending to be searching busily
in all the closets and corners. On the eighth day he
entered the room where the king was sitting. 'Take up
the floor in this place,' he said. The king gave a cry,
but stopped himself, and asked, 'What do you want the
floor up for? There is nothing there.'

But as all his courtiers were watching him he did
not like to make any more objections, and ordered the
floor to be taken up, as the young man desired. The
youth then went straight down the staircase till he
reached the door; then he turned and demanded that the

key should be brought. So the king was forced to unlock
the door, and the next and the next and the next, till all
seven were open, and they entered into the hall where the
twelve maidens were standing all in a row, so like that
none might tell them apart. But as he looked one of
them silently drew a white sash from her pocket and
slipped it round her waist, and the young man sprang to
her and said, ' This is the princess, and I claim her for
my wife.' And the king owned himself beaten, and
commanded that the wedding feast should be held.

After eight days the bridal pair said farewell to the
king, and set sail for the youth's own country, taking with
them a whole shipload of treasures as the princess's dowry.
But they did not forget the old woman who had brought
about all their happiness, and they gave her enough
money to make her comfortable to the end of her days.

THE SPRIG OF ROSEMARY.[1]

ONCE upon a time there lived a man with one daughter, and he made her work hard all the day. One morning, when she had finished everything he had set her to do, he told her to go out into the woods and get some dry leaves and sticks to kindle a fire.

The girl went out, and soon collected a large bundle, and then she plucked at a sprig of sweet-smelling rosemary for herself. But the harder she pulled the firmer seemed the plant, and at last, determined not to be beaten, she gave one great tug, and the rosemary remained in her hands.

Then she heard a voice close to her saying, ' Well? ' and turning she saw before her a handsome young man, who asked why she had come to steal his firewood.

The girl, who felt much confused, only managed to stammer out as an excuse that her father had sent her.

' Very well,' replied the young man ; ' then come with me.'

So he took her through the opening made by the torn-up root, and they travelled till they reached a beautiful palace, splendidly furnished, but only lighted from the top. And when they had entered he told her that he was a great lord, and that never had he seen a maiden so beautiful as she, and that if she would give him her

[1] *Cuentos Populars Catalans*, per lo Dr. D. Francisco de S. Maspons y Labros (Barcelona : Librería de Don Alvar Verdaguer, 1885).

heart they would be married and live happy for ever
after.

And the maiden said 'yes, she would,' and so they
were married.

The next day the old dame who looked after the
house handed her all the keys, but pointed her out one

THE MAIDEN PLUCKS THE ROSEMARY

that she would do well never to use, for if she did the
whole palace would fall to the ground, and the grass
would grow over it, and the damsel herself would be
remembered no more.

The bride promised to be careful, but in a little while,
when there was nothing left for her to do, she began to

wonder what could be in the chest, which was opened by
the key. As everybody knows, if we once begin to think
we soon begin to do, and it was not very long before the
key was no longer in the maiden's hand but in the lock
of the chest.

But the lock was stiff and resisted all her efforts, and
in the end she had to break it. And what was inside after
all? Why, nothing but a serpent's skin, which her husband,
who was, unknown to her, a magician, put on when he
was at work ; and at the sight of it the girl was turning
away in disgust, when the earth shook violently under
her feet, the palace vanished as if it had never been,
and the bride found herself in the middle of a field, not
knowing where she was or whither to go.

She burst into a flood of bitter tears, partly at her
own folly, but more for the loss of her husband, whom
she dearly loved.   Then, breaking a sprig of rosemary off
a bush hard by, she resolved, cost what it might, to seek
him through the world till she found him.

So she walked and she walked and she walked, till
she arrived at a house built of straw. And she knocked
at the door, and asked if they wanted a servant. The
mistress said she did, and if the girl was willing she
might stay.   But day by day the poor maiden grew more
and more sad, till at last her mistress begged her to say
what was the matter. Then she told her story—how she
was going through the world seeking after her husband.

And her mistress answered her, ' Where he is, none
can tell better than the Sun, the Moon, and the Wind,
for they go everywhere ! '

On hearing these words the damsel set forth once
more, and walked till she reached the Golden Castle,
where lived the Sun. And she knocked boldly at the
door, saying, ' All hail, O Sun ! I have come to ask if,
of your charity, you will help me in my need. By my
own fault have I fallen into these straits, and I am
weary, for I seek my husband through the wide world.'

'Indeed!' spoke the Sun. 'Do you, rich as you are, need help? But though you live in a palace without windows, the Sun enters everywhere, and he knows you.'

Then the bride told him the whole story, and did not

The Maiden asks the MOON to help her.

hide her own ill-doing. And the Sun listened, and was sorry for her; and though he could not tell her where to go, he gave her a nut, and bid her open it in a time of great distress. The damsel thanked him with all her heart, and departed, and walked and walked and walked, till she came to another castle, and knocked at the door, which was opened by an old woman.

'All hail!' said the girl. 'I have come, of your charity, to ask your help!'

'It is my mistress, the Moon, you seek. I will tell her of your prayer.'

So the Moon came out, and when she saw the maiden she knew her again, for she had watched her sleeping both in the cottage and in the palace. And she spake to her and said:

'Do you, rich as you are, need help?'

Then the girl told her the whole story, and the Moon listened, and was sorry for her; and though she could not tell her where to find her husband, she gave her an almond, and told her to crack it when she was in great need. So the damsel thanked her, and departed, and walked and walked and walked till she came to another castle. And she knocked at the door, and said:

'All hail! I have come to ask if, of your charity, you will help me in my need.'

'It is my lord, the Wind, that you want,' answered the old woman who opened it. 'I will tell him of your prayer.'

And the Wind looked on her and knew her again, for he had seen her in the cottage and in the palace, and he spake to her and said:

'Do you, rich as you are, want help?'

And she told him the whole story. And the Wind listened, and was sorry for her, and he gave her a walnut that she was to eat in time of need. But the girl did not go as the Wind expected. She was tired and sad, and knew not where to turn, so she began to weep bitterly. The Wind wept too for company, and said:

'Don't be frightened; I will go and see if I can find out something.'

And the Wind departed with a great noise and fuss,

and in the twinkling of an eye he was back again, beaming with delight.

'From what one person and another have let fall,' he exclaimed, 'I have contrived to learn that he is in the palace of the king, who keeps him hidden lest anyone should see him ; and that to-morrow he is to marry the princess, who, ugly creature that she is, has not been able to find any man to wed her.'

Who can tell the despair which seized the poor maiden when she heard this news ! As soon as she could speak she implored the Wind to do all he could to get the wedding put off for two or three days, for it would take her all that time to reach the palace of the king.

The Wind gladly promised to do what he could, and as he travelled much faster than the maiden he soon arrived at the palace, where he found five tailors working night and day at the wedding clothes of the princess.

Down came the Wind right in the middle of their lace and satin and trimmings of pearl ! Away they all went whiz ! through the open windows, right up into the tops of the trees, across the river, among the dancing ears of corn ! After them ran the tailors, catching, jumping, climbing, but all to no purpose ! The lace was torn, the satin stained, the pearls knocked off ! There was nothing for it but to go to the shops to buy fresh, and to begin all over again ! It was plainly quite impossible that the wedding clothes could be ready next day.

However, the king was much too anxious to see his daughter married to listen to any excuses, and he declared that a dress must be put together somehow for the bride to wear. But when he went to look at the princess, she was such a figure that he agreed that it would be unfitting for her position to be seen in such a gown, and he ordered the ceremony and the banquet to be postponed for a few hours, so that the tailors might take the dress to pieces and make it fit.

But by this time the maiden had arrived footsore and

weary at the castle, and as soon as she reached the door she cracked her nut and drew out of it the most beautiful mantle in the world.   Then she rang the bell, and asked :

' Is not the princess to be married to-day ?'

' Yes, she is.'

' Ask her if she would like to buy this mantle.'

And when the princess saw the mantle she was delighted, for her wedding mantle had been spoilt with all the other things, and it was too late to make another. So she told the maiden to ask what price she would, and it should be given her.

The maiden fixed a large sum, many pieces of gold, but the princess had set her heart on the mantle, and gave it readily.

Now the maiden hid her gold in the pocket of her dress, and turned away from the castle.   The moment she was out of sight she broke her almond, and drew from it the most magnificent petticoats that ever were seen.   Then she went back to the castle, and asked if the princess wished to buy any petticoats.   No sooner did the princess cast her eyes on the petticoats than she declared they were even more beautiful than the mantle, and that she would give the maiden whatever price she wanted for them.   And the maiden named many pieces of gold, which the princess paid her gladly, so pleased was she with her new possessions.

Then the girl went down the steps where none could watch her and cracked her walnut, and out came the most splendid court dress that any dressmaker had ever invented ; and, carrying it carefully in her arms, she knocked at the door, and asked if the princess wished to buy a court dress.

When the message was delivered the princess sprang to her feet with delight, for she had been thinking that after all it was not much use to have a lovely mantle and elegant petticoats if she had no dress, and she knew the tailors would never be ready in time. So she sent at once to say she would buy the dress, and what sum did the maiden want for it.

This time the maiden answered that the price of the dress was the permission to see the bridegroom.

The princess was not at all pleased when she heard the maiden's reply, but, as she could not do without the dress, she was forced to give in, and contented herself with thinking that after all it did not matter much.

So the maiden was led to the rooms which had been given to her husband. And when she came near she touched him with the sprig of rosemary that she carried ; and his memory came back, and he knew her, and kissed her, and declared that she was his true wife, and that he loved her and no other.

Then they went back to the maiden's home, and grew to be very old, and lived happy all the days of their life.

THE WHITE DOVE [1]

A KING had two sons. They were a pair of reckless fellows, who always had something foolish to do. One day they rowed out alone on the sea in a little boat. It was beautiful weather when they set out, but as soon as they had got some distance from the shore there arose a terrific storm. The oars went overboard at once, and the little boat was tossed about on the rolling billows like a nut-shell. The princes had to hold fast by the seats to keep from being thrown out of the boat.

In the midst of all this they met a wonderful vessel— it was a dough-trough, in which there sat an old woman. She called to them, and said that they could still get to shore alive if they would promise her the son that was next to come to their mother the queen.

'We can't do that,' shouted the princes; 'he doesn't belong to *us*, so we can't give him away.'

'Then you can rot at the bottom of the sea, both of you,' said the old woman; 'and perhaps it may be the case that your mother would rather keep the two sons she has than the one she hasn't got yet.'

Then she rowed away in her dough-trough, while the storm howled still louder than before, and the water dashed over their boat until it was almost sinking. Then the princes thought that there was something in what the old woman had said about their mother, and being, of course, eager to save their lives, they shouted to her, and

[1] From the Danish.

The Witch comes home

promised that she should have their brother if she would
deliver them from this danger. As soon as they had done
so the storm ceased and the waves fell. The boat drove
ashore below their father's castle, and both princes were
received with open arms by their father and mother, who
had suffered great anxiety for them.

The two brothers said nothing about what they had
promised, neither at that time nor later on when the
queen's third son came, a beautiful boy, whom she loved
more than anything else in the world. He was brought
up and educated in his father's house until he was full
grown, and still his brothers had never seen or heard anything about the witch to whom they had promised him
before he was born.

It happened one evening that there arose a raging
storm, with mist and darkness. It howled and roared
around the king's palace, and in the midst of it there
came a loud knock on the door of the hall where the
youngest prince was. He went to the door and found
there an old woman with a dough-trough on her back,
who said to him that he must go with her at once; his
brothers had promised him to her if she would save their
lives.

'Yes,' said he; 'if you saved my brothers' lives, and
they promised me to you, then I will go with you.'

They therefore went down to the beach together,
where he had to take his seat in the trough, along with the
witch, who sailed away with him, over the sea, home to
her dwelling.

The prince was now in the witch's power, and in her
service. The first thing she set him to was to pick
feathers. 'The heap of feathers that you see here,' said
she, 'you must get finished before I come home in the
evening, otherwise you shall be set to harder work.' He
started to the feathers, and picked and picked until there
was only a single feather left that had not passed through
his hands. But then there came a whirlwind and sent

all the feathers flying, and swept them along the floor into a heap, where they lay as if they were trampled together. He had now to begin all his work over again, but by this time it only wanted an hour of evening, when the witch was to be expected home, and he easily saw that it was impossible for him to be finished by that time.

Then he heard something tapping at the window pane, and a thin voice said, ' Let me in, and I will help you.' It was a white dove, which sat outside the window, and was pecking at it with its beak. He opened the window, and the dove came in and set to work at once, and picked all the feathers out of the heap with its beak. Before the hour was past the feathers were all nicely arranged : the dove flew out at the window, and at the same moment the witch came in at the door.

' Well, well,' said she, ' it was more than I would have expected of you—to get all the feathers put in order so nicely. However, such a prince might be expected to have neat fingers.'

Next morning the witch said to the prince, ' To-day you shall have some easy work to do. Outside the door I have some firewood lying ; you must split that for me into little bits that I can kindle the fire with. That will soon be done, but you must be finished before I come home.'

The prince got a little axe and set to work at once. He split and clove away, and thought that he was getting on fast; but the day wore on until it was long past mid-day, and he was still very far from having finished. He thought, in fact, that the pile of wood rather grew bigger than smaller, in spite of what he took off it ; so he let his hands fall by his side, and dried the sweat from his forehead, and was ill at ease, for he knew that it would be bad for him if he was not finished with the work before the witch came home.

Then the white dove came flying and settled down on the pile of wood, and cooed and said, ' Shall I help you ? '

' Yes,' said the prince, ' many thanks for your help yesterday, and for what you offer to-day.' Thereupon the little dove seized one piece of wood after another and split it with its beak. The prince could not take away the wood as quickly as the dove could split it, and in a short time it was all cleft into little sticks.

The dove then flew up on his shoulder and sat there ; and the prince thanked it, and stroked and caressed its white feathers, and kissed its little red beak. With that it was a dove no longer, but a beautiful young maiden, who stood by his side. She told him then that she was a princess whom the witch had stolen, and had changed to this shape, but with his kiss she had got her human form again ; and if he would be faithful to her, and take her to wife, she could free them both from the witch's power.

The prince was quite captivated by the beautiful princess, and was quite willing to do anything whatsoever to get her for himself.

She then said to him, ' When the witch comes home you must ask her to grant you a wish, when you have accomplished so well all that she has demanded of you. When she agrees to this you must ask her straight out for the princess that she has flying about as a white dove. But just now you must take a red silk thread and tie it round my little finger, so that you may be able to recognise me again, into whatever shape she turns me.'

The prince made haste to get the silk thread tied round her little white finger ; at the same moment the princess became a dove again and flew away, and immediately after that the old witch came home with her dough-trough on her back.

' Well,' said she, ' I must say that you are clever at your work, and it is something, too, that such princely hands are not accustomed to.'

' Since you are so well pleased with my work,' said the prince, ' you will, no doubt, be willing to give me a

The Witch flies into a Rage

little pleasure too, and give me something that I have
taken a fancy to.'

'Oh yes, indeed,' said the old woman ; 'what is it
that you want ? '

'I want the princess here who is in the shape of a
white dove,' said the prince.

'What nonsense ! ' said the witch. ' Why should you
imagine that there are princesses here flying about in the
shape of white doves ?   But if you *will* have a princess,
you can get one such as we have them.'   She then came
to him, dragging a shaggy little grey ass with long ears.
'Will you have this ? ' said she ; 'you can't get any other
princess ! '

The prince used his eyes and saw the red silk thread
on one of the ass's hoofs, so he said, 'Yes, just let me
have it.'

'What will you do with it ? ' asked the witch.

'I will ride on it,' said the prince ; but with that the
witch dragged it away again, and came back with an old,
wrinkled, toothless hag, whose hands trembled with age.
'You can have no other princess,' said she.   'Will you
have *her* ? '

'Yes, I will,' said the prince, for he saw the red silk
thread on the old woman's finger.

At this the witch became so furious that she danced
about and knocked everything to pieces that she could
lay her hands upon, so that the splinters flew about the
ears of the prince and princess, who now stood there in
her own beautiful shape.

Then their marriage had to be celebrated, for the
witch had to stick to what she had promised, and he
must get the princess whatever might happen afterwards.

The princess now said to him, ' At the marriage feast
you may eat what you please, but you must not drink
anything whatever, for if you do that you will forget me.'

This, however, the prince forgot on the wedding day,
and stretched out his hand and took a cup of wine ; but

tne princess was keeping watch over him, and gave him a push with her elbow, so that the wine flew over the table-cloth.

Then the witch got up and laid about her among the plates and dishes, so that the pieces flew about their ears, just as she had done when she was cheated the first time.

They were then taken to the bridal chamber, and the door was shut. Then the princess said, ' Now the witch has kept her promise, but she will do no more if she can help it, so we must fly immediately. I shall lay two pieces of wood in the bed to answer for us when the witch speaks to us. You can take the flower-pot and the glass of water that stands in the window, and we must slip out by that and get away.'

No sooner said than done. They hurried off out into the dark night, the princess leading, because she knew the way, having spied it out while she flew about as a dove.

At midnight the witch came to the door of the room and called in to them, and the two pieces of wood answered her, so that she believed they were there, and went away again. Before daybreak she was at the door again and called to them, and again the pieces of wood answered for them. She thus thought that she had them, and when the sun rose the bridal night was past : she had then kept her promise, and could vent her anger and revenge on both of them. With the first sunbeam she broke into the room, but there she found no prince and no princess—nothing but the two pieces of firewood, which lay in the bed, and stared, and spoke not a word. These she threw on the floor, so that they were splintered into a thousand pieces, and off she hastened after the fugitives.

With the first sunbeam the princess said to the prince, ' Look round ; do you see anything behind us ? '

' Yes, I see a dark cloud, far away,' said he.

' Then throw the flower-pot over your head,' said she

When this was done there was a large thick forest behind them.

When the witch came to the forest she could not get through it until she went home and brought her axe to cut a path.

A little after this the princess said again to the prince, ' Look round ; do you see anything behind us ? '

' Yes,' said the prince, ' the big black cloud is there again.'

' Then throw the glass of water over your head,' said she.

When he had done this there was a great lake behind them, and this the witch could not cross until she ran home again and brought her dough-trough.

Meanwhile the fugitives had reached the castle which was the prince's home. They climbed over the garden wall, ran across the garden, and crept in at an open window. By this time the witch was just at their heels, but the princess stood in the window and blew upon the witch ; hundreds of white doves flew out of her mouth, fluttered and flapped around the witch's head until she grew so angry that she turned into flint, and there she stands to this day, in the shape of a large flint stone, outside the window.

Within the castle there was great rejoicing over the prince and his bride. His two elder brothers came and knelt before him and confessed what they had done, and said that he alone should inherit the kingdom, and they would always be his faithful subjects.

THE TROLL'S DAUGHTER [1]

THERE was once a lad who went to look for a place. As he went along he met a man, who asked him where he was going. He told him his errand, and the stranger said, 'Then you can serve me ; I am just in want of a lad like you, and I will give you good wages—a bushel of money the first year, two the second year, and three the third year, for you must serve me three years, and obey me in everything, however strange it seems to you. You need not be afraid of taking service with me, for there is no danger in it if you only know how to obey.'

The bargain was made, and the lad went home with the man to whom he had engaged himself. It was a strange place indeed, for he lived in a bank in the middle of the wild forest, and the lad saw there no other person than his master. The latter was a great troll, and had marvellous power over both men and beasts.

Next day the lad had to begin his service. The first thing that the troll set him to was to feed all the wild animals from the forest. These the troll had tied up, and there were both wolves and bears, deer and hares, which the troll had gathered in the stalls and folds in his stable down beneath the ground, and that stable was a mile long. The boy, however, accomplished all this work on that day, and the troll praised him and said that it was very well done.

Next morning the troll said to him, 'To-day the

animals are not to be fed; they don't get the like of that every day. You shall have leave to play about for a little, until they are to be fed again.'

Then the troll said some words to him which he did not understand, and with that the lad turned into a hare, and ran out into the wood. He got plenty to run for, too, for all the hunters aimed at him, and tried to shoot him, and the dogs barked and ran after him wherever they got wind of him. He was the only animal that was left in the wood now, for the troll had tied up all the others, and every hunter in the whole country was eager to knock him over. But in this they met with no success; there was no dog that could overtake him, and no marksman that could hit him. They shot and shot at him, and he ran and ran. It was an unquiet life, but in the long run he got used to it, when he saw that there was no danger in it, and it even amused him to befool all the hunters and dogs that were so eager after him.

Thus a whole year passed, and when it was over the troll called him home, for he was now in his power like all the other animals. The troll then said some words to him which he did not understand, and the hare immediately became a human being again. 'Well, how do you like to serve me?' said the troll, 'and how do you like being a hare?'

The lad replied that he liked it very well; he had never been able to go over the ground so quickly before. The troll then showed him the bushel of money that he had already earned, and the lad was well pleased to serve him for another year.

The first day of the second year the boy had the same work to do as on the previous one—namely, to feed all the wild animals in the troll's stable. When he had done this the troll again said some words to him, and with that he became a raven, and flew high up into the air. This was delightful, the lad thought; he could go even faster now than when he was a hare, and the dogs could not

The Troll's Daughter.

come after him here. This was a great delight to him, but he soon found out that he was not to be left quite at peace, for all the marksmen and hunters who saw him aimed at him and fired away, for they had no other birds to shoot at than himself, as the troll had tied up all the others.

This, however, he also got used to, when he saw that they could never hit him, and in this way he flew about all that year, until the troll called him home again, said some strange words to him, and gave him his human shape again. 'Well, how did you like being a raven?' said the troll.

'I liked it very well,' said the lad, 'for never in all my days have I been able to rise so high.' The troll then showed him the two bushels of money which he had earned that year, and the lad was well content to remain in his service for another year.

Next day he got his old task of feeding all the wild beasts. When this was done the troll again said some words to him, and at these he turned into a fish, and sprang into the river. He swam up and he swam down, and thought it was pleasant to let himself drive with the stream. In this way he came right out into the sea, and swam further and further out. At last he came to a glass palace, which stood at the bottom of the sea. He could see into all the rooms and halls, where everything was very grand; all the furniture was of white ivory, inlaid with gold and pearl. There were soft rugs and cushions of all the colours of the rainbow, and beautiful carpets that looked like the finest moss, and flowers and trees with curiously crooked branches, both green and yellow, white and red, and there were also little fountains which sprang up from the most beautiful snail-shells, and fell into bright mussel-shells, and at the same time made a most delightful music, which filled the whole palace.

The most beautiful thing of all, however, was a young girl who went about there, all alone. She went about from one room to another, but did not seem to be happy with all the grandeur she had about her. She walked in solitude and melancholy, and never even thought of looking at her own image in the polished glass walls that were on every side of her, although she was the prettiest creature anyone could wish to see. The lad thought so too while he swam round the palace and peeped in from every side.

'Here, indeed, it would be better to be a man than such a poor dumb fish as I am now,' said he to himself; 'if I could only remember the words that the troll says when he changes my shape, then perhaps I could help myself to become a man again.' He swam and he pondered and he thought over this until he remembered the sound of what the troll said, and then he tried to say it himself. In a moment he stood in human form at the bottom of the sea.

He made haste then to enter the glass palace, and went up to the young girl and spoke to her.

At first he nearly frightened the life out of her, but he talked to her so kindly and explained how he had come down there that she soon recovered from her alarm, and was very pleased to have some company to relieve the terrible solitude that she lived in. Time passed so quickly for both of them that the youth (for now he was quite a young man, and no more a lad) forgot altogether how long he had been there.

One day the girl said to him that now it was close on the time when he must become a fish again—the troll would soon call him home, and he would have to go, but before that he must put on the shape of the fish, otherwise he could not pass through the sea alive. Before this, while he was staying down there, she had told him that she was a daughter of the same troll whom the youth served, and he had shut her up there to keep her away from everyone. She had now devised a plan by which they could perhaps succeed in getting to see each other again, and spending the rest of their lives together. But there was much to attend to, and he must give careful heed to all that she told him.

She told him then that all the kings in the country round about were in debt to her father the troll, and the king of a certain kingdom, the name of which she told him, was the first who had to pay, and if he could not do so at the time appointed he would lose his head. 'And he cannot pay,' said she ; ' I know that for certain. Now you must, first of all, give up your service with my father ; the three years are past, and you are at liberty to go. You will go off, with your six bushels of money, to the kingdom that I have told you of, and there enter the service of the king. When the time comes near for his debt becoming due you will be able to notice by his manner that he is ill at ease. You shall then say to him that you know well enough what it is that is weighing upon him—that it is the debt which he owes to the troll, and cannot pay, but that you can lend him the money. The amount is six bushels—just what you have. You shall, however, only lend them to him on condition that you may accompany him when he goes to make the payment, and that you then have permission to run before him as a fool. When you arrive at the troll's abode, you must perform all kinds of foolish tricks, and see that you break a whole lot of his windows, and do all other damage that you can. My father will then get very angry, and as the king must answer for what his fool does he will sentence him, even although he has paid his debt, either to answer three questions or to lose his life. The first question my father will ask will be, "Where is my daughter?" Then you shall step forward and answer, "She is at the bottom of the sea." He will then ask you whether you can recognise her, and to this you will answer "Yes." Then he will bring forward a whole troop of women, and cause them to pass before you, in order that you may pick out the one that you take for his daughter. You will not be able to recognise me at all, and therefore I will catch hold of you as I go past, so that you can notice it, and you must then make haste to catch me and hold me fast. You have then answered his first question. His next question will be, " Where is my heart ? " You shall then step forward again and answer, " It is in a fish." " Do you know that fish ? " he will say, and you will again answer " Yes." He will then cause all kinds of fish to come before you, and you shall choose between them. I shall take good care to keep by your side, and when the right fish comes I will give you a little push, and with that you will seize the fish and cut it up. Then all will be over with the troll ; he will ask no more questions, and we shall be free to wed.'

When the youth had got all these directions as to what he had to do when he got ashore again the next thing was to remember the words which the troll said when he changed him from a human being to an animal ; but these he had forgotten, and the girl did not know them either. He went about all day in despair, and thought and thought, but he could not remember what they sounded like. During the night he could not sleep, until towards morning he fell into a slumber, and all at once it flashed upon him what the troll used to say. He made haste to repeat the words, and at the same moment he became a fish again and slipped out into the sea. Immediately after this he was called upon, and swam through the sea up the river to where the troll stood on the bank and restored him to human shape with the same words as before.

' Well, how do you like to be a fish ? ' asked the troll.

It was what he had liked best of all, said the youth, and that was no lie, as everybody can guess.

The troll then showed him the three bushels of money which he had earned during the past year ; they stood beside the other three, and all the six now belonged to him.

'Perhaps you will serve me for another year yet,' said the troll, 'and you will get six bushels of money for it; that makes twelve in all, and that is a pretty penny.'

'No,' said the youth; he thought he had done enough, and was anxious to go to some other place to serve, and learn other people's ways; but he would, perhaps, come back to the troll some other time.

The troll said that he would always be welcome; he had served him faithfully for the three years they had agreed upon, and he could make no objections to his leaving now.

The youth then got his six bushels of money, and with these he betook himself straight to the kingdom which his sweetheart had told him of. He got his money buried in a lonely spot close to the king's palace, and then went in there and asked to be taken into service. He obtained his request, and was taken on as stableman, to tend the king's horses.

Some time passed, and he noticed how the king always went about sorrowing and grieving, and was never glad or happy. One day the king came into the stable, where there was no one present except the youth, who said straight out to him that, with his majesty's permission, he wished to ask him why he was so sorrowful.

'It's of no use speaking about that,' said the king; 'you cannot help me, at any rate.'

'You don't know about that,' said the youth; 'I know well enough what it is that lies so heavy on your mind, and I know also of a plan to get the money paid.'

This was quite another case, and the king had more talk with the stableman, who said that he could easily lend the king the six bushels of money, but would only do it on condition that he should be allowed to accompany the king when he went to pay the debt, and that he should then be dressed like the king's court fool, and run before him. He would cause some trouble, for which the king would be severely spoken to, but he would answer for it that no harm would befall him.

The king gladly agreed to all that the youth proposed, and it was now high time for them to set out.

When they came to the troll's dwelling it was no longer in the bank, but on the top of this there stood a large castle which the youth had never seen before. The troll could, in fact, make it visible or invisible, just as he pleased, and, knowing as much as he did of the troll's magic arts, the youth was not at all surprised at this.

When they came near to this castle, which looked as if it was of pure glass, the youth ran on in front as the king's fool. He ran sometimes facing forwards, sometimes backwards, stood sometimes on his head, and sometimes on his feet, and he dashed in pieces so many of the troll's big glass windows and doors that it was something awful to see, and overturned everything he could, and made a fearful disturbance.

The troll came rushing out, and was so angry and furious, and abused the king with all his might for bringing such a wretched fool with him, as he was sure that he could not pay the least bit of all the damage that had been done when he could not even pay off his old debt.

The fool, however, spoke up, and said that he could do so quite easily, and the king then came forward with the six bushels of money which the youth had lent him. They were measured and found to be correct. This the troll had not reckoned on, but he could make no objection against it. The old debt was honestly paid, and the king got his bond back again.

But there still remained all the damage that had been done that day, and the king had nothing with which to pay for this. The troll, therefore, sentenced the king, either to answer three questions that he would put to him, or have his head taken off, as was agreed on in the old bond.

There was nothing else to be done than to try to answer the troll's riddles. The fool then stationed himself just by the king's side while the troll came forward with his questions. He first asked, ' Where is my daughter ? '

The fool spoke up and said, ' She is at the bottom of the sea.'

' How do you know that ? ' said the troll.

' The little fish saw it,' said the fool.

' Would you know her ? ' said the troll.

' Yes, bring her forward,' said the fool.

The troll made a whole crowd of women go past them, one after the other, but all these were nothing but shadows and deceptions. Amongst the very last was the troll's real daughter, who pinched the fool as she went past him to make him aware of her presence. He thereupon caught her round the waist and held her fast, and the troll had to admit that his first riddle was solved.

Then the troll asked again : ' Where is my heart ? '

' It is in a fish,' said the fool.

' Would you know that fish ? ' said the troll.

' Yes, bring it forward,' said the fool.

Then all the fishes came swimming past them, and meanwhile the troll's daughter stood just by the youth's side. When at last the right fish came swimming along she gave him a nudge, and he seized it at once, drove his knife into it, and split it up, took the heart out of it, and cut it through the middle.

At the same moment the troll fell dead and turned into pieces of flint. With that all the bonds that the troll had bound were broken ; all the wild beasts and birds which he had caught and hid under the ground were free now, and dispersed themselves in the woods and in the air.

The youth and his sweetheart entered the castle, which was now theirs, and held their wedding ; and all the kings roundabout, who had been in the troll's debt, and were now out of it, came to the wedding, and saluted the youth as their emperor, and he ruled over them all, and kept peace between them, and lived in his castle with his beautiful empress in great joy and magnificence. And if they have not died since they are living there to this day.

ESBEN AND THE WITCH [1]

THERE was once a man who had twelve sons : the eleven eldest were both big and strong, but the twelfth, whose name was Esben, was only a little fellow. The eleven eldest went out with their father to field and forest, but Esben preferred to stay at home with his mother, and so he was never reckoned at all by the rest, but was a sort of outcast among them.

When the eleven had grown up to be men they decided to go out into the world to try their fortune, and they plagued their father to give them what they required for the journey. The father was not much in favour of this, for he was now old and weak, and could not well spare them from helping him with his work, but in the long run he had to give in. Each one of the eleven got a fine white horse and money for the journey, and so they said farewell to their father and their home, and rode away.

As for Esben, no one had ever thought about him ; his brothers had not even said farewell to him.

After the eleven were gone Esben went to his father and said, ' Father, give me also a horse and money ; I should also like to see round about me in the world.'

' You are a little fool,' said his father. ' If I could have let you go, and kept your eleven brothers at home, it would have been better for me in my old age.'

' Well, you will soon be rid of me at any rate,' said Esben.

---

[1] From the Danish.

THE ELEVEN BROTHERS RIDE OFF.

ESBEN

As he could get no other horse, he went into the forest, broke off a branch, stripped the bark off it, so that it became still whiter than his brothers' horses, and, mounted on this, rode off after his eleven brothers.

The brothers rode on the whole day, and towards evening they came to a great forest, which they entered. Far within the wood they came to a little house, and knocked at the door. There came an old, ugly, bearded hag, and opened it, and they asked her whether all of them could get quarters for the night.

ESBEN GETS A HORSE TOO

'Yes,' said the old, bearded hag, 'you shall all have quarters for the night, and, in addition, each of you shall have one of my daughters.'

The eleven brothers thought that they had come to very hospitable people. They were well attended to, and when they went to bed, each of them got one of the hag's daughters.

Esben had been coming along behind them, and had followed the same way, and had also found the same house in the forest. He slipped into this, without either the witch or her daughters noticing him, and hid himself under one of the beds. A little before midnight he crept quietly out and wakened his brothers. He told these to change night-caps with the witch's daughters. The brothers saw no reason for this, but, to get rid of Esben's persistence, they made the exchange, and slept soundly again.

When midnight came Esben heard the old witch come creeping along. She had a broad-bladed axe in her hand, and went over all the eleven beds. It was so dark that she could not see a hand's breadth before her, but she felt her way, and hacked the heads off all the sleepers who had the men's night-caps on—and these were her own daughters. As soon as she had gone her way Esben wakened his brothers, and they hastily took their horses and rode off from the witch's house, glad that they had escaped so well. They quite forgot to thank Esben for what he had done for them.

When they had ridden onwards for some time they reached a king's palace, and inquired there whether they could be taken into service. Quite easily, they were told, if they would be stablemen, otherwise the king had no use for them. They were quite ready for this, and got the task of looking after all the king's horses.

Long after them came Esben riding on his stick, and he also wanted to get a place in the palace, but no one had any use for him, and he was told that he could just go back the way he had come. However, he stayed there and occupied himself as best he could. He got his food, but nothing more, and by night he lay just where he could.

At this time there was in the palace a knight who was called Sir Red. He was very well liked by the king, but hated by everyone else, for he was wicked both in will and deed. This Sir Red became angry with the eleven brothers, because they would not always stand at attention for him, so he determined to avenge himself on them.

One day, therefore, he went to the king, and said that the eleven brothers who had come to the palace a little while ago, and served as stablemen, could do a great deal more than they pretended. One day he had heard them say that if they liked they could get for the king a wonderful dove which had a feather of gold and a feather of silver time about. But they would not procure it unless they were threatened with death.

The king then had the eleven brothers called before him, and said to them, 'You have said that you can get me a dove which has feathers of gold and silver time about.'

All the eleven assured him that they had never said anything of the kind, and they did not believe that such a dove existed in the whole world.

'Take your own mind of it,' said the king; 'but if you don't get that dove within three days you shall lose your heads, the whole lot of you.'

With that the king let them go, and there was great grief among them; some wept and others lamented.

At that moment Esben came along, and, seeing their sorrowful looks, said to them, 'Hallo, what's the matter with you?'

'What good would it do to tell you, you little fool? *You* can't help us.'

'Oh, you don't know that,' answered Esben. 'I have helped you before.'

In the end they told him how unreasonable the king was, and how he had ordered them to get for him a dove with feathers of gold and silver time about.

'Give me a bag of peas' said Esben, 'and I shall see what I can do for you.'

Esben got his bag of peas; then he took his white stick, and said,

> Fly quick, my little stick,
> Carry me across the stream.

Straightway the stick carried him across the river and straight into the old witch's courtyard. Esben had noticed that she had such a dove; so when he arrived in the courtyard he shook the peas out of the bag, and the dove came fluttering down to pick them up. Esben caught it at once, put it into the bag, and hurried off before the witch caught sight of him; but the next moment she came running, and shouted after him, ' Hey is that you, Esben? '

' Ye—e—s! '

' Is it you that has taken my dove? '

' Ye—e—s! '

' Was it you that made me kill my eleven daughters? '

' Ye—e—s! '

' Are you coming back again? '

' That may be,' said Esben.

' Then you'll catch it,' shouted the witch.

The stick carried Esben with the dove back to the king's palace, and his brothers were greatly delighted. The king thanked them many times for the dove, and gave them in return both silver and gold. At this Sir Red

became still more embittered, and again thought of how to avenge himself on the brothers.

One day he went to the king and told him that the dove was by no means the best thing that the brothers could get for him ; for one day he had heard them talking quietly among themselves, and they had said that they could procure a boar whose bristles were of gold and silver time about.

The king again summoned the brothers before him, and asked whether it was true that they had said that they could get for him a boar whose bristles were of gold and silver time about.

'No,' said the brothers ; they had never said nor thought such a thing, and they did not believe that there was such a boar in the whole world.

'You must get me that boar within three days,' said the king, ' or it will cost you your heads.'

With that they had to go. This was still worse than before, they thought. Where could they get such a marvellous boar ? They all went about hanging their heads ; but when only one day remained of the three Esben came along. When he saw his brothers' sorrowful looks he cried, ' Hallo, what's the matter now ? '

' Oh, what's the use of telling you ? ' said his brothers. ' *You* can't help us, at any rate.'

' Ah, you don't know that,' said Esben ; ' I've helped you before.'

In the end they told him how Sir Red had stirred up the king against them, so that he had ordered them to get for him a boar with bristles of gold and silver time about.

' That's all right,' said Esben ; ' give me a sack of malt, and it is not quite impossible that I may be able to help you.'

Esben got his sack of malt ; then he took his little white stick, set himself upon it, and said,

> Fly quick, my little stick,
> Carry me across the stream.

Off went the stick with him, and very soon he was again in the witch's courtyard. There he emptied out the malt, and next moment came the boar, which had every second bristle of gold and of silver. Esben at once put it into his sack and hurried off before the witch should catch sight of him ; but the next moment she came running, and shouted after him, ' Hey ! is that you, Esben ? '

' Ye—e—s ! '

' Is it you that has taken my pretty boar ? '

' Ye—e—s ! '

' It was also you that took my dove ? '

' Ye—e—s ! '

' And it was you that made me kill my eleven daughters ? '

' Ye—e—s ! '

' Are you coming back again ? '

' That may be,' said Esben.

' Then you'll catch it,' said the witch.

Esben was soon back at the palace with the boar, and

his brothers scarcely knew which leg to stand on, so rejoiced were they that they were safe again. Not one of them, however, ever thought of thanking Esben for what he had done for them.

The king was still more rejoiced over the boar than he had been over the dove, and did not know what to give the brothers for it. At this Sir Red was again possessed with anger and envy, and again he went about and planned how to get the brothers into trouble.

One day he went again to the king and said, ' These eleven brothers have now procured the dove and the boar, but they can do much more than that ; I know they have said that if they liked they could get for the king a lamp that can shine over seven kingdoms.'

' If they have said that,' said the king, ' they shall also be made to bring it to me. *That* would be a glorious lamp for me.'

Again the king sent a message to the brothers to come up to the palace. They went accordingly, although very unwillingly, for they suspected that Sir Red had fallen on some new plan to bring them into trouble.

As soon as they came before the king he said to them, ' You brothers have said that you could, if you liked, get for me a lamp that can shine over seven kingdoms. That lamp must be mine within three days, or it will cost you your lives.'

The brothers assured him that they had never said so, and they were sure that no such lamp existed, but their words were of no avail.

' The lamp ! ' said the king, ' or it will cost you your heads.'

The brothers were now in greater despair than ever. They did not know what to do, for such a lamp no one had ever heard of. But just as things looked their worst along came Esben.

' Something wrong again ? ' said he. ' What's the matter with you now ? '

' Oh, it's no use telling you,' said they. ' *You* can't help us, at any rate.'

' Oh, you might at least tell me,' said Esben ; ' I have helped you before.'

In the end they told him that the king had ordered them to bring him a lamp which could shine over seven kingdoms, but such a lamp no one had ever heard tell of.

' Give me a bushel of salt,' said Esben, ' and we shall see how matters go.'

He got his bushel of salt, and then mounted his little white stick, and said,

> Fly quick, my little stick,
> Carry me across the stream.

With that both he and his bushel of salt were over beside the witch's courtyard. But now matters were less easy, for he could not get inside the yard, as it was evening and the gate was locked. Finally he hit upon a plan ; he got up on the roof and crept down the chimney.

He searched all round for the lamp, but could find it nowhere, for the witch always had it safely guarded, as it was one of her most precious treasures. When he became tired of searching for it he crept into the baking-oven, intending to lie down there and sleep till morning ; but just at that moment he heard the witch calling from her bed to one of her daughters, and telling her to make some porridge for her. She had grown hungry, and had taken such a fancy to some porridge. The daughter got out of bed, kindled the fire, and put on a pot with water in it.

' You mustn't put any salt in the porridge, though,' cried the witch.

' No, neither will I,' said the daughter ; but while she was away getting the meal Esben slipped out of the oven and emptied the whole bushel of salt into the pot. The daughter came back then and put in the meal, and after it had boiled a little she took it in to her mother. The witch took a spoonful and tasted it.

'Uh!' said she; 'didn't I tell you not to put any salt
in it, and it's just as salt as the sea.'

So the daughter had to go and make new porridge,
and her mother warned her strictly not to put any salt in
it. But now there was no water in the house, so she
asked her mother to give her the lamp, so that she could
go to the well for more.

'There you have it, then,' said the witch; 'but take
good care of it.'

The daughter took the lamp which shone over seven
kingdoms, and went out to the well for water, while

HOW ESBEN STOLE THE WITCH'S LAMP

Esben slipped out after her. When she was going to draw
the water from the well she set the lamp down on a stone
beside her. Esben watched his chance, seized the lamp,
and gave her a push from behind, so that she plumped
head first into the well. Then he made off with the lamp.
But the witch got out of her bed and ran after him,
crying:

'Hey! is that you again, Esben?'

'Ye—e—s!'

'Was it you that took my dove?'

'Ye—e—s!'

' Was it also you that took my boar ? '

' Ye—e—s ! '

'And it was you that made me kill my eleven daughters ? '

' Ye—e—s ! '

' And now you have taken my lamp, and drowned my twelfth daughter in the well ? '

' Ye—e—s ! '

' Are you coming back again ? '

' That may be,' said Esben.

' Then you'll catch it,' said the witch.

It was only a minute before the stick had again landed Esben at the king's palace, and the brothers were then freed from their distress. The king gave them many fine presents, but Esben did not get even so much as thanks from them.

Never had Sir Red been so eaten up with envy as he was now, and he racked his brain day and night to find something quite impossible to demand from the brothers.

One day he went to the king and told him that the lamp the brothers had procured was good enough, but they could still get for him something that was far better. The king asked what that was.

' It is,' said Sir Red, ' the most beautiful coverlet that any mortal ever heard tell of. It also has the property that, when anyone touches it, it sounds so that it can be heard over eight kingdoms.'

' That must be a splendid coverlet,' said the king, and he at once sent for the brothers.

' You have said that you know of a coverlet, the most beautiful in the whole world, and which sounds over eight kingdoms when anyone touches it. You shall procure it for me, or else lose your lives,' said he.

The brothers answered him that they had never said a word about such a coverlet, did not believe it existed, and that it was quite impossible for them to procure it. But the king would not hear a word ; he drove them

away, telling them that if they did not get it very soon
it would cost them their heads.

Things looked very black again for the brothers, for
they were sure there was no escape for them. The
youngest of them, indeed, asked where Esben was, but
the others said that that little fool could scarcely keep
himself in clothes, and it was not to be expected that
he could help them. Not one of them thought it worth
while to look for Esben, but he soon came along of
himself.

' Well, what's the matter now?' said he.

' Oh, what's the use of telling you?' said the brothers.
' *You* can't help us, at any rate.'

' Ah! who knows that?' said Esben. 'I have helped
you before.'

In the end the brothers told him about the coverlet
which, when one touched it, sounded so that it could be
heard over eight kingdoms. Esben thought that this was
the worst errand that he had had yet, but he could not do
worse than fail, and so he would make the attempt.

He again took his little white stick, set himself on it,
and said,

> Fly quick, my little stick,
> Carry me across the stream.

Next moment he was across the river and beside the
witch's house. It was evening, and the door was locked,
but he knew the way down the chimney. When he had
got into the house, however, the worst yet remained to do,
for the coverlet was on the bed in which the witch lay
and slept. He slipped into the room without either she
or her daughter wakening; but as soon as he touched the
coverlet to take it it sounded so that it could be heard
over eight kingdoms. The witch awoke, sprang out of
bed, and caught hold of Esben. He struggled with her,
but could not free himself, and the witch called to her
daughter, ' Come and help me; we shall put him into the

little dark room to be fattened. Ho, ho! now I have him!'

Esben was now put into a little dark hole, where he neither saw sun nor moon, and there he was fed on sweet milk and nut-kernels. The daughter had enough to do cracking nuts for him, and at the end of fourteen days she had only one tooth left in her mouth; she had broken all the rest with the nuts. In this time, however, she had taken a liking to Esben, and would willingly have set him free, but could not

HOW THE WITCH CAUGHT ESBEN

When some time had passed the witch told her daughter to go and cut a finger off Esben, so that she could see whether he was nearly fat enough yet. The daughter went and told Esben, and asked him what she should do. Esben told her to take an iron nail and wrap a piece of skin round it: she could then give her mother this to bite at.

The daughter did so, but when the witch bit it she cried, 'Uh! no, no! This is nothing but skin and bone; he must be fattened much longer yet.'

So Esben was fed for a while longer on sweet milk

and nut-kernels, until one day the witch thought that
now he must surely be fat enough, and told her daughter
again to go and cut a finger off him. By this time
Esben was tired of staying in the dark hole, so he told her
to go and cut a teat off a cow, and give it to the witch to
bite at. This the daughter did, and the witch cried, 'Ah!
now he is fat—so fat that one can scarcely feel the bone
in him. Now he shall be killed.'

Now this was just the very time that the witch had
to go to Troms Church, where all the witches gather once
every year, so she had no time to deal with Esben herself.
She therefore told her daughter to heat up the big oven
while she was away, take Esben out of his prison, and
roast him in there before she came back. The daughter
promised all this, and the witch went off on her journey.

The daughter then made the oven as hot as could be,
and took Esben out of his prison in order to roast him.
She brought the oven spade, and told Esben to seat himself on it, so that she could shoot him into the oven.
Esben accordingly took his seat on it, but when she had
got him to the mouth of the oven he spread his legs out
wide, so that she could not get him pushed in.

'You mustn't sit like that,' said she.

'How then?' said Esben.

'You must cross your legs,' said the daughter; but
Esben could not understand what she meant by this.

'Get out of the way,' said she, 'and I will show you
how to place yourself.'

She seated herself on the oven spade, but no sooner
had she done so than Esben laid hold of it, shot her into
the oven, and fastened the door of it. Then he ran and
seized the coverlet, but as soon as he did so it sounded
so that it could be heard over eight kingdoms, and the
witch, who was at Troms Church, came flying home, and
shouted, 'Hey! is that you again, Esben?'

'Ye—e—s!'

'It was you that made me kill my eleven daughters?'

'Ye—e—s!'

'And took my dove?'

'Ye—e—s!'

'And my beautiful boar?'

'Ye—e—s!'

'And drowned my twelfth daughter in the well, and took my lamp?'

'Ye—e—s!'

'And now you have roasted my thirteenth and last daughter in the oven, and taken my coverlet?'

'Ye—e—s!'

'Are you coming back again?'

'No, never again,' said Esben.

At this the witch became so furious that she sprang into numberless pieces of flint, and from this come all the flint stones that one finds about the country.

Esben had found again his little stick, which the witch had taken from him, so he said,

> Fly quick, my little stick,
> Carry me across the stream.

Next moment he was back at the king's palace. Here things were in a bad way, for the king had thrown all the eleven brothers into prison, and they were to be executed very shortly because they had not brought him the coverlet. Esben now went up to the king and gave him the coverlet, with which the king was greatly delighted. When he touched it it could be heard over eight kingdoms, and all the other kings sat and were angry because they had not one like it.

Esben also told how everything had happened, and how Sir Red had done the brothers all the ill he could devise because he was envious of them. The brothers were at once set at liberty, while Sir Red, for his wickedness, was hanged on the highest tree that could be found, and so he got the reward he deserved.

Much was made of Esben and his brothers, and these

now thanked him for all that he had done for them. The twelve of them received as much gold and silver as they could carry, and betook themselves home to their old father. When he saw again his twelve sons, whom he

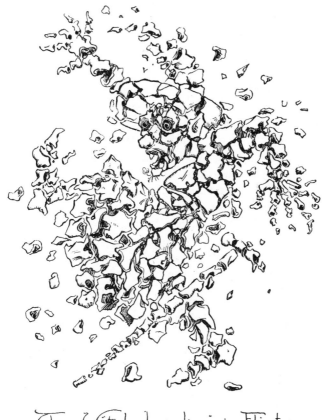

The Witch breaks into Flints

had never expected to see more, he was so glad that he wept for joy. The brothers told him how much Esben had done, and how he had saved their lives, and from that time forward he was no longer the butt of the rest at home.

PRINCESS MINON-MINETTE [1]

ONCE upon a time there lived a young king whose name
was Souci, and he had been brought up, ever since he
was a baby, by the fairy Inconstancy. Now the fairy
Girouette had a kind heart, but she was a very trying
person to live with, for she never knew her own mind for
two minutes together, and as she was the sole ruler at
Court till the prince grew up everything was always at
sixes and sevens. At first she determined to follow the
old custom of keeping the young king ignorant of the
duties he would have to perform some day ; then, quite
suddenly, she resigned the reins of government into his
hands ; but, unluckily, it was too late to train him properly
for the post. However, the fairy did not think of that,
but, carried away by her new ideas, she hastily formed a
Council, and named as Prime Minister the excellent
' Ditto,' so called because he had never been known to
contradict anybody.

Young Prince Souci had a handsome face, and at the
bottom a good deal of common sense ; but he had never
been taught good manners, and was shy and awkward ;
and had, besides, never learned how to use his brains.

Under these circumstances it is not surprising that
the Council did not get through much work. Indeed, the
affairs of the country fell into such disorder that at last
the people broke out into open rebellion, and it was only
the courage of the king, who continued to play the flute

---

[1] *Bibliothèque des Fées et des Génies.*

PRINCESS DIAPHANA is carried off by the BREEZE

while swords and spears were flashing before the palace gate, that prevented civil war from being declared.

No sooner was the revolt put down than the Council turned their attention to the question of the young king's marriage. Various princesses were proposed to him, and the fairy, who was anxious to get the affair over before she left the Court for ever, gave it as her opinion that the Princess Diaphana would make the most suitable wife. Accordingly envoys were sent to bring back an exact report of the princess's looks and ways, and they returned saying that she was tall and well made, but so very light that the equerries who accompanied her in her walks had to be always watching her, lest she should suddenly be blown away. This had happened so often that her subjects lived in terror of losing her altogether, and tried everything they could think of to keep her to the ground. They even suggested that she should carry weights in her pockets, or have them tied to her ankles; but this idea was given up, as the princess found it so uncomfortable. At length it was decided that she was never to go out in a wind, and in order to make matters surer still the equerries each held the end of a string which was fastened to her waist.

The Council talked over this report for some days, and then the king made up his mind that he would judge for himself, and pretend to be his own ambassador. This plan was by no means new, but it had often succeeded, and, anyhow, they could think of nothing better.

Such a splendid embassy had never before been seen in any country. The kingdom was left in the charge of the Prime Minister, who answered ' Ditto ' to everything; but the choice was better than it seemed, for the worthy man was much beloved by the people, as he agreed with all they said, and they left him feeling very pleased with themselves and their own wisdom.

When the king arrived at Diaphana's Court he found a magnificent reception awaiting him, for, though they pretended not to know who he was, secrets like this are never hidden. Now the young king had a great dislike to long ceremonies, so he proposed that his second interview with the princess should take place in the garden. The princess made some difficulties, but, as the weather was lovely and very still, she at last consented to the king's wishes. But no sooner had they finished their first bows and curtseys than a slight breeze sprung up, and began to sway the princess, whose equerries had retired out of respect. The king went forward to steady her, but the wind that he caused only drove her further away from him. He rushed after her exclaiming, ' O princess ! are you really running away from me ? '

' Good gracious, no ! ' she replied. ' Run a little quicker and you will be able to stop me, and I shall be for ever grateful. That is what comes of talking in a garden,' she added in disgust ; ' as if one wasn't much better in a room that was tightly closed all round.'

The king ran as fast as he could, but the wind ran faster still, and in a moment the princess was whirled to the bottom of the garden, which was bounded by a ditch. She cleared it like a bird, and the king, who was obliged to stop short at the edge, saw the lovely Diaphana flying over the plain, sometimes driven to the right, sometimes to the left, till at last she vanished out of sight.

By this time the whole court were running over the plain, some on foot and some on horseback, all hurrying to the help of their princess, who really was in some danger, for the wind was rising to the force of a gale. The king looked on for a little, and then returned with his attendants to the palace, reflecting all the while on the extreme lightness of his proposed bride and the absurdity of having a wife that rose in the air better than any kite. He thought on the whole that it would be wiser not to wait longer, but to depart at once, and he started on horseback at the very moment when the princess had been found by her followers, wet to the

skin, and blown against a rick. Souci met the carriage
which was bringing her home, and stopped to congratu-
late her on her escape, and to advise her to put on dry
clothes. Then he continued his journey.

It took a good while for the king to get home again,
and he was rather cross at having had so much trouble
for nothing. Besides which, his courtiers made fun at
his adventure, and he did not like being laughed at,
though of course they did not dare to do it before his
face. And the end of it was that very soon he started
on his travels again, only allowing one equerry to accompany him, and even this attendant he managed to lose
the moment he had left his own kingdom behind him.

Now it was the custom in those days for princes and
princesses to be brought up by fairies, who loved them
as their own children, and did not mind what incon-
venience they put other people to for their sakes, for all
the world as if they had been real mothers. The fairy
Aveline, who lived in a country that touched at one point
the kingdom of King Souci, had under her care the lovely
Princess Minon-Minette, and had made up her mind to
marry her to the young king, who, in spite of his awkward
manners, which could be improved, was really very much
nicer than most of the young men she was likely to meet.

So Aveline made her preparations accordingly, and
began by arranging that the equerry should lose himself
in the forest, after which she took away the king's sword
and his horse while he lay asleep under a tree. Her
reason for this was that she felt persuaded that, finding
himself suddenly alone and robbed of everything, the
king would hide his real birth, and would have to fall
back on his powers of pleasing, like other men, which
would be much better for him.

When the king awoke and found that the tree to
which he had tied his horse had its lowest branch broken,
and that nothing living was in sight, he was much dis-
mayed, and sought high and low for his lost treasure, but

Princess Diaphana blown against the haystack

all in vain. After a time he began to get hungry, so he decided that he had better try to find his way out of the forest, and perhaps he might have a chance of getting something to eat. He had only gone a few steps when he met Aveline, who had taken the shape of an old woman with a heavy bundle of faggots on her back. She staggered along the path and almost fell at his feet, and Souci, afraid that she might have hurt herself, picked her up and set her on her feet again before passing on his way. But he was not to be let off so easy.

'What about my bundle?' cried the old woman. 'Where is your politeness? Really, you seem to have been very nicely brought up! What have they taught you?'

'Taught me? Nothing,' replied he.

'I can well believe it!' she said. 'You don't know even how to pick up a bundle. Oh, you can come near; I am cleverer than you, and know how to pick up a bundle very well.'

The king blushed at her words, which he felt had a great deal of truth in them, and took up the bundle meekly.

Aveline, delighted at the success of her first experiment, hobbled along after him, chattering all the while, as old women do.

'I wish,' she said, 'that all kings had done as much once in their lives. Then they would know what a lot of trouble it takes to get wood for their fires.'

Souci felt this to be true, and was sorry for the old woman.

'Where are we going to?' asked he.

'To the castle of the White Demon; and if you are in want of work I will find you something to do.'

'But I can't do anything,' he said, 'except carry a bundle, and I shan't earn much by that.'

'Oh, you are learning,' replied the old woman, 'and it isn't bad for a first lesson.' But the king was paying very little attention to her, for he was rather cross and very tired. Indeed, he felt that he really could not carry the bundle any further, and was about to lay it down when up came a young maiden more beautiful than the day, and covered with precious stones. She ran to them, exclaiming to the old woman,

'Oh, you poor thing! I was just coming after you to see if I could help you.'

'Here is a young man,' replied the old woman, 'who will be quite ready to give you up the bundle. You see he does not look as if he enjoyed carrying it.'

'Will you let me take it, sir?' she asked.

But the king felt ashamed of himself, and held on to it tightly, while the presence of the princess put him in a better temper.

So they all travelled together till they arrived at a very ordinary-looking house, which Aveline pointed out as the castle of the White Demon, and told the king that he might put down his bundle in the courtyard. The young man was terribly afraid of being recognised by someone in this strange position, and would have turned on his heel and gone away had it not been for the thought of Minon-Minette. Still, he felt very awkward and lonely, for both the princess and the old woman had entered the castle without taking the slightest notice of the young man, who remained where he was for some time, not quite knowing what he had better do. At length a servant arrived and led him up into a beautiful room filled with people, who were either playing on musical instruments or talking in a lively manner, which astonished the king, who stood silently listening, and not at all pleased at the want of attention paid him.

Matters went on this way for some time. Every day the king fell more and more in love with Minon-Minette, and every day the princess seemed more and more taken up with other people. At last, in despair, the prince sought out the old woman, to try to get some advice

from her as to his conduct, or, anyway, to have the pleasure of talking about Minon-Minette.

He found her spinning in an underground chamber,
but quite ready to tell him all he wanted to know. In
answer to his questions he learned that in order to win
the hand of the princess it was not enough to be born a
prince, for she would marry nobody who had not proved
himself faithful, and had, besides, all those talents and
accomplishments which help to make people happy.

For a moment Souci was very much cast down on
hearing this, but then he plucked up. 'Tell me what I
must do in order to win the heart of the princess, and no
matter how hard it is I will do it. And show me how I
can repay you for your kindness, and you shall have anything I can give you. Shall I bring in your bundle of
faggots every day ?'

'It is enough that you should have made the offer,'
replied the old woman; and she added, holding out a
skein of thread, 'Take this; one day you will be thankful
for it, and when it becomes useless your difficulties will
be past.'

'Is it the skein of my life ?' he asked.

'It is the skein of your love's ill-luck,' she said.

And he took it and went away.

Now the fairy Girouette, who had brought up Souci,
had an old friend called Grimace, the protectress of
Prince Fluet. Grimace often talked over the young
prince's affairs with Girouette, and, when she decided
that he was old enough to govern his own kingdom, consulted Girouette as to a suitable wife. Girouette, who
never stopped to think or to make inquiries, drew such a
delightful picture of Minon-Minette that Grimace determined to spare no pains to bring about the marriage, and
accordingly Fluet was presented at court. But though
the young man was pleasant and handsome, the princess
thought him rather womanish in some ways, and displayed
her opinion so openly as to draw upon herself and Aveline

the anger of the fairy, who declared that Minon-Minette should never know happiness till she had found a bridge without an arch and a bird without feathers. So saying, she also went away.

Before the king set out afresh on his travels Aveline had restored to him his horse and his sword, and though these were but small consolation for the absence of the princess, they were better than nothing, for he felt that somehow they might be the means of leading him back to her.

After crossing several deserts the king arrived at length in a country that seemed inhabited, but the instant he stepped over the border he was seized and flung into chains, and dragged at once to the capital. He asked his guards why he was treated like this, but the only answer he got was that he was in the territory of the Iron King, for in those days countries had no names of their own, but were called after their rulers.

The young man was led into the presence of the Iron King, who was seated on a black throne in a hall also hung with black, as a token of mourning for all the relations whom he had put to death.

'What are you doing in my country?' he cried fiercely.

'I came here by accident,' replied Souci, 'and if I ever escape from your clutches I will take warning by you and treat my subjects differently.'

'Do you dare to insult me in my own court?' cried the king. 'Away with him to Little Ease!'

Now Little Ease was an iron cage hung by four thick chains in the middle of a great vaulted hall, and the prisoner inside could neither sit, nor stand, nor lie; and, besides that, he was made to suffer by turns unbearable heat and cold, while a hundred heavy bolts kept everything safe. Girouette, whose business it was to see after Souci, had forgotten his existence in the excitement of some new idea, and he would not have been alive long to trouble anybody if Aveline had not come to the rescue and whispered in his ear, ' And the skein of thread ? ' He took it up obediently, though he did not see how it would help him ; but he tied it round one of the iron bars of his cage, which seemed the only thing he could do, and gave a pull. To his surprise the bar gave way at once, and he found he could break it into a thousand pieces. After this it did not take him long to get out of his cage, or to treat the closely barred windows of the hall in the same manner. But even after he had done all this freedom appeared as far from him as ever, for between him and the open country was a high wall, and so smooth that not even a monkey could climb it. Then Souci's heart died within him. He saw nothing for it but to submit to some horrible death, but he determined that the Iron King should not profit more than he could help, and flung his precious thread into the air, saying, as he did so, ' O fairy, my misfortunes are greater than your power. I am grateful for your goodwill, but take back your gift ! ' The fairy had pity on his youth and want of faith, and took care that one end of the thread remained in his hand. He suddenly felt a jerk, and saw that the thread must have caught on something, and this thought filled him with the daring that is born of despair. ' Better,' he said to himself, ' trust to a thread than to the mercies of a king ; ' and, gliding down, he found himself safe on the other side of the wall. Then he rolled up the thread and put it carefully into his pocket, breathing silent thanks to the fairy.

Now Minon-Minette had been kept informed by Aveline of the prince's adventures, and when she heard of the way in which he had been treated by the Iron King she became furious, and began to prepare for war. She made her plans with all the secresy she could, but when great armies are collected people are apt to suspect a storm is brewing, and of course it is very difficult to keep anything hidden from fairy godmothers. Anyway,

Grimace soon heard of it, and as she had never forgiven
Minon-Minette for refusing Prince Fluet, she felt that
here was her chance of revenge.

Up to this time Aveline had been able to put a stop
to many of Grimace's spiteful tricks, and to keep guard
over Minon-Minette, but she had no power over anything
that happened at a distance; and when the princess
declared her intention of putting herself at the head of
her army, and began to train herself to bear fatigue by
hunting daily, the fairy entreated her to be careful never
to cross the borders of her dominions without Aveline to
protect her. The princess at once gave her promise, and
all went well for some days. Unluckily one morning, as
Minon-Minette was cantering slowly on her beautiful
white horse, thinking a great deal about Souci and not at
all of the boundaries of her kingdom (of which, indeed,
she was very ignorant), she suddenly found herself
in front of a house made entirely of dead leaves, which
somehow brought all sorts of unpleasant things into her
head. She remembered Aveline's warning, and tried
to turn her horse, but it stood as still as if it had been
marble. Then the princess felt that she was slowly, and
against her will, being dragged to the ground. She
shrieked, and clung tightly to the saddle, but it was
all in vain; she longed to fly, but something outside
herself proved too strong for her, and she was forced
to take the path that led to the House of Dead
Leaves.

Scarcely had her feet touched the threshold than
Grimace appeared. ' So here you are at last, Minon-
Minette ! I have been watching for you a long time, and
my trap was ready for you from the beginning. Come
here, my darling ! I will teach you to make war on my
friends ! Things won't turn out exactly as you fancied.
What you have got to do now is to go on your knees to
the king and crave his pardon, and before he consents to
a peace you will have to implore him to grant you the

favour of becoming his wife. Meanwhile you will have to be my servant.'

From that day the poor princess was put to the hardest and dirtiest work, and each morning something more disagreeable seemed to await her. Besides which, she had no food but a little black bread, and no bed but a little straw. Out of pure spite she was sent in the heat of the day to look after the geese, and would most likely have got a sunstroke if she had not happened to pick up in the fields a large fan, with which she sheltered her face. To be sure, a fan seems rather an odd possession for a goose girl, but the princess did not think of that, and she forgot all her troubles when, on opening the fan to use it as a parasol, out tumbled a letter from her lover. Then she felt sure that the fairy had not forgotten her, and took heart.

When Grimace saw that Minon-Minette still managed to look as white as snow, instead of being burnt as brown as a berry, she wondered what could have happened, and began to watch her closely. The following day, when the sun was at its highest and hottest, she noticed her draw a fan from the folds of her dress and hold it before her eyes. The fairy, in a rage, tried to snatch it from her, but the princess would not let it go. ' Give me that fan at once ! ' cried Grimace.

' Never while I live ! ' answered the princess, and, not knowing where it would be safest, placed it under her feet. In an instant she felt herself rising from the ground, with the fan always beneath her, and while Grimace was too much blinded by her fury to notice what was going on the princess was quickly soaring out of her reach.

All this time Souci had been wandering through the world with his precious thread carefully fastened round him, seeking every possible and impossible place where his beloved princess might chance to be. But though he sometimes found traces of her, or even messages scratched on a rock, or cut in the bark of a tree, she herself was

BEHOLD·THE·
BIRD·WITHOUT·
FEATHERS·&·
THE·BRIDGE·
WITHOUT·AN·
ARCH·

nowhere to be found. ' If she is not on the earth,' said
Souci to himself, 'perhaps she is hiding somewhere in
the air. It is there that I shall find her.' So, by the help
of his thread, he tried to mount upwards, but he could go
such a little way, and hurt himself dreadfully when he
tumbled back to earth again. Still he did not give up,
and after many days of efforts and tumbles he found to
his great joy that he could go a little higher and stay up
a little longer than he had done at first, and by-and-bye
he was able to live in the air altogether. But alas! the
world of the air seemed as empty of her as the world
below, and Souci was beginning to despair, and to think
that he must go and search the world that lay in the sea.
He was floating sadly along, not paying any heed to
where he was going, when he saw in the distance a
beautiful, bright sort of bird coming towards him. His
heart beat fast—he did not know why—and as they both
drew near the voice of the princess exclaimed, ' Behold
the bird without feathers and the bridge without an arch ! '

So their first meeting took place in the air, but it was
none the less happy for that ; and the fan grew big
enough to hold the king as well as Aveline, who had
hastened to give them some good advice. She guided
the fan above the spot where the two armies lay encamped
before each other ready to give battle. The fight was
long and bloody, but in the end the Iron King was obliged
to give way and surrender to the princess, who set him
to keep King Souci's sheep, first making him swear a
solemn oath that he would treat them kindly.

Then the marriage took place, in the presence of
Girouette, whom they had the greatest trouble to find,
and who was much astonished to discover how much
business had been got through in her absence.

MAIDEN BRIGHT-EYE [1]

ONCE upon a time there was a man and his wife who had
two children, a boy and a girl. The wife died, and the
man married again. His new wife had an only daughter,
who was both ugly and untidy, whereas her stepdaughter
was a beautiful girl, and was known as Maiden Bright-
eye. Her stepmother was very cruel to her on this
account; she had always to do the hardest work, and got
very little to eat, and no attention paid to her; but to her
own daughter she was all that was good. She was spared
from all the hardest of the housework, and had always
the prettiest clothes to wear.

Maiden Bright-eye had also to watch the sheep, but
of course it would never do to let her go idle and enjoy
herself too much at this work, so she had to pull heather
while she was out on the moors with them. Her stepmother gave her pancakes to take with her for her
dinner, but she had mixed the flour with ashes, and made
them just as bad as she could.

The little girl came out on the moor and began to pull
heather on the side of a little mound, but next minute a
little fellow with a red cap on his head popped up out of
the mound and said:

' Who's that pulling the roof off my house? '

' Oh, it's me, a poor little girl,' said she; ' my mother
sent me out here, and told me to pull heather. If you
will be good to me I will give you a bit of my dinner.'

[1] From the Danish.

The little fellow was quite willing, and she gave him the biggest share of her pancakes. They were not particularly good, but when one is hungry anything tastes well. After he had got them all eaten he said to her :

'Now, I shall give you three wishes, for you are a very nice little girl ; but I will choose the wishes for you. You are beautiful, and much more beautiful shall you be ; yes, so lovely that there will not be your like in the

world. The next wish shall be that every time you open your mouth a gold coin shall fall out of it, and your voice shall be like the most beautiful music. The third wish shall be that you may be married to the young king, and become the queen of the country. At the same time I shall give you a cap, which you must carefully keep, for it can save you, if you ever are in danger of your life, if you just put it on your head.

Maiden Bright-eye thanked the little bergman ever so

often, and drove home her sheep in the evening. By that time she had grown so beautiful that her people could scarcely recognise her. Her stepmother asked her how it had come about that she had grown so beautiful. She told the whole story—for she always told the truth—that a little man had come to her out on the moor and had given her all this beauty. She did not tell, however, that she had given him a share of her dinner.

The stepmother thought to herself, 'If one can become so beautiful by going out there, my own daughter shall also be sent, for she can well stand being made a little prettier.'

Next morning she baked for her the finest cakes, and dressed her prettily to go out with the sheep. But she was afraid to go away there without having a stick to defend herself with if anything should come near her.

She was not very much inclined for pulling the heather, as she never was in the habit of doing any work, but she was only a minute or so at it when up came the same little fellow with the red cap, and said :

' Who's that pulling the roof off my house ? '

' What's that to you ? ' said she.

' Well, if you will give me a bit of your dinner I won't do you any mischief,' said he.

' I will give you something else in place of my dinner,' said she. ' I can easily eat it myself ; but if you *will* have something you can have a whack of my stick,' and with that she raised it in the air and struck the bergman over the head with it.

' What a wicked little girl you are ! ' said he ; ' but you shall be none the better of this. I shall give you three wishes, and choose them for you. First, I shall say, " Ugly are you, but you shall become so ugly that there will not be an uglier one on earth." Next I shall wish that every time you open your mouth a big toad may fall out of it, and your voice shall be like the roaring of a bull. In the third place I shall wish for you a violent death.'

The girl went home in the evening, and when her mother saw her she was as vexed as she could be, and with good reason, too ; but it was still worse when she saw the toads fall out of her mouth and heard her voice.

Now we must hear something about the stepson. He had gone out into the world to look about him, and took service in the king's palace. About this time he got permission to go home and see his sister, and when he saw how lovely and beautiful she was, he was so pleased and delighted that when he came back to the king's palace everyone there wanted to know what he was always so happy about. He told them that it was because he had such a lovely sister at home.

At last it came to the ears of the king what the brother said about his sister, and, besides that, the report of her beauty spread far and wide, so that the youth was summoned before the king, who asked him if everything was true that was told about the girl. He said it was quite true, for he had seen her beauty with his own eyes, and had heard with his own ears how sweetly she could sing and what a lovely voice she had.

The king then took a great desire for her, and ordered her brother to go home and bring her back with him, for he trusted no one better to accomplish that errand. He got a ship, and everything else that he required, and sailed home for his sister. As soon as the stepmother heard what his errand was she at once said to herself, 'This will never come about if I can do anything to hinder it. She must not be allowed to come to such honour.'

She then got a dress made for her own daughter, like the finest robe for a queen, and she had a mask prepared and put upon her face, so that she looked quite pretty, and gave her strict orders not to take it off until the king had promised to wed her.

The brother now set sail with his two sisters, for the stepmother pretended that the ugly one wanted to see the other a bit on her way. But when they got out to sea,

and Maiden Bright-eye came up on deck, the sister did as
her mother had instructed her— she gave her a push and
made her fall into the water. When the brother learned

The Ugly & Wicked Sister

what had happened he was greatly distressed, and did
not know what to do. He could not bring himself to tell
the truth about what had happened, nor did he expect

that the king would believe it. In the long run he decided to hold on his way, and let things go as they liked. What he had expected happened—the king received his sister and wedded her at once, but repented it after the first night, as he could scarcely put down his foot in the morning for all the toads that were about the room, and when he saw her real face he was so enraged against the brother that he had him thrown into a pit full of serpents. He was so angry, not merely because he had been deceived, but because he could not get rid of the ugly wretch that was now tied to him for life.

Now we shall hear a little about Maiden Bright-eye. When she fell into the water she was fortunate enough to get the bergman's cap put on her head, for now she was in danger of her life, and she was at once transformed into a duck. The duck swam away after the ship, and came to the king's palace on the next evening. There it waddled up the drain, and so into the kitchen, where her little dog lay on the hearth-stone; it could not bear to stay in the fine chambers along with the ugly sister, and had taken refuge down here. The duck hopped up till it could talk to the dog.

'Good evening,' it said.

'Thanks, Maiden Bright-eye,' said the dog.

'Where is my brother?'

'He is in the serpent-pit.'

'Where is my wicked sister?'

'She is with the noble king.'

'Alas! alas! I am here this evening, and shall be for two evenings yet, and then I shall never come again.'

When it had said this the duck waddled off again. Several of the servant girls heard the conversation, and were greatly surprised at it, and thought that it would be worth while to catch the bird next evening and see into the matter a little more closely. They had heard it say that it would come again.

Next evening it appeared as it had said, and a great

many were present to see it. It came waddling in by the drain, and went up to the dog, which was lying on the hearth-stone.

'Good evening,' it said.

'Thanks, Maiden Bright-eye,' said the dog.

'Where is my brother?'

'He is in the serpent-pit.'

'Where is my wicked sister?'

'She is with the noble king.'

'Alas! alas! I am here this evening, and shall be for one evening yet, and then I shall never come again.'

After this it slipped out, and no one could get hold of it. But the king's cook thought to himself, 'I shall see if I can't get hold of you to-morrow evening.'

On the third evening the duck again came waddling in by the drain, and up to the dog on the hearth-stone.

'Good evening,' it said.

'Thanks, Maiden Bright-eye,' said the dog.

'Where is my brother?'

'He is in the serpent-pit.'

'Where is my wicked sister?

'She is with the noble king.'

'Alas! alas! now I shall never come again.'

With this it slipped out again, but in the meantime the cook had posted himself at the outer end of the drain with a net, which he threw over it as it came out. In this way he caught it, and came in to the others with the most beautiful duck they had ever seen—with so many golden feathers on it that everyone marvelled. No one, however, knew what was to be done with it; but after what they had heard they knew that there was something uncommon about it, so they took good care of it.

At this time the brother in the serpent-pit dreamed that his right sister had come swimming to the king's palace in the shape of a duck, and that she could not regain her own form until her beak was cut off. He got this dream told to some one, so that the king at last came to hear of it, and had him taken up out of the pit and brought before him. The king then asked him if he could produce to him his sister as beautiful as he had formerly described her. The brother said he could if they would bring him the duck and a knife.

Both of them were brought to him, and he said, ' I wonder how you would look if I were to cut the point off your beak.'

With this he cut a piece off the beak, and there came a voice which said, ' Oh, oh, you cut my little finger ! '

Next moment Maiden Bright-eye stood there, as lovely and beautiful as he had seen her when he was home. This was his sister now, he said ; and the whole story now came out of how the other had behaved to her. The wicked sister was put into a barrel with spikes round it, which was dragged off by six wild horses, and so she came to her end. But the king was delighted with Maiden Bright-eye, and immediately made her his queen, while her brother became his prime minister.

THE MERRY WIVES [1]

THERE lay three houses in a row, in one of which there lived a tailor, in another a carpenter, and in the third a smith. All three were married, and their wives were very good friends. They often talked about how stupid their husbands were, but they could never agree as to which of them had the most stupid one; each one stuck up for her own husband, and maintained that it was he.

The three wives went to church together every Sunday, and had a regular good gossip on the way, and when they were coming home from church they always turned into the tavern which lay by the wayside and drank half a pint together. This was at the time when half a pint of brandy cost threepence, so that was just a penny from each of them.

But the brandy went up in price, and the taverner said that he must have fourpence for the half-pint.

They were greatly annoyed at this, for there were only the three of them to share it, and none of them was willing to pay the extra penny.

As they went home from the church that day they decided to wager with each other as to whose husband was the most stupid, and the one who, on the following Sunday, should be judged to have played her husband the greatest trick should thereafter go free from paying, and each of the two others would give twopence for their Sunday's half-pint.

---

[1] From the Danish.

Next day the tailor's wife said to her husband, 'I have some girls coming to-day to help to card my wool; there is a great deal to do, and we must be very busy. I am so annoyed that our watchdog is dead, for in the evening the young fellows will come about to get fun with the girls, and they will get nothing done. If we had only had a fierce watchdog he would have kept them away.'

'Yes,' said the man, 'that would have been a good thing.'

'Listen, good man,' said the wife, 'you must just be the watchdog yourself, and scare the fellows away from the house.'

The husband was not very sure about this, although otherwise he was always ready to give in to her.

'Oh yes, you will see it will work all right,' said the wife.

And so towards evening she got the tailor dressed up in a shaggy fur coat, tied a black woollen cloth round his head, and chained him up beside the dog's kennel.'

There he stood and barked and growled at everyone that moved in his neighbourhood. The neighbour wives knew all about this, and were greatly amused at it.

On the day after this the carpenter had been out at work, and came home quite merry; but as soon as he entered the house his wife clapped her hands together and cried, 'My dear, what makes you look like that? You are ill.'

The carpenter knew nothing about being ill; he only thought that he wanted something to eat, so he sat down at the table and began his dinner.

His wife sat straight in front of him, with her hands folded, and shook her head, and looked at him with an anxious air.

'You are getting worse, my dear,' she said; 'you are quite pale now; you have a serious illness about you; I can see it by your looks.'

The husband now began to grow anxious, and thought that perhaps he was not quite well.

' No, indeed,' said she ; ' it's high time that you were in bed.'

She then got him to lie down, and piled above him all the bedclothes she could find, and gave him various medicines, while he grew worse and worse.

' You will never get over it,' said she ; ' I am afraid you are going to die.'

' Do you think so ? ' said the carpenter ; ' I can well believe it, for I am indeed very poorly.'

In a little while she said again, ' Ah, now I must part with you. Here comes Death. Now I must close your eyes.' And she did so.

The carpenter believed everything that his wife said, and so he believed now that he was dead, and lay still and let her do as she pleased.

She got her neighbours summoned, and they helped to lay him in the coffin—it was one of those he himself had made ; but his wife had bored holes in it to let him get some air. She made a soft bed under him, and put a coverlet over him, and she folded his hands over his breast ; but instead of a flower or a psalm-book, she gave him a pint-bottle of brandy in his hands. After he had lain for a little he took a little pull at this, and then another and another, and he thought this did him good, and soon he was sleeping sweetly, and dreaming that he was in heaven.

Meanwhile word had gone round the village that the carpenter was dead, and was to be buried next day.

It was now the turn of the smith's wife. Her husband was lying sleeping off the effects of a drinking bout, so she pulled off all his clothes and made him black as coal from head to foot, and then let him sleep till far on in the day.

The funeral party had already met at the carpenter's, and marched off towards the church with the coffin, when the smith's wife came rushing in to her husband.

' Gracious, man,' said she, ' you are lying there yet? You are sleeping too long. You know you are going to the funeral.'

The smith was quite confused ; he knew nothing about any funeral.

' It's our neighbour the carpenter,' said his wife, ' who is to be buried to-day. They are already half-way to church with him.'

' All right,' said the smith, ' make haste to help me on with my black clothes.'

' What nonsense ! ' said his wife, ' you have them on already. Be off with you now.'

The smith looked down at his person and saw that he was a good deal blacker than he usually was, so he caught up his hat and ran out after the funeral. This was already close to the church, and the smith wanted to take part in carrying the coffin, like a good neighbour. So he ran with all his might, and shouted after them, ' Hey! wait a little ; let me get a hold of him ! '

The people turned round and saw the black figure coming, and thought it was the devil himself, who wanted to get hold of the carpenter, so they threw down the coffin and took to their heels.

The lid sprang off the coffin with the shock, and the carpenter woke up and looked out. He remembered the whole affair ; he knew that he was dead and was going to be buried, and recognising the smith, he said to him, in a low voice, ' My good neighbour, if I hadn't been dead already, I should have laughed myself to death now to see you coming like this to my funeral.'

From that time forth the carpenter's wife drank free of expense every Sunday, for the others had to admit that she had fooled her husband the best.

KING LINDORM

THERE once lived a king and a queen who ruled over a
very great kingdom. They had large revenues, and lived
happily with each other; but, as the years went past, the
king's heart became heavy, because the queen had no
children. She also sorrowed greatly over it, because,
although the king said nothing to her about this trouble,
yet she could see that it vexed him that they had no heir
to the kingdom; and she wished every day that she
might have one.

One day a poor old woman came to the castle and
asked to speak with the queen. The royal servants
answered that they could not let such a poor beggar-
woman go in to their royal mistress. They offered her a
penny, and told her to go away. Then the woman desired
them to tell the queen that there stood at the palace gate
one who would help her secret sorrow. This message was
taken to the queen, who gave orders to bring the old
woman to her. This was done, and the old woman said
to her :

' I know your secret sorrow, O queen, and am come
to help you in it. You wish to have a son ; you shall
have two if you follow my instructions.'

The queen was greatly surprised that the old woman
knew her secret wish so well, and promised to follow her
advice.

' You must have a bath set in your room, O queen,'

<hr>

¹ From the Swedish.

said she, ' and filled with running water. When you have bathed in this you will find under the bath two red onions. These you must carefully peel and eat, and in time your wish will be fulfilled.'

The queen did as the poor woman told her; and after she had bathed she found the two onions under the bath. They were both alike in size and appearance. When she saw these she knew that the woman had been something more than she seemed to be, and in her delight she ate up one of the onions, skin and all. When she had done so she remembered that the woman had told her to peel them carefully before she ate them. It was now too late for the one of them, but she peeled the other and then ate it too.

In due time it happened as the woman had said; but the first that the queen gave birth to was a hideous lindorm, or serpent. No one saw this but her waiting-woman, who threw it out of the window into the forest beside the castle. The next that came into the world was the most beautiful little prince, and he was shown to the king and queen, who knew nothing about his brother the lindorm.

There was now joy in all the palace and over the whole country on account of the beautiful prince; but no one knew that the queen's first-born was a lindorm, and lay in the wild forest. Time passed with the king, the queen, and the young prince in all happiness and prosperity, until he was twenty years of his age. Then his parents said to him that he should journey to another kingdom and seek for himself a bride, for they were beginning to grow old, and would fain see their son married before they were laid in their grave. The prince obeyed, had his horses harnessed to his gilded chariot, and set out to woo his bride. But when he came to the first cross-ways there lay a huge and terrible lindorm right across the road, so that his horses had to come to a standstill.

'Where are you driving to?' asked the lindorm with a hideous voice.

'That does not concern you,' said the prince. 'I am the prince, and can drive where I please.'

'Turn back,' said the lindorm. 'I know your errand, but you shall get no bride until I have got a mate and slept by her side.'

The prince turned home again, and told the king and the queen what he had met at the cross-roads; but they thought that he should try again on the following day, and see whether he could not get past it, so that he might seek a bride in another kingdom.

The prince did so, but got no further than the first cross-roads; there lay the lindorm again, who stopped him in the same way as before.

The same thing happened on the third day when the prince tried to get past: the lindorm said, with a threatening voice, that before the prince could get a bride he himself must find a mate.

When the king and queen heard this for the third time they could think of no better plan than to invite the lindorm to the palace, and they would find him a mate. They thought that a lindorm would be quite well satisfied with anyone that they might give him, and so they would get some slave-woman to marry the monster. The lindorm came to the palace and received a bride of this kind, but in the morning she lay torn in pieces. So it happened every time that the king and queen compelled any woman to be his bride.

The report of this soon spread over all the country. Now it happened that there was a man who had married a second time, and his wife heard of the lindorm with great delight. Her husband had a daughter by his first wife who was more beautiful than all other maidens, and so gentle and good that she won the heart of all who knew her. His second wife, however, had also a grown-up daughter, who by herself would have been ugly and disagreeable enough, but beside her good and beautiful stepsister seemed still more ugly and wicked, so that all turned from her with loathing.

The stepmother had long been annoyed that her husband's daughter was so much more beautiful than her own, and in her heart she conceived a bitter hatred for her stepdaughter. When she now heard that there was in the king's palace a lindorm which tore in pieces all the women that were married to him, and demanded a beautiful maiden for his bride, she went to the king, and said that her stepdaughter wished to wed the lindorm, so that the country's only prince might travel and seek a bride. At this the king was greatly delighted, and gave orders that the young girl should be brought to the palace.

When the messengers came to fetch her she was terribly frightened, for she knew that it was her wicked stepmother who in this way was aiming at her life. She begged that she might be allowed to spend another night in her father's house. This was granted her, and she went to her mother's grave. There she lamented her hard fate in being given over to the lindorm, and earnestly prayed her mother for counsel. How long she lay there by the grave and wept one cannot tell, but sure it is that she fell asleep and slept until the sun rose. Then she rose up from the grave, quite happy at heart, and began to search about in the fields. There she found three nuts, which she carefully put away in her pocket.

'When I come into very great danger I must break one of these,' she said to herself. Then she went home, and set out quite willingly with the king's messengers.

When these arrived at the palace with the beautiful young maiden everyone pitied her fate ; but she herself was of good courage, and asked the queen for another bridal chamber than the one the lindorm had had before. She got this, and then she requested them to put a pot full of strong lye on the fire and lay down three new scrubbing brushes. The queen gave orders that every-thing should be done as she desired; and then the maiden dressed herself in seven clean snow-white shirts, and held her wedding with the lindorm.

When they were left alone in the bridal chamber the lindorm, in a threatening voice, ordered her to undress herself.

'Undress yourself first!' said she.

'None of the others bade me do that,' said he in surprise.

'But I bid you,' said she.

Then the lindorm began to writhe, and groan, and breathe heavily; and after a little he had cast his outer skin, which lay on the floor, hideous to behold. Then his bride took off one of her snow-white shirts, and cast it on the lindorm's skin. Again he ordered her to un-dress, and again she commanded him to do so first. He had to obey, and with groaning and pain cast off one skin after another, and for each skin the maiden threw off one of her shirts, until there lay on the floor seven lindorm skins and six snow-white shirts; the seventh she still had on. The lindorm now lay before her as a formless, slimy mass, which she with all her might began to scrub with the lye and new scrubbing brushes.

When she had nearly worn out the last of these there stood before her the loveliest youth in the world. He thanked her for having saved him from his enchantment, and told her that he was the king and queen's eldest son, and heir to the kingdom. Then he asked her whether she would keep the promise she had made to the lindorm, to share everything with him. To this she was well content to answer 'Yes.'

Each time that the lindorm had held his wedding one of the king's retainers was sent next morning to open the door of the bridal chamber and see whether the bride was alive. This next morning also he peeped in at the door, but what he saw there surprised him so much that he shut the door in a hurry, and hastened to the king and queen, who were waiting for his report. He told them of the wonderful sight he had seen. On the floor lay seven lindorm skins and six snow-white shirts, and beside these three worn-out scrubbing brushes, while in the bed a beautiful youth was lying asleep beside the fair young maiden.

The king and queen marvelled greatly what this could mean; but just then the old woman who was spoken of in the beginning of the story was again brought in to the queen. She reminded her how she had not followed her instructions, but had eaten the first onion with all its skins, on which account her first-born had been a lindorm. The waiting-woman was then summoned, and admitted that she had thrown it out through the window into the forest. The king and queen now sent for their eldest son and his young bride. They took them both in their arms, and asked him to tell about his sorrowful lot during the twenty years he had lived in the forest as a hideous lindorm. This he did, and then his parents had it proclaimed over the whole country that he was their eldest son, and along with his spouse should inherit the country and kingdom after them.

Prince Lindorm and his beautiful wife now lived in joy and prosperity for a time in the palace; and when his father was laid in the grave, not long after this, he obtained the whole kingdom. Soon afterwards his mother also departed from this world.

Now it happened that an enemy declared war against the young king; and, as he foresaw that it would be three years at the least before he could return to his country and his queen, he ordered all his servants who remained at home to guard her most carefully. That they might be able to write to each other in confidence, he had two seal rings made, one for himself and one for his young queen, and issued an order that no one, under pain of death, was to open any letter that was sealed with one of

The Bride & The Lindorm

these. Then he took farewell of his queen, and marched out to war.

The queen's wicked stepmother had heard with great grief that her beautiful stepdaughter had prospered so well that she had not only preserved her life, but had even become queen of the country. She now plotted continually how she might destroy her good fortune. While King Lindorm was away at the war the wicked woman came to the queen, and spoke fair to her, saying that she had always foreseen that her stepdaughter was destined to be something great in the world, and that she had on this account secured that she should be the enchanted prince's bride. The queen, who did not imagine that any person could be so deceitful, bade her stepmother welcome, and kept her beside her.

Soon after this the queen had two children, the prettiest boys that anyone could see. When she had written a letter to the king to tell him of this her stepmother asked leave to comb her hair for her, as her own mother used to do. The queen gave her permission, and the stepmother combed her hair until she fell asleep. Then she took the seal ring off her neck, and exchanged the letter for another, in which she had written that the queen had given birth to two whelps.

When the king received this letter he was greatly distressed, but he remembered how he himself had lived for twenty years as a lindorm, and had been freed from the spell by his young queen. He therefore wrote back to his most trusted retainer that the queen and her two whelps should be taken care of while he was away.

The stepmother, however, took this letter as well, and wrote a new one, in which the king ordered that the queen and the two little princes should be burnt at the stake. This she also sealed with the queen's seal, which was in all respects like the king's.

The retainer was greatly shocked and grieved at the king's orders, for which he could discover no reason ; but, as he had not the heart to destroy three innocent beings, he had a great fire kindled, and in this he burned a sheep and two lambs, so as to make people believe that he had carried out the king's commands. The stepmother had made these known to the people, adding that the queen was a wicked sorceress.

The faithful servant, however, told the queen that it was the king's command that during the years he was absent in the war she should keep herself concealed in the castle, so that no one but himself should see her and the little princes.

The queen obeyed, and no one knew but that both she and her children had been burned. But when the time came near for King Lindorm to return home from the war the old retainer grew frightened because he had not obeyed his orders. He therefore went to the queen, and told her everything, at the same time showing her the king's letter containing the command to burn her and the princes. He then begged her to leave the palace before the king returned.

The queen now took her two little sons, and wandered out into the wild forest. They walked all day without finding a human habitation, and became very tired. The queen then caught sight of a man who carried some venison. He seemed very poor and wretched, but the queen was glad to see a human being, and asked him whether he knew where she and her little children could get a house over their heads for the night.

The man answered that he had a little hut in the forest, and that she could rest there; but he also said that he was one who lived entirely apart from men, and owned no more than the hut, a horse, and a dog, and supported himself by hunting.

The queen followed him to the hut and rested there overnight with her children, and when she awoke in the morning the man had already gone out hunting. The queen then began to put the room in order and prepare food, so that when the man came home he found every-thing neat and tidy, and this seemed to give him some pleasure. He spoke but little, however, and all that he said about himself was that his name was Peter.

Later in the day he rode out into the forest, and the queen thought that he looked very unhappy. While he was away she looked about her in the hut a little more closely, and found a tub full of shirts stained with blood, lying among water. She was surprised at this, but thought that the man would get the blood on his shirt when he was carrying home venison. She washed the shirts, and hung them up to dry, and said nothing to Peter about the matter.

After some time had passed she noticed that every day he came riding home from the forest he took off a blood-stained shirt and put on a clean one. She then saw that it was something else than the blood of the deer that stained his shirts, so one day she took courage and asked him about it.

At first he refused to tell her, but she then related to him her own story, and how she had succeeded in deliver-ing the lindorm. He then told her that he had formerly lived a wild life, and had finally entered into a written com-pact with the Evil Spirit. Before this contract had expired he had repented and turned from his evil ways, and with-drawn himself to this solitude. The Evil One had then lost all power to take him, but so long as he had the contract he could compel him to meet him in the forest each day at a certain time, where the evil spirits then scourged him till he bled.

Next day, when the time came for the man to ride into the forest, the queen asked him to stay at home and look after the princes, and she would go to meet the evil spirits in his place. The man was amazed, and said that this would not only cost her her life, but would also bring upon him a greater misfortune than the one he was already under. She bade him be of good courage, looked to see that she had the three nuts which she had found beside her mother's grave, mounted her horse, and rode out into the forest. When she had ridden for some time the evil spirits came forth and said, ' Here comes Peter's horse and Peter's hound; but Peter himself is not with them.'

Then at a distance she heard a terrible voice demanding to know what she wanted.

' I have come to get Peter's contract,' said she.

At this there arose a terrible uproar among the evil spirits, and the worst voice among them all said, ' Ride home and tell Peter that when he comes to-morrow he shall get twice as many strokes as usual.'

The queen then took one of her nuts and cracked it, and turned her horse about. At this sparks of fire flew out of all the trees, and the evil spirits howled as if they were being scourged back to their abode.

Next day at the same time the queen again rode out into the forest; but on this occasion the spirits did not dare to come so near her. They would not, however, give up the contract, but threatened both her and the man. Then she cracked her second nut, and all the forest behind her seemed to be in fire and flames, and the evil spirits howled even worse than on the previous day; but the contract they would not give up.

The queen had only one nut left now, but even that she was ready to give up in order to deliver the man. This time she cracked the nut as soon as she came near the place where the spirits appeared, and what then happened to them she could not see, but amid wild screams and howls the contract was handed to her at the end of a long branch. The queen rode happy home to the hut, and happier still was the man, who had been sitting there in great anxiety, for now he was freed from all the power of the evil spirits.

Meanwhile King Lindorm had come home from the war, and the first question he asked when he entered the palace was about the queen and the whelps. The attendants were surprised: they knew of no whelps. The queen had had two beautiful princes; but the king had sent orders that all these were to be burned.

The king grew pale with sorrow and anger, and ordered them to summon his trusted retainer, to whom he had sent the instructions that the queen and the whelps were to be carefully looked after. The retainer, however, showed him the letter in which there was written that the queen and her children were to be burned, and everyone then understood that some great treachery had been enacted.

When the king's trusted retainer saw his master's deep sorrow he confessed to him that he had spared the lives of the queen and the princes, and had only burned a sheep and two lambs, and had kept the queen and her children hidden in the palace for three years, but had sent her out into the wild forest just when the king was expected home. When the king heard this his sorrow was lessened, and he said that he would wander out into the forest and search for his wife and children. If he found them he would return to his palace; but if he did not find them he would never see it again, and in that case the faithful retainer who had saved the lives of the queen and the princes should be king in his stead.

The king then went forth alone into the wild forest, and wandered there the whole day without seeing a single human being. So it went with him the second day also, but on the third day he came by roundabout ways to the little hut. He went in there, and asked for leave to rest himself for a little on the bench. The queen and the princes were there, but she was poorly clad and so sorrowful that the king did not recognise her, neither did he think for a moment that the two children, who were dressed only in rough skins, were his own sons.

He lay down on the bench, and, tired as he was, he soon fell asleep. The bench was a narrow one,

THE QUEEN RECOVERS THE CONTRACT

and as he slept his arm fell down and hung by the side of it.

'My son, go and lift your father's arm up on the bench,' said the queen to one of the princes, for she easily knew the king again, although she was afraid to make herself known to him. The boy went and took the king's arm, but, being only a child, he did not lift it up very gently on to the bench.

The king woke at this, thinking at first that he had fallen into a den of robbers, but he decided to keep quiet and pretend that he was asleep until he should find out what kind of folk were in the house. He lay still for a little, and, as no one moved in the room, he again let his arm glide down off the bench. Then he heard a woman's voice say, 'My son, go you and lift your father's arm up on the bench, but don't do it so roughly as your brother did.' Then he felt a pair of little hands softly clasping his arm; he opened his eyes, and saw his queen and her children.

He sprang up and caught all three in his arms, and afterwards took them, along with the man and his horse and his hound, back to the palace with great joy. The most unbounded rejoicing reigned there then, as well as over the whole kingdom, but the wicked stepmother was burned.

King Lindorm lived long and happily with his queen, and there are some who say that if they are not dead now they are still living to this day.

THE JACKAL, THE DOVE, AND
THE PANTHER [1]

THERE was once a dove who built a nice soft nest as a home for her three little ones. She was very proud of their beauty, and perhaps talked about them to her neighbours more than she need have done, till at last everybody for miles round knew where the three prettiest baby doves in the whole country-side were to be found.

One day a jackal who was prowling about in search of a dinner came by chance to the foot of the rock where the dove's nest was hidden away, and he suddenly bethought himself that if he could get nothing better he might manage to make a mouthful of one of the young doves. So he shouted as loud as he could, 'Ohé, ohé, mother dove.'

And the dove replied, trembling with fear, 'What do you want, sir?'

'One of your children,' said he; 'and if you don't throw it to me I will eat up you and the others as well.'

Now, the dove was nearly driven distracted at the jackal's words; but, in order to save the lives of the other two, she did at last throw the little one out of the nest. The jackal ate it up, and went home to sleep.

Meanwhile the mother dove sat on the edge of her nest, crying bitterly, when a heron, who was flying slowly

[1] *Contes populaires des Bassoutos.* Recueillis et traduits par E. Jacottet. Paris: Leroux, Editeur.

past the rock, was filled with pity for her, and stopped to ask, ' What is the matter, you poor dove ? '

And the dove answered, ' A jackal came by, and asked me to give him one of my little ones, and said that if I refused he would jump on my nest and eat us all up.'

But the heron replied, ' You should not have believed him. He could never have jumped so high. He only deceived you because he wanted something for supper.' And with these words the heron flew off.

He had hardly got out of sight when again the jackal came creeping slowly round the foot of the rock. And when he saw the dove he cried out a second time, ' Ohé, ché, mother dove ! give me one of your little ones, or I will jump on your nest and eat you all up.'

This time the dove knew better, and she answered boldly, ' Indeed, I shall do nothing of the sort,' though her heart beat wildly with fear when she saw the jackal preparing for a spring.

However, he only cut himself against the rock, and thought he had better stick to threats, so he started again with his old cry, ' Mother dove, mother dove ! be quick and give me one of your little ones, or I will eat you all up.'

But the mother dove only answered as before, ' Indeed, I shall do nothing of the sort, for I know we are safely out of your reach.'

The jackal felt it was quite hopeless to get what he wanted, and asked, ' Tell me, mother dove, how have you suddenly become so wise ? '

' It was the heron who told me,' replied she.

' And which way did he go ? ' said the jackal.

' Down there among the reeds. You can see him if you look,' said the dove.

Then the jackal nodded good-bye, and went quickly after the heron. He soon came up to the great bird, who was standing on a stone on the edge of the river watching for a nice fat fish. ' Tell me, heron,' said he, ' when the wind blows from that quarter, to which side do you turn ? '

'And which side do *you* turn to ? ' asked the heron.

The jackal answered, ' I always turn to *this* side.'

' Then that is the side *I* turn to,' remarked the heron.

' And when the rain comes from that quarter, which side do you turn to ? '

And the heron replied, ' And which side do *you* turn to ? '

' Oh, *I* always turn to this side,' said the jackal.

' Then that is the side *I* turn to,' said the heron.

' And when the rain comes straight down, what do you do ? '

' What do you do yourself ? ' asked the heron.

' I do this,' answered the jackal. ' I cover my head with my paws.'

' Then that is what I do,' said the heron. ' I cover my head with my wings,' and as he spoke he lifted his large wings and spread them completely over his head.

With one bound the jackal had seized him by the neck, and began to shake him.

' Oh, have pity, have pity ! ' cried the heron. ' I never did you any harm.'

' You told the dove how to get the better of me, and I am going to eat you for it.'

' But if you will let me go,' entreated the heron, ' I will show you the place where the panther has her lair.'

' Then you had better be quick about it,' said the jackal, holding tight on to the heron until he had pointed out the panther's den. ' Now you may go, my friend, for there is plenty of food here for me.'

So the jackal came up to the panther, and asked politely, ' Panther, would you like me to look after your children while you are out hunting ? '

' I should be very much obliged,' said the panther ; ' but be sure you take care of them. They always cry all the time that I am away.'

So saying she trotted off, and the jackal marched into the cave, where he found ten little panthers, and instantly ate one up. By-and-bye the panther returned from hunting, and said to him, 'Jackal, bring out my little ones for their supper.'

The jackal fetched them out one by one till he had brought out nine, and he took the last one and brought it out again, so the whole ten seemed to be there, and the panther was quite satisfied.

Next day she went again to the chase, and the jackal ate up another little panther, so now there were only eight. In the evening, when she came back, the panther said, 'Jackal, bring out my little ones!'

And the jackal brought out first one and then another, and the last one he brought out three times, so that the whole ten seemed to be there.

The following day the same thing happened, and the next and the next and the next, till at length there was not even one left, and the rest of the day the jackal busied himself with digging a large hole at the back of the den.

That night, when the panther returned from hunting, she said to him as usual, 'Jackal, bring out my little ones.'

But the jackal replied: 'Bring out your little ones, indeed! Why, you know as well as I do that you have eaten them all up.'

Of course the panther had not the least idea what the jackal meant by this, and only repeated, 'Jackal, bring out my children.' As she got no answer she entered the cave, but found no jackal, for he had crawled through the hole he had made and escaped. And, what was worse, she did not find the little ones either.

Now the panther was not going to let the jackal .get off like that, and set off at a trot to catch him. The jackal, however, had got a good start, and he reached a place where a swarm of bees deposited their honey in the cleft of a rock. Then he stood still and waited till the

panther came up to him : ' Jackal, where are my little
ones ? ' she asked.

And the jackal answered : ' They are up there. It
is where I keep school.'

The panther looked about, and then inquired, ' But
where ? I see nothing of them.'

° THE ° BABOON ° WISHES ° TO ° SEE ° THE ° PANTHER'S ° CHILDREN °

' Come a little this way,' said the jackal, ' and you will
hear how beautifully they sing.'

So the panther drew near the cleft of the rock.

' Don't you hear them ? ' said the jackal ; ' they are in
there,' and slipped away while the panther was listening
to the song of the children.

She was still standing in the same place when a baboon went by. ' What are you doing there, panther ? '

' I am listening to my children singing. It is here that the jackal keeps his school.'

Then the baboon seized a stick, and poked it in the cleft of the rock, exclaiming, ' Well, then, I should like to see your children ! '

The bees flew out in a huge swarm, and made furiously for the panther, whom they attacked on all sides, while the baboon soon climbed up out of the way, crying, as he perched himself on the branch of a tree, ' I wish you joy of your children ! ' while from afar the jackal's voice was heard exclaiming : ' Sting her well ! don't let her go ! '

The panther galloped away as if she was mad, and flung herself into the nearest lake, but every time she raised her head, the bees stung her afresh so at last the poor beast was drowned altogether.

THE LITTLE HARE [1]

A LONG, long way off, in a land where water is very scarce, there lived a man and his wife and several children. One day the wife said to her husband, ' I am pining to have the liver of a *nyamatsané* for my dinner. If you love me as much as you say you do, you will go out and hunt for a *nyamatsané*, and will kill it and get its liver. If not, I shall know that your love is not worth having.'

' Bake some bread,' was all her husband answered, ' then take the crust and put it in this little bag.'

The wife did as she was told, and when she had finished she said to her husband, ' The bag is all ready and quite full.'

' Very well,' said he, ' and now good-bye ; I am going after the *nyamatsané*.'

But the *nyamatsané* was not so easy to find as the woman had hoped. The husband walked on and on and on without ever seeing one, and every now and then he felt so hungry that he was obliged to eat one of the crusts of bread out of his bag. At last, when he was ready to drop from fatigue, he found himself on the edge of a great marsh, which bordered on one side the country of the *nyamatsanés*. But there were no more *nyamatsanés* here than anywhere else. They had all gone on a hunt-

---

[1] *Contes populaires des Bassoutos.* Recueillis et traduits par E. Jacottet. Paris : Leroux, Editeur.

ing expedition, as their larder was empty, and the only person left at home was their grandmother, who was so feeble she never went out of the house. Our friend looked on this as a great piece of luck, and made haste to kill her before the others returned, and to take out her liver, after which he dressed himself in her skin as well as he could. He had scarcely done this when he heard the noise of the *nyamatsanès* coming back to their grandmother, for they were very fond of her, and never stayed away from her longer than they could help. They rushed clattering into the hut, exclaiming, 'We smell human flesh! Some man is here,' and began to look about for him; but they only saw their old grandmother, who answered, in a trembling voice, 'No, my children, no! What should any man be doing here?' The *nyamatsanès* paid no attention to her, and began to open all the cupboards, and peep under all the beds, crying out all the while, 'A man is here! a man is here!' but they could find nobody, and at length, tired out with their long day's hunting, they curled themselves up and fell asleep.

Next morning they woke up quite refreshed, and made ready to start on another expedition; but as they did not feel happy about their grandmother they said to her, 'Grandmother, won't you come to-day and feed with us?' And they led their grandmother outside, and all of them began hungrily to eat pebbles. Our friend pretended to do the same, but in reality he slipped the stones into his pouch, and swallowed the crusts of bread instead. However, as the *nyamatsanès* did not see this they had no idea that he was not really their grandmother. When they had eaten a great many pebbles they thought they had done enough for that day, and all went home together and curled themselves up to sleep. Next morning when they woke they said, 'Let us go and amuse ourselves by jumping over the ditch,' and every time they cleared it with a bound. Then they begged their grandmother to jump over it too, and with a tremendous effort she managed to spring right over to the other side. After this they had no doubt at all of its being their true grandmother, and went off to their hunting, leaving our friend at home in the hut.

As soon as they had gone out of sight our hero made haste to take the liver from the place where he had hid it, threw off the skin of the old *nyamatsané*, and ran away as hard as he could, only stopping to pick up a very brilliant and polished little stone, which he put in his bag by the side of the liver.

Towards evening the *nyamatsanés* came back to the hut full of anxiety to know how their grandmother had got on during their absence. The first thing they saw on entering the door was her skin lying on the floor, and then they knew that they had been deceived, and they said to each other, ' So we were right, after all, and it was human flesh we smelt.' Then they stooped down to find traces of the man's footsteps, and when they had got them instantly set out in hot pursuit.

Meanwhile our friend had journeyed many miles, and was beginning to feel quite safe and comfortable, when, happening to look round, he saw in the distance a thick cloud of dust moving rapidly. His heart stood still within him, and he said to himself, ' I am lost. It is the *nyamatsanés*, and they will tear me in pieces,' and indeed the cloud of dust was drawing near with amazing quickness, and the *nyamatsanés* almost felt as if they were already devouring him. Then as a last hope the man took the little stone that he had picked up out of his bag and flung it on the ground. The moment it touched the soil it became a huge rock, whose steep sides were smooth as glass, and on the top of it our hero hastily seated himself. It was in vain that the *nyamat-sanés* tried to climb up and reach him ; they slid down again much faster than they had gone up ; and by sunset they were quite worn out, and fell asleep at the foot of the rock.

No sooner had the *nyamatsanès* tumbled off to sleep than the man stole softly down and fled away as fast as his legs would carry him, and by the time his enemies were awake he was a very long way off. They sprang quickly to their feet and began to sniff the soil round the rock, in order to discover traces of his footsteps, and they galloped after him with terrific speed. The chase continued for several days and nights ; several times the *nyamatsanès* almost reached him, and each time he was saved by his little pebble.

Between his fright and his hurry he was almost dead of exhaustion when he reached his own village, where the *nyamatsanès* could not follow him, because of their enemies the dogs, which swarmed over all the roads. So they returned home.

Then our friend staggered into his own hut and called to his wife : ' Ichou ! how tired I am ! Quick, give me something to drink. Then go and get fuel and light a fire.'

So she did what she was bid, and then her husband took the *nymatsanè's* liver from his pouch and said to her, ' There, I have brought you what you wanted, and now you know that I love you truly.'

And the wife answered, ' It is well. Now go and take out the children, so that I may remain alone in the hut,' and as she spoke she lifted down an old stone pot and put on the liver to cook. Her husband watched her for a moment, and then said, ' Be sure you eat it all yourself. Do not give a scrap to any of the children, but eat every morsel up.' So the woman took the liver and ate it all herself.

Directly the last mouthful had disappeared she was seized with such violent thirst that she caught up a great pot full of water and drank it at a single draught. Then, having no more in the house, she ran in next door and said, ' Neighbour, give me, I pray you, something to drink.' The neighbour gave her a large vessel quite full,

and the woman drank it off at a single draught, and held
it out for more.

But the neighbour pushed her away, saying, 'No, I
shall have none left for my children.'

So the woman went into another house, and drank all
the water she could find; but the more she drank the
more thirsty she became. She wandered in this manner
through the whole village till she had drunk every
water-pot dry. Then she rushed off to the nearest

THE NYAMATSANES RETURN HOME

spring, and swallowed that, and when she had finished all
the springs and wells about she drank up first the river
and then a lake. But by this time she had drunk so
much that she could not rise from the ground.

In the evening, when it was time for the animals to
have their drink before going to bed, they found the lake
quite dry, and they had to make up their minds to be
thirsty till the water flowed again and the streams were
full. Even then, for some time, the lake was very dirty,

and the lion, as king of the beasts, commanded that no one should drink till it was quite clear again.

But the little hare, who was fond of having his own way, and was very thirsty besides, stole quietly off when all the rest were asleep in their dens, and crept down to the margin of the lake and drank his fill. Then he smeared the dirty water all over the rabbit's face and paws, so that it might look as if it were he who had been disobeying Big Lion's orders.

The next day, as soon as it was light, Big Lion marched straight for the lake, and all the other beasts followed him. He saw at once that the water had been troubled again, and was very angry.

' Who has been drinking my water ? ' said he ; and the little hare gave a jump, and, pointing to the rabbit, he answered, ' Look there ! it must be he ! Why, there is mud all over his face and paws ! '

The rabbit, frightened out of his wits, tried to deny the fact, exclaiming, ' Oh, no, indeed I never did ; ' but Big Lion would not listen, and commanded them to cane him with a birch rod.

Now the little hare was very much pleased with his cleverness in causing the rabbit to be beaten instead of himself, and went about boasting of it. At last one of the other animals overheard him, and called out, ' Little hare, little hare ! what is that you are saying ? '

But the little hare hastily replied, ' I only asked you to pass me my stick.'

An hour or two later, thinking that no one was near him, he said to himself again, ' It was really I who drank up the water, but I made them think it was the rabbit.'

But one of the beasts whose ears were longer than the rest caught the words, and went to tell Big Lion about it. ' Do you hear what the little hare is saying ? '

So Big Lion sent for the little hare, and asked him what he meant by talking like that.

The little hare saw that there was no use trying to hide it, so he answered pertly, ' It was I who drank the water, but I made them think it was the rabbit.' Then he turned and ran as fast as he could, with all the other beasts pursuing him.

They were almost up to him when he dashed into a very narrow cleft in the rock, much too small for them to follow ; but in his hurry he had left one of his long ears sticking out, which they just managed to seize. But pull as hard as they might they could not drag him out of the hole, and at last they gave it up and left him, with his ear very much torn and scratched.

When the last tail was out of sight the little hare crept cautiously out, and the first person he met was the rabbit. He had plenty of impudence, so he put a bold face on the matter, and said, ' Well, my good rabbit, you see I have had a beating as well as you.'

But the rabbit was still sore and sulky, and he did not care to talk, so he answered, coldly, ' You have treated me very badly. It was really you who drank that water, and you accused me of having done it.'

' Oh, my good rabbit, never mind that ! I've got such a wonderful secret to tell you ! Do you know what to do so as to escape death ? '

' No, I don't.'

' Well, we must begin by digging a hole.'

So they dug a hole, and then the little hare said, ' The next thing is to make a fire in the hole,' and they set to work to collect wood, and lit quite a large fire.

When it was burning brightly the little hare said to the rabbit, ' Rabbit, my friend, throw me into the fire, and when you hear my fur crackling, and I call " Itchi, Itchi," then be quick and pull me out.'

The rabbit did as he was told, and threw the little hare into the fire ; but no sooner did the little hare begin to feel the heat of the flames than he took some green bay leaves he had plucked for the purpose and held them in the middle of the fire, where they crackled and made a great noise. Then he called loudly 'Itchi, Itchi! Rabbit, my friend, be quick, be quick! Don't you hear how my skin is crackling?'

And the rabbit came in a great hurry and pulled him out.

Then the little hare said, 'Now it is your turn!' and he threw the rabbit in the fire. The moment the rabbit felt the flames he cried out 'Itchi, Itchi, I am burning; pull me out quick, my friend!'

But the little hare only laughed, and said, 'No, you may stay there! It is your own fault. Why were you such a fool as to let yourself be thrown in? Didn't you know that fire burns?' And in a very few minutes nothing was left of the rabbit but a few bones.

When the fire was quite out the little hare went and picked up one of these bones, and made a flute out of it, and sang this song:

> Pii, pii, O flute that I love,
> Pii, pii, rabbits are but little boys.
> Pii, pii, he would have burned me if he could;
> Pii, pii, but I burned him, and he crackled finely.

When he got tired of going through the world singing this the little hare went back to his friends and entered the service of Big Lion. One day he said to his master, 'Grandfather, shall I show you a splendid way to kill game?'

'What is it?' asked Big Lion.

'We must dig a ditch, and then you must lie in it and pretend to be dead.'

Big Lion did as he was told, and when he had lain down the little hare got up on a wall blew a trumpet and shouted—

> Pii, pii, all you animals come and see,
> Big Lion is dead, and now peace will be.

Directly they heard this they all came running. The little hare received them and said, 'Pass on, this way

to the lion.' So they all entered into the Animal Kingdom. Last of all came the monkey with her baby on
her back. She approached the ditch, and took a blade
of grass and tickled Big Lion's nose, and his nostrils
moved in spite of his efforts to keep them still. Then
the monkey cried, 'Come, my baby, climb on my back
and let us go. What sort of a dead body is it that can
still feel when it is tickled?' And she and her baby went
away in a fright. Then the little hare said to the other

beasts, 'Now, shut the gate of the Animal Kingdom.'
And it was shut, and great stones were rolled against it.
When everything was tight closed the little hare turned
to Big Lion and said '*Now!*' and Big Lion bounded out
of the ditch and tore the other animals in pieces.

But Big Lion kept all the choice bits for himself, and
only gave away the little scraps that he did not care about
eating; and the little hare grew very angry, and determined to have his revenge. He had long ago found out

that Big Lion was very easily taken in ; so he laid his plans accordingly. He said to him, as if the idea had just come into his head, ' Grandfather, let us build a hut,' and Big Lion consented. And when they had driven the stakes into the ground, and had made the walls of the hut, the little hare told Big Lion to climb upon the top while he stayed inside. When he was ready he called out, ' Now, grandfather, begin,' and Big Lion passed his rod through the reeds with which the roofs are always covered in that country. The little hare took it and cried, ' Now it is my turn to pierce them,' and as he spoke he passed the rod back through the reeds and gave Big Lion's tail a sharp poke.

' What is pricking me so ? ' asked Big Lion.

' Oh, just a little branch sticking out. I am going to break it,' answered the little hare ; but of course he had done it on purpose, as he wanted to fix Big Lion's tail so firmly to the hut that he would not be able to move. In a little while he gave another prick, and Big Lion called again, ' What is pricking me so ? '

This time the little hare said to himself, ' He will find out what I am at. I must try some other plan.' So he called out, ' Grandfather, you had better put your tongue here, so that the branches shall not touch you.' Big Lion did as he was bid, and the little hare tied it tightly to the stakes of the wall. Then he went outside and shouted, ' Grandfather, you can come down now,' and Big Lion tried, but he could not move an inch.

Then the little hare began quietly to eat Big Lion's dinner right before his eyes, and paying no attention at all to his growls of rage. When he had quite done he climbed up on the hut, and, blowing his flute, he chanted ' Pii, pii, fall rain and hail,' and directly the sky was full of clouds, the thunder roared, and huge hailstones whitened the roof of the hut. The little hare, who had taken refuge within, called out again, ' Big Lion, be quick and come down and dine with me.' But there was no answer, not even a growl, for the hailstones had killed Big Lion.

The little hare enjoyed himself vastly for some time, living comfortably in the hut, with plenty of food to eat and no trouble at all in getting it. But one day a great wind arose, and flung down the Big Lion's half-dried skin from the roof of the hut. The little hare bounded with terror at the noise, for he thought Big Lion must have come to life again ; but on discovering what had happened he set about cleaning the skin, and propped the mouth open with sticks so that he could get through. So, dressed in Big Lion's skin, the little hare started on his travels.

The first visit he paid was to the hyænas, who trem-bled at the sight of him, and whispered to each other, ' How shall we escape from this terrible beast ? ' Mean-while the little hare did not trouble himself about them, but just asked where the king of the hyænas lived, and made himself quite at home there. Every morning each hyæna thought to himself, ' To-day he is certain to eat me ; ' but several days went by, and they were all still alive. At length, one evening, the little hare, looking round for something to amuse him, noticed a great pot full of boiling water, so he strolled up to one of the hyænas and said, ' Go and get in.' The hyæna dared not disobey, and in a few minutes was scalded to death. Then the little hare went the round of the village, saying to every hyæna he met, ' Go and get into the boiling water,' so that in a little while there was hardly a male left in the village.

One day all the hyænas that remained alive went out very early into the fields, leaving only one little daughter at home. The little hare, thinking he was all alone, came into the enclosure, and, wishing to feel what it was like to be a hare again, threw off Big Lion's skin, and began to jump and dance, singing—

I am just the little hare, the little hare, the little hare ;
I am just the little hare who killed the great hyænas.

The little hyæna gazed at him in surprise, saying to herself, 'What! was it really this tiny beast who put to death all our best people?' when suddenly a gust of wind rustled the reeds that surrounded the enclosure, and the little hare, in a fright, hastily sprang back into Big Lion's skin.

When the hyænas returned to their homes the little hyæna said to her father: 'Father, our tribe has very nearly been swept away, and all this has been the work of a tiny creature dressed in the lion's skin.'

But her father answered, 'Oh, my dear child, you don't know what you are talking about.'

She replied, 'Yes, father, it is quite true. I saw it with my own eyes.'

The father did not know what to think, and told one of his friends, who said, 'To-morrow we had better keep watch ourselves.'

And the next day they hid themselves and waited till the little hare came out of the royal hut. He walked gaily towards the enclosure, threw off Big Lion's skin, and sang and danced as before—

I am just the little hare, the little hare, the little hare,
I am just the little hare, who killed the great hyænas.

That night the two hyænas told all the rest, saying, 'Do you know that we have allowed ourselves to be trampled on by a wretched creature with nothing of the lion about him but his skin?'

When supper was being cooked that evening, before they all went to bed, the little hare, looking fierce and terrible in Big Lion's skin, said as usual to one of the hyænas, 'Go and get into the boiling water.' But the hyæna never stirred. There was silence for a moment; then a hyæna took a stone, and flung it with all his force against the lion's skin. The little hare jumped out through the mouth with a single spring, and fled away like lightning, all the hyænas in full pursuit uttering great

cries.   As he turned a corner the little hare cut off both
his ears, so that they should not know him, and pretended
to be working at a grindstone which lay there.

The hyænas soon came up to him and said, 'Tell
me, friend, have you seen the little hare go by?

'No, I have seen no one.'

'Where can he be?' said the hyænas one to another.
'Of course, this creature is quite different, and not at all
like the little hare.' Then they went on their way, but,
finding no traces of the little hare, they returned sadly to
their village, saying, 'To think we should have allowed
ourselves to be swept away by a wretched creature like
that!'

THE SPARROW WITH THE SLIT TONGUE [1]

A LONG long time ago, an old couple dwelt in the very heart of a high mountain. They lived together in peace and harmony, although they were very different in character, the man being good-natured and honest, and the wife being greedy and quarrelsome when anyone came her way that she could possibly quarrel with.

One day the old man was sitting in front of his cottage, as he was very fond of doing, when he saw flying towards him a little sparrow, followed by a big black raven. The poor little thing was very much frightened and cried out as it flew, and the great bird came behind it terribly fast, flapping its wings and craning its beak, for it was hungry and wanted some dinner. But as they drew near the old man, he jumped up, and beat back the raven, which mounted, with hoarse screams of disappointment, into the sky, and the little bird, freed from its enemy, nestled into the old man's hand, and he carried it into the house. He stroked its feathers, and told it not to be afraid, for it was quite safe; but as he still felt its heart beating, he put it into a cage, where it soon plucked up courage to twitter and hop about. The old man was fond of all creatures, and every morning he used to open the cage door, and the sparrow flew happily about until it caught sight of a cat or a rat or some other fierce beast, when it would instantly return to the cage, knowing that there no harm could come to it.

The woman, who was always on the look-out for something to grumble at, grew very jealous of her

[1] From the *Japanische Märchen und Sagen*.

husband's affection for the bird, and would gladly have done it some harm had she dared. At last, one morning her opportunity came. Her husband had gone to the town some miles away down the mountain, and would not be back for several hours, but before he left he did not forget to open the door of the cage. The sparrow hopped about as usual, twittering happily, and thinking no evil, and all the while the woman's brow became blacker and blacker, and at length her fury broke out. She threw her broom at the bird, who was perched on a bracket high up on the wall. The broom missed the bird, but knocked down and broke the vase on the bracket, which did not soothe the angry woman. Then she chased it from place to place, and at last had it safe between her fingers, almost as frightened as on the day that it had made its first entrance into the hut.

By this time the woman was more furious than ever. If she had dared, she would have killed the sparrow then and there, but as it was she only ventured to slit its tongue. The bird struggled and piped, but there was no one to hear it, and then, crying out loud with the pain, it flew from the house and was lost in the depths of the forest.

By-and-bye the old man came back, and at once began to ask for his pet. His wife, who was still in a very bad temper, told him the whole story, and scolded him roundly for being so silly as to make such a fuss over a bird. But the old man, who was much troubled, declared she was a bad, hard-hearted woman, to have behaved so to a poor harmless bird ; then he left the house, and went into the forest to seek for his pet. He walked many hours, whistling and calling for it, but it never came, and he went sadly home, resolved to be out with the dawn and never to rest till he had brought the wanderer back. Day after day he searched and called ; and evening after evening he returned in despair. At length he gave up hope, and made up his mind that he should see his little friend no more.

One hot summer morning, the old man was walking slowly under the cool shadows of the big trees, and without thinking where he was going, he entered a bamboo thicket. As the bamboos became thinner, he found himself opposite to a beautiful garden, in the centre of which stood a tiny spick-and-span little house, and out of the house came a lovely maiden, who unlatched the gate and invited him in the most hospitable way to enter and rest. 'Oh, my dear old friend,' she exclaimed, 'how glad I am you have found me at last! I am your little sparrow, whose life you saved, and whom you took such care of.'

The old man seized her hands eagerly, but no time was given him to ask any questions, for the maiden drew him into the house, and set food before him, and waited on him herself.

While he was eating, the damsel and her maids took their lutes, and sang and danced to him, and altogether the hours passed so swiftly that the old man never saw that darkness had come, or remembered the scolding he would get from his wife for returning home so late.

Thus, in dancing and singing, and talking over the days when the maiden was a sparrow hopping in and out of her cage, the night passed away, and when the first rays of sun broke through the hedge of bamboo, the old man started up, thanked his hostess for her friendly welcome, and prepared to say farewell. 'I am not going to let you depart like that,' said she; 'I have a present for you, which you must take as a sign of my gratitude.' And as she spoke, her servants brought in two chests, one of them very small, the other large and heavy. 'Now choose which of them you will carry with you.' So the old man chose the small chest, and hid it under his cloak, and set out on his homeward way.

But as he drew near the house his heart sank a little, for he knew what a fury his wife would be in, and how she would abuse him for his absence. And it was even

worse than he expected. However, long experience had
taught him to let her storm and say nothing, so he lit his
pipe and waited till she was tired out. The woman was
still raging, and did not seem likely to stop, when her
husband, who by this time had forgotten all about her,
drew out the chest from under his cloak, and opened it.
Oh, what a blaze met his eyes! gold and precious stones
were heaped up to the very lid, and lay dancing in he
sunlight. At the sight of these wonders even the
scolding tongue ceased, and the woman approached, and
took the stones in her hand, setting greedily aside those
that were the largest and most costly. Then her voice
softened, and she begged him quite politely to tell her
where he had spent his evening, and how he had come
by these wonderful riches. So he told her the whole
story, and she listened with amazement, till he came to
the choice which had been given him between the two
chests. At this her tongue broke loose again, as she
abused him for his folly in taking the little one, and she
never rested till her husband had described the exact way
which led to the sparrow-princess's house. When she had
got it into her head, she put on her best clothes and set
out at once. But in her blind haste she often missed the
path, and she wandered for several hours before she at
length reached the little house. She walked boldly up to
the door and entered the room as if the whole place
belonged to her, and quite frightened the poor girl, who
was startled at the sight of her old enemy. However,
she concealed her feelings as well as she could, and bade
the intruder welcome, placing before her food and wine,
hoping that when she had eaten and drunk she might
take her leave. But nothing of the sort.

'You will not let me go without a little present?' said
the greedy wife, as she saw no signs of one being offered
her. 'Of course not,' replied the girl, and at her orders
two chests were brought in, as they had been before. The
old woman instantly seized the bigger, and staggering

under the weight of it, disappeared into the forest, hardly waiting even to say good-bye.

It was a long way to her own house, and the chest seemed to grow heavier at every step. Sometimes she felt as if it would be impossible for her to get on at all, but her greed gave her strength, and at last she arrived at her own door. She sank down on the threshold, overcome with weariness, but in a moment was on her feet

The OLD WOMAN OPENS The BOX

again, fumbling with the lock of the chest. But by this time night had come, and there was no light in the house, and the woman was in too much hurry to get to her treasures, to go and look for one. At length, however, the lock gave way, and the lid flew open, when, O horror! instead of gold and jewels, she saw before her serpents with glittering eyes and forky tongues. And they twined themselves about her and darted poison into her veins, and she died, and no man regretted her.

THE STORY OF CICCU [1]

ONCE upon a time there lived a man who had three
sons. The eldest was called Peppe, the second Alfin, and
the youngest Ciccu. They were all very poor, and at
last things got so bad that they really had not enough to
eat. So the father called his sons, and said to them,
' My dear boys, I am too old to work any more, and there
is nothing left for me but to beg in the streets.'

' No, no!' exclaimed his sons; ' that you shall never
do. Rather, if it must be, would we do it ourselves.
But we have thought of a better plan than that.'

' What is it?' asked the father.

' Well, we will take you in the forest, where you shall
cut wood, and then we will bind it up in bundles and sell
it in the town.' So their father let them do as they said,
and they all made their way into the forest; and as the
old man was weak from lack of food his sons took it in
turns to carry him on their backs. Then they built a
little hut where they might take shelter, and set to work.
Every morning early the father cut his sticks, and the
sons bound them in bundles, and carried them to the
town, bringing back the food the old man so much
needed.

Some months passed in this way, and then the father
suddenly fell ill, and knew that the time had come when
he must die. He bade his sons fetch a lawyer, so that
he might make his will, and when the man arrived he
explained his wishes.

[1] From *Sicilianische Mährchen.*

'I have,' said he, 'a little house in the village, and over it grows a fig-tree. The house I leave to my sons, who are to live in it together; the fig-tree I divide as follows. To my son Peppe I leave the branches. To my son Alfin I leave the trunk. To my son Ciccu I leave the fruit. Besides the house and tree, I have an old coverlet, which I leave to my eldest son. And an old purse, which I leave to my second son. And a horn, which I leave to my youngest son. And now farewell.'

Thus speaking, he laid himself down, and died quietly. The brothers wept bitterly for their father, whom they loved, and when they had buried him they began to talk over their future lives. 'What shall we do now?' said they. 'Shall we live in the wood, or go back to the village?' And they made up their minds to stay where they were and continue to earn their living by selling firewood.

One very hot evening, after they had been working hard all day, they fell asleep under a tree in front of the hut. And as they slept there came by three fairies, who stopped to look at them.

'What fine fellows!' said one. 'Let us give them a present.'

'Yes, what shall it be?' asked another.

'This youth has a coverlet over him,' said the first fairy. 'When he wraps it round him, and wishes himself in any place, he will find himself there in an instant.'

Then said the second fairy: 'This youth has a purse in his hand. I will promise that it shall always give him as much gold as he asks for.'

Last came the turn of the third fairy. 'This one has a horn slung round him. When he blows at the small end the seas shall be covered with ships. And if he blows at the wide end they shall all be sunk in the waves.' So they vanished, without knowing that Ciccu had been awake and heard all they said.

The next day, when they were all cutting wood, he

The Enchantment

said to his brothers, 'That old coverlet and the purse are no use to you; I wish you would give them to me. I have a fancy for them, for the sake of old times.' Now Peppe and Alfin were very fond of Ciccu, and never refused him anything, so they let him have the coverlet and the purse without a word. When he had got them safely Ciccu went on, 'Dear brothers, I am tired of the forest. I want to live in the town, and work at some trade.'

'O Ciccu! stay with us,' they cried. 'We are very happy here; and who knows how we shall get on elsewhere?'

'We can always try,' answered Ciccu; 'and if times are bad we can come back here and take up wood-cutting.' So saying he picked up his bundle of sticks, and his brothers did the same.

But when they reached the town they found that the market was overstocked with firewood, and they did not sell enough to buy themselves a dinner, far less to get any food to carry home. They were wondering sadly what they should do when Ciccu said, 'Come with me to the inn and let us have something to eat.' They were so hungry by this time that they did not care much whether they paid for it or not, so they followed Ciccu, who gave his orders to the host. 'Bring us three dishes, the nicest that you have, and a good bottle of wine.'

'Ciccu! Ciccu!' whispered his brothers, horrified at this extravagance, 'are you mad? How do you ever mean to pay for it?'

'Let me alone,' replied Ciccu; 'I know what I am about.' And when they had finished their dinner Ciccu told the others to go on, and he would wait to pay the bill.

The brothers hurried on, without needing to be told twice, 'for,' thought they, 'he has no money, and of course there will be a row.'

When they were out of sight Ciccu asked the landlord how much he owed, and then said to his purse, 'Dear purse, give me, I pray you, six florins,' and instantly six florins were in the purse. Then he paid the bill and joined his brothers.

'How did you manage?' they asked.

'Never you mind,' answered he. 'I have paid every penny,' and no more would he say. But the other two were very uneasy, for they felt sure something must be wrong, and the sooner they parted company with Ciccu the better. Ciccu understood what they were thinking, and, drawing forty gold pieces from his pocket, he held out twenty to each, saying, 'Take these and turn them to good account. I am going away to seek my own fortune.' Then he embraced them, and struck down another road.

He wandered on for many days, till at length he came to the town where the king had his court. The first thing Ciccu did was to order himself some fine clothes, and then buy a grand house, just opposite the palace.

Next he locked his door, and ordered a shower of gold to cover the staircase, and when this was done, the door was flung wide open, and everyone came and peeped at the shining golden stairs. Lastly the rumour of these wonders reached the ears of the king, who left his palace to behold these splendours with his own eyes. And Ciccu received him with all respect, and showed him over the house.

When the king went home he told such stories of what he had seen that his wife and daughter declared that they must go and see them too. So the king sent to ask Ciccu's leave, and Ciccu answered that if the queen and the princess would be pleased to do him such great honour he would show them anything they wished. Now the princess was as beautiful as the sun, and when Ciccu looked upon her his heart went out to her, and he longed to have her to wife. The princess saw what was passing in his mind, and how she could make use of it to satisfy her curiosity as to the golden stairs; so she praised him and flattered him, and put cunning questions,

till at length Ciccu's head was quite turned, and he told
her the whole story of the fairies and their gifts. Then
she begged him to lend her the purse for a few days, so
that she could have one made like it, and so great was
the love he had for her that he gave it to her at once.

The princess returned to the palace, taking with her
the purse, which she had not the smallest intention of
ever restoring to Ciccu. Very soon Ciccu had spent all
the money he had by him, and could get no more without
the help of his purse. Of course, he went at once to the
king's daughter, and asked her if she had done with it,
but she put him off with some excuse, and told him to
come back next day. The next day it was the same
thing, and the next, till a great rage filled Ciccu's heart
instead of the love that had been there. And when night
came he took in his hand a thick stick, wrapped himself
in the coverlet, and wished himself in the chamber of the
princess. The princess was asleep, but Ciccu seized her
arm and pulled her out of bed, and beat her till she gave
back the purse. Then he took up the coverlet, and
wished he was safe in his own house.

No sooner had he gone than the princess hastened to
her father and complained of her sufferings. Then the
king rose up in a fury, and commanded Ciccu to be
brought before him. 'You richly deserve death,' said he,
'but I will allow you to live if you will instantly hand
over to me the coverlet, the purse, and the horn.'

What could Ciccu do? Life was sweet, and he was
in the power of the king; so he gave up silently his ill-
gotten goods, and was as poor as when he was a boy.

While he was wondering how he was to live it
suddenly came into his mind that this was the season
for the figs to ripen, and he said to himself, 'I will go
and see if the tree has borne well.' So he set off home,
where his brothers still lived, and found them living very
uncomfortably, for they had spent all their money, and
did not know how to make any more. However, he was

pleased to see that the fig-tree looked in splendid condition, and was full of fruit.   He ran and fetched a basket,
and was just feeling the figs, to make sure which of them
were ripe, when his brother Peppe called to him, ' Stop !
The figs of course are yours, but the branches they grow
on are mine, and I forbid you to touch them.'

Ciccu did not answer, but set a ladder against the tree,
so that he could reach the topmost branches, and had his
foot already on the first rung when he heard the voice of
his brother Alfin : ' Stop ! the trunk belongs to me, and I
forbid you to touch it ! '

Then they began to quarrel violently, and there seemed
no chance that they would ever cease, till one of them said,
' Let us go before a judge.'   The others agreed, and when
they had found a man whom they could trust Ciccu told
him the whole story.

' This is my verdict,' said the judge.   ' The figs in
truth belong to you, but you cannot pluck them without
touching both the trunk and the branches.   Therefore you
must give your first basketful to your brother Peppe, as
the price of his leave to put your ladder against the tree ;
and the second basketful to your brother Alfin, for leave
to shake his boughs.   The rest you can keep for yourself.'

And the brothers were contented, and returned home,
saying one to the other, ' We will each of us send a
basket of figs to the king.   Perhaps he will give us
something in return, and if he does we will divide
it faithfully between us.'   So the best figs were carefully
packed in a basket, and Peppe set out with it to the castle.

On the road he met a little old man who stopped and
said to him, ' What have you got there, my fine fellow ? '

' What is that to you ? ' was the answer ; ' mind your
own business.'   But the old man only repeated his
question, and Peppe, to get rid of him, exclaimed in
anger, ' Dirt.'

' Good,' replied the old man ; ' dirt you have said, and
dirt let it be.'

Peppe only tossed his head and went on his way till he got to the castle, where he knocked at the door. 'I have a basket of lovely figs for the king,' he said to the servant who opened it, 'if his majesty will be graciously pleased to accept them with my humble duty.'

The king loved figs, and ordered Peppe to be admitted to his presence, and a silver dish to be brought on which to put the figs. When Peppe uncovered his basket sure enough a layer of beautiful purple figs met the king's eyes, but underneath there was nothing but dirt. 'How dare you play me such a trick?' shrieked the king in a rage. 'Take him away, and give him fifty lashes.' This was done, and Peppe returned home, sore and angry, but determined to say nothing about his adventure. And when his brothers asked him what had happened he only answered, 'When we have all three been I will tell you.'

A few days after this more figs were ready for plucking, and Alfin in his turn set out for the palace. He had not gone far down the road before he met the old man, who asked him what he had in his basket.

'Horns,' answered Alfin, shortly.

'Good,' replied the old man; 'horns you have said, and horns let it be.'

When Alfin reached the castle he knocked at the door and said to the servant: 'Here is a basket of lovely figs, if his majesty will be good enough to accept them with my humble duty.'

The king commanded that Alfin should be admitted to his presence, and a silver dish to be brought on which to lay the figs. When the basket was uncovered some beautiful purple figs lay on the top, but underneath there was nothing but horns. Then the king was beside himself with passion, and screamed out, 'Is this a plot to mock me? Take him away, and give him a hundred and fifty lashes!' So Alfin went sadly home, but would not tell anything about his adventures, only saying grimly, 'Now it is Ciccu's turn.'

Ciccu had to wait a little before he gathered the last figs on the tree, and these were not nearly so good as the first set. However, he plucked them, as they had agreed, and set out for the king's palace. The old man was still on the road, and he came up and said to Ciccu, 'What have you got in that basket?'

'Figs for the king,' answered he.

'Let me have a peep,' and Ciccu lifted the lid. 'Oh, do give me one, I am so fond of figs,' begged the little man.

'I am afraid if I do that the hole will show,' replied Ciccu, but as he was very good-natured he gave him one. The old man ate it greedily and kept the stalk in his hand, and then asked for another and another and another till he had eaten half the basketful. 'But there are not enough left to take to the king,' murmured Ciccu.

'Don't be anxious,' said the old man, throwing the stalks back into the basket; 'just go on and carry the basket to the castle, and it will bring you luck.'

Ciccu did not much like it; however, he went on his way, and with a trembling heart rang the castle bell. 'Here are some lovely figs for the king,' said he, 'if his majesty will graciously accept them with my humble duty.'

When the king was told that there was another man with a basket of figs he cried out, 'Oh, have him in, have him in! I suppose it is a wager!' But Ciccu uncovered the basket, and there lay a pile of beautiful ripe figs. And the king was delighted, and emptied them himself on the silver dish, and gave five florins to Ciccu, and offered besides to take him into his service. Ciccu accepted gratefully, but said he must first return home and give the five florins to his brothers.

When he got home Peppe spoke: 'Now we will see what we each have got from the king. I myself received from him fifty lashes.'

'And I a hundred and fifty,' added Alfin.

' And I five florins and some sweets, which you can divide between you, for the king has taken me into his service.' Then Ciccu went back to the Court and served the king, and the king loved him.

The other two brothers heard that Ciccu had become quite an important person, and they grew envious, and thought how they could put him to shame. At last they came to the king and said to him, ' O king! your palace is beautiful indeed, but to be worthy of you it lacks one thing—the sword of the Man-eater.'

' How can I get it?' asked the king.

' Oh, Ciccu can get it for you; ask him.'

So the king sent for Ciccu and said to him, ' Ciccu, you must at any price manage to get the sword of the Man-eater.'

Ciccu was very much surprised at this sudden command, and he walked thoughtfully away to the stables and began to stroke his favourite horse, saying to himself, ' Ah, my pet, we must bid each other good-bye, for the king has sent me away to get the sword of the Man-eater.' Now this horse was not like other horses, for it was a talking horse, and knew a great deal about many things, so it answered, ' Fear nothing, and do as I tell you. Beg the king to give you fifty gold pieces and leave to ride me, and the rest will be easy.' Ciccu believed what the horse said, and prayed the king to grant him what he asked. Then the two friends set out, but the horse chose what roads he pleased, and directed Ciccu in everything.

It took them many days' hard riding before they reached the country where the Man-eater lived, and then the horse told Ciccu to stop a group of old women who were coming chattering through the wood, and offer them each a shilling if they would collect a number of mosquitos and tie them up in a bag. When the bag was full Ciccu put it on his shoulder and stole into the house of the Man-eater (who had gone to look for his dinner) and let them all out in his bedroom. He himself hid carefully under the bed and waited. The Man-eater came in late, very tired with his long walk, and flung himself on the bed, placing his sword with its shining blade by his side. Scarcely had he lain down than the mosquitos began to buzz about and bite him, and he rolled from side to side trying to catch them, which he never could do, though they always seemed to be close to his nose. He was so busy over the mosquitos that he did not hear Ciccu steal softly out, or see him catch up the sword. But the horse heard and stood ready at the door, and as Ciccu came flying down the stairs and jumped on his back he sped away like the wind, and never stopped till they arrived at the king's palace.

The king had suffered much pain in his absence, thinking that if the Man-eater ate Ciccu, it would be all his fault. And he was so overjoyed to have him safe that he almost forgot the sword which he had sent him to bring. But the two brothers did not love Ciccu any better because he had succeeded when they hoped he would have failed, and one day they spoke to the king. 'It is all very well for Ciccu to have got possession of the sword, but it would have been far more to your majesty's honour if he had captured the Man-eater himself.' The king thought upon these words, and at last he said to Ciccu, ' Ciccu, I shall never rest until you bring me back the Man-eater himself. You may have any help you like, but somehow or other you must manage to do it.' Ciccu felt very much cast down at these words, and went to the stable to ask advice of his friend the horse. 'Fear nothing,' said the horse; 'just say you want me and fifty pieces of gold.' Ciccu did as he was bid, and the two set out together.

When they reached the country of the Man-eater, Ciccu made all the church bells toll and a proclamation to be made. ' Ciccu, the servant of the king, is dead.' The Man-eater soon heard what everyone was saying, and was glad in his heart, for he thought, ' Well, it is good news that the thief who stole my sword is dead.' But Ciccu bought an axe and a saw, and cut down a pine tree in the nearest wood, and began to hew it into planks.

' What are you doing in my wood ? ' asked the Man-eater, coming up.

' Noble lord,' answered Ciccu, ' I am making a coffin for the body of Ciccu, who is dead.'

' Don't be in a hurry,' answered the Man-eater, who of course did not know whom he was talking to, ' and perhaps I can help you ; ' and they set to work sawing and fitting, and very soon the coffin was finished.

Then Ciccu scratched his ear thoughtfully, and cried, ' Idiot that I am ! I never took any measures. How am I to know if it is big enough ? But now I come to think of it, Ciccu was about your size. I wonder if you would be so good as just to put yourself in the coffin, and see if there is enough room.'

' Oh, delighted ! ' said the Man-eater, and laid himself at full length in the coffin. Ciccu clapped on the lid, put a strong cord round it, tied it fast on his horse, and rode back to the king. And when the king saw that he really had brought back the Man-eater, he commanded a huge iron chest to be brought, and locked the coffin up inside.

Just about this time the queen died, and soon after the king thought he should like to marry again. He sought everywhere, but he could not hear of any princess that took his fancy. Then the two envious brothers came to him and said, ' O king ! there is but one woman that is worthy of being your wife, and that is she who is the fairest in the whole world.'

' But where can I find her ? ' asked the king.

' Oh, Ciccu will know, and he will bring her to you.'

Now the king had got so used to depending on Ciccu, that he really believed he could do everything. So he sent for him and said, ' Ciccu, unless within eight days

you bring me the fairest in the whole world, I will have
you hewn into a thousand pieces.' This mission seemed
to Ciccu a hundred times worse than either of the others,
and with tears in his eyes he took his way to the stables.

'Cheer up,' laughed the horse; 'tell the king you
must have some bread and honey, and a purse of gold,
and leave the rest to me.'

Ciccu did as he was bid, and they started at a gallop.

After they had ridden some way, they saw a swarm of
bees lying on the ground, so hungry and weak that they
were unable to fly. 'Get down, and give the poor things
some honey,' said the horse, and Ciccu dismounted. By-
and-bye they came to a stream, on the bank of which was
a fish, flapping feebly about in its efforts to reach the
water. 'Jump down, and throw the fish into the water;
he will be useful to us,' and Ciccu did so. Farther along
the hillside they saw an eagle whose leg was caught in a
snare. 'Go and free that eagle from the snare; he will
be useful to us;' and in a moment the eagle was soaring
up into the sky.

At length they came to the castle where the fairest in
the world lived with her parents. Then said the horse,
'You must get down and sit upon that stone, for I must
enter the castle alone. Directly you see me come
tearing by with the princess on my back, jump up
behind, and hold her tight, so that she does not escape
you. If you fail to do this, we are both lost.' Ciccu
seated himself on the stone, and the horse went on to the
courtyard of the castle, where he began to trot round in
a graceful and elegant manner. Soon a crowd collected
first to watch him and then to pat him, and the king and
queen and princess came with the rest. The eyes of the
fairest in the world brightened as she looked, and she
sprang on the horse's saddle, crying, 'Oh, I really must
ride him a little!' But the horse made one bound
forward, and the princess was forced to hold tight by his
mane, lest she should fall off. And as they dashed past

the stone where Ciccu was waiting for them, he swung himself up and held her round the waist. As he put his arms round her waist, the fairest in the world unwound the veil from her head and cast it to the ground, and then she drew a ring from her finger and flung it into the stream. But she said nothing, and they rode on fast, fast.

The king of Ciccu's country was watching for them from the top of a tower, and when he saw in the distance a cloud of dust, he ran down to the steps so as to be ready to receive them. Bowing low before the fairest in the world, he spoke: 'Noble lady, will you do me the honour to become my wife?'

But she answered, 'That can only be when Ciccu brings me the veil that I let fall on my way here.'

And the king turned to Ciccu and said, 'Ciccu, if you do not find the veil at once, you shall lose your head.'

Ciccu, who by this time had hoped for a little peace, felt his heart sink at this fresh errand, and he went into the stable to complain to the faithful horse.

'It will be all right,' answered the horse when he had heard his tale; 'just take enough food for the day for both of us, and then get on my back.'

They rode back all the way they had come till they reached the place where they had found the eagle caught in the snare; then the horse bade Ciccu to call three times on the king of the birds, and when he replied, to beg him to fetch the veil which the fairest in the world had let fall.

'Wait a moment,' answered a voice that seemed to come from somewhere very high up indeed. 'An eagle is playing with it just now, but he will be here with it in an instant;' and a few minutes after there was a sound of wings, and an eagle came fluttering towards them with the veil in his beak. And Ciccu saw it was the very same eagle that he had freed from the snare. So he took the veil and rode back to the king.

Now the king was enchanted to see him so soon, and

· CICCU · CARRIES · OFF · THE · FAIREST · ONE ·

took the veil from Ciccu and flung it over the princess, crying, 'Here is the veil you asked for, so I claim you for my wife.'

'Not so fast,' answered she. 'I can never be your wife till Ciccu puts on my finger the ring I threw into the stream. Ciccu, who was standing by expecting something of the sort, bowed his head when he heard her words, and went straight to the horse.

'Mount at once,' said the horse; 'this time it is very simple,' and he carried Ciccu to the banks of the little stream. 'Now, call three times on the emperor of the fishes, and beg him to restore you the ring that the princess dropped.

Ciccu did as the horse told him, and a voice was heard in answer that seemed to come from a very long way off.

'What is your will?' it asked; and Ciccu replied that he had been commanded to bring back the ring that the princess had flung away, as she rode past.

'A fish is playing with it just now,' replied the voice; 'however, you shall have it without delay.'

And sure enough, very soon a little fish was seen rising to the surface with the lost ring in his mouth. And Ciccu knew him to be the fish that he had saved from death, and he took the ring and rode back with it to the king.

'That is not enough,' exclaimed the princess when she saw the ring; 'before we can be man and wife, the oven must be heated for three days and three nights, and Ciccu must jump in.' And the king forgot how Ciccu had served him, and desired him to do as the princess had said.

This time Ciccu felt that no escape was possible, and he went to the horse and laid his hand on his neck. 'Now it is indeed good-bye, and there is no help to be got even from you,' and he told him what fate awaited him.

But the horse said, 'Oh, never lose heart, but jump

on my back, and make me go till the foam flies in flecks all about me. Then get down, and scrape off the foam with a knife. This you must rub all over you, and when you are quite covered, you may suffer yourself to be cast into the oven, for the fire will not hurt you, nor anything else.' And Ciccu did exactly as the horse bade him, and went back to the king, and before the eyes of the fairest in the world he sprang into the oven.

And when the fairest in the world saw what he had done, love entered into her heart, and she said to the king, ' One thing more : before I can be your wife, you must jump into the oven as Ciccu has done.'

' Willingly,' replied the king, stooping over the oven. But on the brink he paused a moment and called to Ciccu, ' Tell me, Ciccu, how did you manage to prevent the fire burning you ? '

Now Ciccu could not forgive his master, whom he had served so faithfully, for sending him to his death without a thought, so he answered, ' I rubbed myself over with fat, and I am not even singed.'

When he heard these words, the king, whose head was full of the princess, never stopped to inquire if they could be true, and smeared himself over with fat, and sprang into the oven. And in a moment the fire caught him, and he was burned up.

Then the fairest in the world held out her hand to Ciccu and smiled, saying, ' Now we will be man and wife.' So Ciccu married the fairest in the world, and became king of the country.

DON GIOVANNI DE LA FORTUNA [1]

THERE was once a man whose name was Don Giovanni
de la Fortuna, and he lived in a beautiful house that his
father had built, and spent a great deal of money.
Indeed, he spent so much that very soon there was
none left, and Don Giovanni, instead of being a rich man
with everything he could wish for, was forced to put on
the dress of a pilgrim, and to wander from place to place
begging his bread.

One day he was walking down a broad road when he
was stopped by a handsome man he had never seen
before, who, little as Don Giovanni knew it, was the devil
himself.

'Would you like to be rich,' asked the devil, 'and to
lead a pleasant life?'

'Yes, of course I should,' replied the Don.

'Well, here is a purse; take it and say to it, "Dear
purse, give me some money," and you will get as much
as you can want. But the charm will only work if you
promise to remain three years, three months, and three
days without washing and without combing and without shaving your beard or changing your clothes. If you
do all this faithfully, when the time is up you shall keep
the purse for yourself, and I will let you off any other
conditions.'

Now Don Giovanni was a man who never troubled his
head about the future. He did not once think how very

[1] *Sicilianische Mährchen.*

uncomfortable he should be all those three years, but only that he should be able, by means of the purse, to have all sorts of things he had been obliged to do without; so he joyfully put the purse in his pocket and went on his way. He soon began to ask for money for the mere pleasure of it, and there was always as much as he needed. For a little while he even forgot to notice how dirty he was getting, but this did not last long, for his hair became matted with dirt and hung over his eyes, and his pilgrim's dress was a mass of horrible rags and tatters.

He was in this state when, one morning, he happened to be passing a fine palace; and, as the sun was shining bright and warm, he sat down on the steps and tried to shake off some of the dust which he had picked up on the road. But in a few minutes a maid saw him, and said to her master, 'I pray you, sir, to drive away that beggar who is sitting on the steps, or he will fill the whole house with his dirt.'

So the master went out and called from some distance off, for he was really afraid to go near the man, 'You filthy beggar, leave my house at once!'

'You need not be so rude,' said Don Giovanni; 'I am not a beggar, and if I chose I could force you and your wife to leave your house.'

'What is that you can do?' laughed the gentleman.

'Will you sell me your house?' asked Don Giovanni. 'I will buy it from you on the spot.'

'Oh, the dirty creature is quite mad!' thought the gentleman. 'I shall just accept his offer for a joke.' And aloud he said: 'All right; follow me, and we will go to a lawyer and get him to make a contract.' And Don Giovanni followed him, and an agreement was drawn up by which the house was to be sold at once, and a large sum of money paid down in eight days. Then the Don went to an inn, where he hired two rooms, and, standing in one of them, said to his purse, 'Dear purse, fill this room with gold; ' and when the eight days were up it was so full you could not have put in another sovereign.

When the owner of the house came to take away his money Don Giovanni led him into the room and said: 'There, just pocket what you want.' The gentleman stared with open mouth at the astonishing sight; but he had given his word to sell the house, so he took his money, as he was told, and went away with his wife to look for some place to live in. And Don Giovanni left the inn and dwelt in the beautiful rooms, where his rags and dirt looked sadly out of place. And every day these got worse and worse.

By-and-bye the fame of his riches reached the ears of the king, and, as he himself was always in need of money, he sent for Don Giovanni, as he wished to borrow a large sum. Don Giovanni readily agreed to lend him what he wanted, and sent next day a huge waggon laden with sacks of gold.

'Who can he be?' thought the king to himself. 'Why, he is much richer than I!'

The king took as much as he had need of; then ordered the rest to be returned to Don Giovanni, who refused to receive it, saying, 'Tell his majesty I am much hurt at his proposal. I shall certainly not take back that handful of gold, and, if he declines to accept it, keep it yourself.'

The servant departed and delivered the message, and the king wondered more than ever how anyone could be so rich. At last he spoke to the queen: 'Dear wife, this man has done me a great service, and has, besides, behaved like a gentleman in not allowing me to send back the money. I wish to give him the hand of our eldest daughter.'

The queen was quite pleased at this idea, and again a messenger was sent to Don Giovanni, offering him the hand of the eldest princess.

'His majesty is too good,' he replied. 'I can only humbly accept the honour.'

The messenger took back this answer, but a second time returned with the request that Don Giovanni would present them with his picture, so that they might know what sort of a person to expect. But when it came, and the princess saw the horrible figure, she screamed out, ' What ! marry this dirty beggar ? Never, never ! '

' Ah, child,' answered the king, ' how could I ever guess that the rich Don Giovanni would ever look like that ? But I have passed my royal word, and I cannot break it, so there is no help for you.'

' No, father ; you may cut off my head, if you choose, but marry that horrible beggar—I never will ! '

And the queen took her part, and reproached her husband bitterly for wishing his daughter to marry a creature like that.

Then the youngest daughter spoke : ' Dear father, do not look so sad. As you have given your word, *I* will marry Don Giovanni.' The king fell on her neck, and thanked her and kissed her, but the queen and the elder girl had nothing for her but laughs and jeers.

So it was settled, and then the king bade one of his lords go to Don Giovanni and ask him when the wedding day was to be, so that the princess might make ready.

' Let it be in two months,' answered Don Giovanni, for the time was nearly up that the devil had fixed, and he wanted a whole month to himself to wash off the dirt of the past three years.

The very minute that the compact with the devil had come to an end his beard was shaved, his hair was cut, and his rags were burned, and day and night he lay in a bath of clear warm water. At length he felt he was clean again, and he put on splendid clothes, and hired a beautiful ship, and arrived in state at the king's palace.

The whole of the royal family came down to the ship to receive him, and the whole way the queen and the elder princess teased the sister about the dirty husband she was going to have. But when they saw how handsome he really was their hearts were filled with envy and anger, so that their eyes were blinded, and they fell over into the sea and were drowned. And the youngest daughter rejoiced in the good luck that had come to her, and they had a splendid wedding when the days of mourning for her mother and sister were ended.

Soon after the old king died, and Don Giovanni became king. And he was rich and happy to the end of his days, for he loved his wife, and his purse always gave him money.